TIME IS THE SIMPLEST THING

For thirty hours he had roamed the alien planet. All around was a howling wilderness of sand. Suddenly Blaine realized he had entered some sort of dwelling place. The floor was hard and smooth, and of a bright blue colour. And then he saw the life – the thing that sprawled limply on the floor. Fully twelve feet high, it was pink, an exciting pink. And it was aware of him.

He sensed the flutter of a thought half-formed, and had to fight down the elation that surged inside him, for it was seldom that one contacted a telepathic creature.

Hang on, he told himself, hang on!

And the creature spoke.

Hi, pal, it said. *I trade with you my mind.*

Also by Clifford D. Simak
in Magnum Books

WAY STATION
CEMETERY WORLD
TIME AND AGAIN
A CHOICE OF GODS
SO BRIGHT THE VISION
SHAKESPEARE'S PLANET
ALL FLESH IS GRASS
A HERITAGE OF STARS

Clifford D. Simak

Time is the
Simplest Thing

MAGNUM BOOKS
Methuen Paperbacks Ltd

A Magnum Book

TIME IS THE SIMPLEST THING

ISBN 0 417 05630 3

First published in Great Britain 1962
by Victor Gollancz Ltd
First paperback edition by Pan 1964
Methuen Paperbacks first edition published 1977
Reprinted (Magnum Books) 1980

Copyright © 1961 by Clifford D. Simak

Magnum Books are published
by Methuen Paperbacks Ltd
11 New Fetter Lane, London EC4P 4EE

Set, printed and bound in Great Britain
by Cox & Wyman Ltd, Reading

1

Finally there came a time when Man was ready to admit that he was barred from space. He had first suspected it in that day when Van Allen found the radiation belts that encircled Earth, and the men at Minnesota used balloons to trap the solar protons. But Man had dreamed so long that even in the face of this he could not forsake the dream without giving it a try.

So he went ahead and tried — and he kept on trying even after astronauts had died to prove he couldn't do it. Man was too frail for space. He died too easily. He died either of the primary radiations hurled out by the sun or of the secondaries to which the metal of his ship gave birth.

At length Man knew the dream had failed and there was a bitterness and a disillusion in looking at the stars, for the stars were farther now than they had ever been.

After many years, after great thundering in the sky, after a hundred million heartbreaks, Man finally gave up.

It was just as well he did.

There was a better way.

2

Shepherd Blaine sensed that he was in some sort of house, or, if not a house exactly, in something's dwelling place. For there was an orderliness and a sense of proportion and of form which did not occur in nature, even in an alien nature on the planet of an unknown star far removed from Earth.

His treads left no tracks upon the floor as they had left tracks upon the sand dunes before he had come upon this dwelling place, if that was what it was. The wind was a whisper only as compared with the howling of the desert storm through which he'd forged for hours.

The floor was hard and smooth and of a bright blue color and very easy for him to roll along. There were forms scattered here and there that might have been furniture or equipment or artifacts of some aesthetic value and they all were blue as well and the shape of them was not the wild, haphazard shape of a surface carved by wind or sun or weather, but the clean-cut lines, straight or curved as they might be, of functional apparatus.

And yet the stars still shone and the distant sun was there, dim as it might be, and so this place he had stumbled on was certainly no enclosure.

Blaine moved forward slowly with all his sensors out, turned up to full capacity, and the sense of *house* persisted and, a little after that, the sense of life as well.

He felt a thin thread of excitement mount inside himself. For it was not often that one found life at all. It was a memorable occasion when one found intelligence. And here, from the smoothness of the bright blue floor, from these artifacts, was intelligence.

His pace slowed to a crawl, his treads whispering on the floor, his sensors out and working, and the whirring of the tape that sucked up sight and sound and shape and smell and form, recording temperature and time and magnetics and all the other phenomena which existed on this planet.

Far off he saw the life – the thing that sprawled limply on the floor, as a lazy man might sprawl, not doing anything, not expecting to do anything, but just lying there.

Blaine moved toward it, still keeping his slow pace, and the sensors gathered in the knowledge of this sprawling life and the recorders sucked it up.

It was pink; an exciting pink, not a disgusting pink as pink so often can be, not a washed-out pink, nor an anatomical pink, but a very pretty pink, the kind of pink the little girl next door might wear at her seventh birthday party.

It was looking at him – maybe not with eyes – but it was looking at him. It was aware of him. And it was not afraid.

Finally he reached it. He came up to within six feet of it and there he stopped and waited.

It was a fairly massive thing, twelve feet high or so in the middle of it, and it sprawled across an area twenty feet or more in diameter. It towered above the smallness of the machine that happened to be Blaine, but there was no menace in it. Nor a friendliness. There was nothing yet. It was just a lump.

And this was the tough part of it, Blaine reminded himself. This was the moment when you could make or break. The move that he made now might set the pattern for all his future relationship with this thing he faced.

So he stayed perfectly still and did not a single thing. The sensors pulled back in and barely kept alive, the tape scarcely moved at all.

And it was tough to wait, for he was running out of time. There was very little left.

Then he sensed the flutter, picked up by the sophisticated electronic innards of the machine which for the moment was his body; the flutter of the being that sprawled pinkly on the floor – the flutter of a thought half-formed, the beginning of communication, the breaking of the ice.

Blaine tensed, fighting down the elation that surged inside of him. For it was foolish to become elated yet – there was no certain indication of telepathic power. Although the flutter had the feeling of it, a certain connotation . . .

Hang on, he told himself, hang on!

Hold onto that time!

Just thirty seconds left!

The flutter stirred again, louder and sharper now, as if the creature squatting there before him had cleared its mental throat before attempting speech.

It was seldom that one contacted a telepathic creature. Other abilities and traits and idiosyncrasies that made telepathy seem a pallid thing were not at all uncommon, but only rarely did they prove as useful as the plain, old-fashioned telepathic art.

And the creature spoke.

Hi, pal, it said. *I trade with you my mind.*

Blaine's mind screamed soundlessly in outraged surprise that came very close to panic. For, suddenly, without warning, he was a double thing – himself and this other creature. For one chaotic instant he saw as the creature saw, felt as the creature felt, knew what the creature knew. And in that same instant he was likewise Shepherd Blaine, Fishhook explorer, a mind from out of Earth and very far from home.

And in that same instant, as well, his time clicked to an end.

There was a sense of rushing, as if space itself might be thundering past at a fantastic rate of speed. Shepherd Blaine, protesting, was jerked across five thousand light years into one specific spot in northern Mexico.

3

He crawled upward from the well of darkness into which he had been plunged, groping his way with a blind persistence that was almost driven instinct. And he knew where he was – he was sure he knew – but he could not grasp the knowledge. He had been in this well before, many times before, and it was familiar to him, but there was a strangeness now that had never been before.

It was himself, he knew, in which the strangeness lay – almost as if he were another, as if he were only half himself, and the other half of him were tenanted by an unknown being that was backed against a wall and spat in overriding fear and mewled in loneliness.

He clawed his way upward from the well, and his mind fought in frantic urgency against the mewling strangeness in him even as he sensed that it was no use to fight, that the strangeness was a thing that had come to live with him and be a part of him so long as he existed.

He rested for a moment from the climbing and tried to sort out himself, but he was too many things and in too many places and it was utterly confusing. He was a human being (whatever that might be) and he was a scurrying machine and he was an alien Pinkness sprawling on a bright blue floor and he was a mindlessness that fell through aeons of screaming time which finally figured out, when one nailed down the mathematics of it, to the fraction of a second.

He crawled out of the well, and the blackness went away and there was soft light. He was lying flat upon his back and he finally was home and he felt the old, old thankfulness that he'd made it once again.

And finally he knew.

He was Shepherd Blaine and he was an explorer for Fishhook, and he went far out in space to nose out stranger stars. He went out many light years and at times he found certain things of some significance and other times he didn't. But this time he had found a thing, and a part of it had come back home with him.

He sought for it and found it in the corner of his mind, rolled tight against its fear, and he tried to comfort it even as he feared it. For it was a terrible thing, he told himself, to be caught inside an alien mind. And, on the other hand, it was a lousy deal to have a thing like this trapped inside his mind.

It's tough on both of us, he said, talking to himself and to this other thing which was a part of him.

He lay there quietly – wherever he was lying – and tried to put himself in order. He had gone out some thirty hours before – not he, himself, of course, for his body had stayed here – but his mind had gone out, and with it the little scurrying machine, to this unguessed planet that spun an unknown sun.

The planet had been no different than a lot of other planets, just a howling wilderness, and that was what a lot of them turned out to be when you came stumbling down upon them. This time a howling wilderness of sand although it could just as well have been a jungle or a desert of ice or a bare and naked place of nothing but primeval rock.

For almost thirty hours he had roamed the sand and there had been nothing there. Then suddenly he had come upon the great blue room with the Pinkness sprawling in it, and when he had come home the Pinkness, or a shadow of the Pinkness, had come back with him.

It crawled out from where it had been hiding, and he felt the touch of it again, the knowing and the feeling and the knowledge. His blood crawled like icy slush gurgling in his veins, and he went rigid with the musty smell and the slimy feel of alienness, and he could have shouted in pure terror, but he did not shout. He lay there, quite unstirring, and the Pinkness scurried back to its nook once more and lay there tightly curled.

Blaine opened his eyes and saw that the lid of the place in which he lay had been tilted back, and the glare of brightness that was a hooded light bulb was stabbing down at him.

He took inventory of his body and it was all right. There was no reason for it not to be all right, for it had lain here and rested for all of thirty hours.

He stirred and raised himself so that he sat up, and there were faces, staring at him, faces swimming in the light.

'A tough one?' asked one face.

'They all are tough,' said Blaine.

He climbed from the coffinlike machine and shivered, for he suddenly was cold.

'Here's your jacket, sir,' one of the faces said, a face that surmounted a white smock.

She held it for him, and he shrugged into it.

She handed him a glass, and he took a sip of it and knew that it was milk. He should have known it would be. As soon as anyone got back they gave him a glass of milk. With something in it, maybe? He had never thought to ask. It was just one of the many little things that spelled out Fishhook to him and to all the others like him. Fishhook, in its century or more, had managed to accumulate an entire host of moldy traditions, all of them fuddy-duddy in varying degrees.

It was coming back – familiar now as he stood there sipping at his glass of milk – the great operations room with its rows of glistening star machines, some of which were closed while the rest stood open. And in the closed ones lay others like himself, their bodies left behind and their minds far out in space.

'What time is it?' he asked.

'Nine P.M.,' said a man who held a clipboard in his hand.

The alienness was creeping in his mind again, and the words were there once more: *Hi, pal. I trade with you my mind!*

And now, in the light of human reason, it was crazier than hell. A form of greeting more than likely. A sort of shaking hands. A shaking of the minds. And when one thought of it, a lot more sensible than the shaking of the hands.

The girl reached out and touched him on the arm. 'Finish up your milk,' she said.

If it were a mind-shake, it was a lasting one, for the mind was staying on. He could feel it now, an alien dirtiness, lurking just below the level of his consciousness.

'The machine got back O.K.?' he asked.

The man with the clipboard nodded. 'Not a bit of trouble. We sent down the tapes.'

Half an hour, Blaine thought calmly, and was surprised that he could be so calm. Half an hour was all he had, for that was the length of time required to process the tapes. They always, he knew, ran through the exploratory tapes as soon as they came in.

It would all be there; all the data would be down, telling all the story. There would be no question of it, no doubt of what had happened. And before they read it, he must be out of reach.

He looked around the room and once again he felt the satisfaction and the thrill and pride that he had felt, years ago, when he'd first been brought into this room. For here was the heart-throb of Fishhook itself; here was the reaching out, here the dipping into distant places.

It would be hard to leave, he knew; hard to turn his back upon, for much of him was here.

But there was no question of it – he simply had to go.

He finished up the milk and handed the waiting girl the glass. He turned toward the door.

'Just a minute,' said the man, holding out the clipboard. 'You forgot to sign out, sir.'

Grumbling, Blaine pulled the pencil from beneath the clip and signed. It was a lot of foolishness, but you went through the motions. You signed in and you signed out and you kept your mouth tight shut, and all of Fishhook acted as if the place would fall into a heap of dust if you missed a single lick.

He handed back the board.

'Excuse me, Mr Blaine, but you failed to note when you would return for evaluation.'

'Make it nine tomorrow morning,' Blaine told him curtly.

They could put down anything they wished, for he wasn't coming back. He had thirty minutes left – less than thirty minutes now – and he needed all of it.

For the memory of that night of three years ago was becoming sharper with every passing second. He could remember, not the words alone, but the very tone of them. When Godfrey Stone had phoned that night there had been a sound of sobbing in his breath, as if he had been running, and there had been a sense of panic.

'Good night, everyone,' said Blaine.

He went out into the corridor and closed the door behind him, and the place was empty. The flanking doors were closed, although lights burned in some of them. The corridor was deserted and everything was quiet. But even in the quietness and the emptiness there was still a sense of massive vitality, as if all of Fishhook might have stood on watch. As if all the mighty complex never slept at all – all the laboratories and experimental stations, all the factories and the universities, all the planning boards and the vast libraries and repositories and all the rest of it never closed an eye.

He stood for a moment, considering. And it all was simple. He could walk out of here and there was not a thing to stop him. He could get his car out of the parking lot just five blocks away and head northward for the border. But it was, he told himself, too simple and direct. It was too obvious. It was just the thing that Fishhook would figure him to do.

And there was something else – the nagging thought, the clinging, monstrous doubt: Did he really need to run?

Five men in the three years since Godfrey Stone – and was that evidence?

He went striding down the corridor, and his mind was busy sorting out the doubts, but even as he sorted he knew there was no room for doubts. Whatever doubt might rise, he knew that he was right. But the rightness was an intellectual rightness and the doubt emotional.

He admitted to himself that it all boiled down to a single factor: he did not want to flee from Fishhook. He liked being here; he liked the work he did; he didn't want to leave.

But he had fought that out with himself many months ago. He'd reached decision then. When the time came, he would go. No matter how much he might want to stay, he'd drop everything and run.

For Godfrey Stone had known and in his desperate fleeing he had taken out the time to make one desperate call – not a call for help, but a cry of warning.

'Shep,' he had said, sobbing out the words as if he had been running. 'Shep, listen to me and don't interrupt. If you ever should go alien, take it on the lam. Don't wait around a minute. Just take it on the lam.'

And then the receiver had crashed down and that was all there was.

Blaine remembered how he'd stood there, with the phone still in his fist.

'Yes, Godfrey,' he had said into the silence at the other end. 'Yes, Godfrey, I'll remember. Thank you and good luck.'

And there'd not been word again. He had never heard from Godfrey Stone again.

If you ever should turn alien, Godfrey Stone had said. And now he had turned alien, for he could feel the alienness, like a lurking second self crouched inside his brain. And that had been the manner in which he had turned alien. But what about the others? Certainly not all of them had met a Pinkness, five thousand light years distant. How many other ways might a man turn alien?

Fishhook would know that he was alien. There was no way to stop them knowing. They'd know when they processed the tapes. Then they'd have him in and turn a peeper on him – for while the tapes might say that he was alien, they could not tell in what manner or to what extent he might have turned an alien. The peeper would talk very friendly to him even sympathetically, and all the time he would be rooting out the alien in his mind – rooting it out of hiding to find out what it was.

He reached the elevator and was punching at the button when a door just down the hall came open.

'Oh, Shep, I see it's you,' said the man standing in the door. 'I heard you going down the hall. I wondered who it was.'

Blaine swung around. 'I just got back,' he said.

'Why don't you come in for a while?' Kirby Rand invited. 'I was getting ready to open up a bottle.'

There was no time to hesitate. Blaine knew. He either went in and had a drink or two or he gave a curt refusal. And if there were a curt refusal, Rand would become suspicious. For suspicion was Rand's business. He was section chief of Fishhook security.

'Thanks,' said Blaine, as unruffled as he could. 'For a short one only. There's a girl. I shouldn't keep her waiting.'

And that, he told himself, would block any well-intentioned invitation to take him out to dinner or to go out and see a show.

He heard the elevator coming up, but he walked away from it. There was nothing he could do. It was a dirty break, but there was no help for it.

As he walked through the door, Rand thumped him on the shoulder in round good fellowship.

'Good trip?' he asked.

'Not a bit of trouble.'

'How far out?'

'About five thousand.'

Rand wagged his head. 'I guess that's a foolish one to ask,' he said. 'They all are far out now. We've just about finished off all the near-by ones. Another hundred years from now, we'll be going out ten thousand.'

'It makes no difference,' Blaine told him. 'Once you get going, you are there. Distance seems to be no factor. Maybe when we get way out we may pick up a lag. Halfway across the galaxy. But I doubt it even then.'

'The theoretical boys think not,' said Rand.

He walked across the office to the massive desk and picked up the bottle that was standing there. He broke the seal and spun the cap.

'You know, Shep,' he said, 'this is a fantastic business we are in. We tend to take it in our stride and it becomes at times a bit humdrum to us. But the fantasy is there.'

'Just because it came so late to us,' said Blaine. 'Just because we passed up the ability so long. It was in us all the time and we never used it. Because it wasn't practical. Because it was fantastic. Because we couldn't quite believe it. The ancients grabbed the edge of it, but they didn't understand it. They thought that it was magic.'

'That's what a lot of folks still think,' said Rand.

He rustled up two glasses and got ice out of the wall refrigerator. He poured out generous helpings.

'Drink up,' he said, handing Blaine a glass.

Rand lowered himself into the chair behind the desk.

'Sit down,' he said to Blaine. 'You aren't in that much of a rush. And you lose something in the drinking when you stay standing up.'

Blaine sat down.

Rand put his feet up on the desk, settled back in comfort.

No more than twenty minutes left!

And sitting there, with the glass clutched in his hand, in that second of silence before Rand should speak again, it seemed to Blaine once more that he could hear the throbbing of the huge thing that was Fishhook, as if it were one great sentient being lying here against the nighttime mother earth of northern Mexico, as if it had heart and lungs and many throbbing veins and it was this throbbing which he heard.

Across the desk Rand crinkled his face into a gracious mask of geniality.

'You guys have all the fun,' he said. 'I sometimes envy you.'

'It's a job,' Blaine told him carelessly.

'You went out five thousand years today. You got something out of it.'

'I suppose there was some satisfaction,' Blaine admitted. 'The intellectual thrill of knowing where you were. Actually, it was better than the usual run. I think I rustled up some life.'

'Tell me,' said Rand.

'Not a thing to tell. I found this thing when time was running out. I didn't have a chance to do anything at all before I was jerked back home. You've got to do something about that, Kirby. It can get damn embarrassing.'

Rand shook his head. 'I'm afraid that's out,' he said.

'You should give us some discretion,' Blaine insisted. 'The time limit should not be so arbitrary. You keep a man out the total length of time – the entire thirty hours – when there is no earthly reason for him staying on. Then you yank him back when he's on the very verge of something.'

Rand grinned at him.

'Don't tell me you can't do it,' said Blaine. 'Don't pretend that it's impossible. Fishhook has cords of scientists, stacked up in solid rows—'

'Oh, I suppose it's possible,' Rand told him. 'We just like to keep control.'

'Afraid of someone staying?'

'That's possible,' said Rand.

'What for?' demanded Blaine. 'You're not a man out there. You're nothing but a human mind caged in a smart machine.'

'We like it as it is,' said Rand. 'After all, you guys are valuable.

We must take safety measures. What if you got into a jam five thousand years from home? What if something happened and you were unable to exercise control? We would lose you then. But this way it's automatic. When we send you out, we know you're coming back.'

'You value us too highly,' Blaine told him dryly.

'Not at all,' said Rand. 'Do you realize how much we have invested in you? Do you realize how many men we sift through before we find one that we can use? One who is both a telepath and a rather special kind of teleporter, one who has the mental balance to stand up to the impact of some of the things he finds out there, and, finally, one who is capable of loyalty to Fishhook.'

'You buy the loyalty,' said Blaine. 'There is no one of us who ever claimed he was underpaid.'

'That,' Rand told him, 'is not what I am talking about and you know it isn't.'

And you, Blaine asked inaudibly – what are the qualifications for security? Peeping could be one of them – the ability to look into another's mind – but there'd never been any evidence in all the years he had known Rand that the man actually was a peeper. If he were a peeper, then why should he use men in his department whose sole purpose consisted of their ability to peep?

'I can't see what all this has to do,' said Blaine, 'with not giving us some time control. We could—'

'And I don't see why you should fret yourself,' Rand countered. 'You'll be going back to your precious planet. You can pick up where you left off.'

'Of course, I'm going back. I found it, didn't I? That sort of makes it mine.'

He finished off the drink, put the glass down on the desk.

'Well, I'm off,' he said. 'Thank you for the drink.'

'Of course,' said Rand. 'Wouldn't think of keeping you. You'll be back tomorrow?'

'Nine o'clock,' said Blaine.

4

Blaine walked through the massive, ornate entrance that fronted on the plaza and under ordinary circumstance he would have stopped there for a moment to soak in this best part of the day.

The street lamps were soft blobs of light, and the fronds were rustling in the evening breeze. The strollers on the walks seemed disembodied shadows, and the cars went sliding past in a sort of breathless haste, but quietly, very quietly. And over all of it hung the magic haze of an autumn night.

Tonight he did not stop. There was no time to stop.

Eight minutes now. Eight little lousy minutes.

Five blocks to get his car out of the parking lot and he didn't have the time. He couldn't take the chance. He had to leave the car.

And there was something else – there was Kirby Rand. Why, on this of all nights, had Rand popped out his door and asked him in to have a drink?

There was nothing that he could put his finger on, but he felt a vague disquiet at his talk with Rand. It was almost as if the man had known he was stealing time from him, as if he might have sensed that there was something wrong.

But all of that was past, Blaine told himself. It had been hard luck, of course, but it was not disastrous. In fact, there might even be some advantage to it. If he had got his car, Fishhook would have known exactly where to look for him. But forced to stay within the city, he could vanish in a matter of ten minutes.

He strode swiftly down the walk and turned in a direction away from the parking lot.

Give me ten minutes more, he told himself, almost as if it were a prayer. With a ten-minute start, there were a dozen places he could hide himself – hide himself to gain a little breathing space, to do a little thinking and to make some plans. For now, without a car, he simply had no plans.

He'd get those ten minutes, he was sure, if he only could be so lucky as to meet no one who might recognize him.

He felt the terror welling up as he strode along, a terror rising like a froth foaming in his skull. And it was not his terror; it was not human terror. It was abysmal and black, a screaming, clawing terror that had its origin in a mind that could hide no longer from the horrors of an alien planet, that could no longer huddle inside an alien brain, that finally found it unbearable to face up to a frightening situation that was made almost unendurable by a total lack of background.

Blaine fought against the terror, teeth gritted in his mind, knowing with one thin, undulled edge of understanding that it was not himself who had tripped the terror, but this other, this lurker in the brain.

And realized, even as he thought it, that he could scarcely

separate the two of them – that they were bound inexorably together, that they shared a common fate.

He started to run but forced himself to stop with the last ounce of resolution in him. For he must not run; he must in no wise attract attention to himself.

He lurched off the walk and collided with the trunk of a massive tree, and his hands went out to grasp and hug it, as if by the mere act of contact with something earthly he might gain some strength.

He stood there against the tree, hanging on as best he could – and hanging on was all. Slowly the terror began to drain back into some inner recess of his skull, crawling back into its hole, hiding piteously again.

It's all right, he told the thing. *You stay right where you are. Don't worry. Leave everything to me. I will handle this.*

It had tried to get away. It had tried its best to burst free of where it was and, having failed, now was pulling back into the one safe corner of the pen in which it found itself.

No more of this, Blaine thought. I can't afford another one like this. If another came, he knew, he could not stand against it. He could not keep himself from running from the terror, slobbering and screaming in horror as he ran. And that would be the end for him.

He let loose of the tree and stood stiff and straight beside it, forcing himself to stand stiff and straight against his weakness and his rubber legs. He felt the chill dampness of the perspiration which had started out on him and he was panting like a man who had run a race.

How could he run and hide, he asked himself; how could he get away with this monkey on his back? Himself alone was bad enough. He could not hope to do it if he had to drag along a frightened, whimpering alien.

But there was no way to lose the alien, no way he knew of at the moment to shake it loose of him. He was stuck with it and he must get along with it the best way that he could.

He moved out from the tree and went on down the walk, but more slowly and less surely, trying to still the shaking in him, trying to pump some strength into his wobbly legs. And through it all, he suddenly realized that he was ravenous with hunger. The wonder was, he told himself, that he had not sooner been aware of it, for except for the glass of milk, he had had no food for more than thirty hours. Rest – rest that had amounted to a deep, unbroken sleep – but not a bite of food.

The cars went sliding past, whispering on their airjets, with the soft, low murmur of the nuclear engines like an undertone.

One pulled to the curb just ahead of him, and a head stuck out.

'Shep,' said the head, 'how lucky! I was hoping I would find you.'

Blaine stood in panic for an instant and he felt the alien terror rising once again, but he crammed it back into its corner with every shred of mental power he had.

He made his voice calm and fought to keep it even. .

'Freddy,' he said. 'It's a long time since I've seen you.'

For it was Freddy Bates, man of no apparent occupation, although it was vaguely understood that he represented someone or other in this place where almost every other person was a lobbyist or representative or petty diplomat or undercover agent.

Freddy opened the door.

'Hop in,' he said. 'We're going to a party.'

And this might be it, thought Blaine. This might be the way to start where he was going. It was better, certainly, than anything he had in mind. Fishhook would never in a million years think to find him at a party. And another thing: A party would be an easy place to slip away from. There would be so many people that none of them would notice when or where one of them might go. There would be, he was almost certain, at least one car with the key left carelessly in its ignition lock. There would be food – and he needed food.

'Come on,' said Freddy. 'It is one of Charline's parties.'

Blaine slid into the car and sank into the seat. The door hissed shut, and Freddy swung the car into a traffic lane.

'I told Charline,' said Freddy, settling down to chatter, 'that a party simply could not be a party without a soul from Fishhook. I volunteered to go out and snare a Fishhook personage.'

'You goofed,' Blaine told him shortly. 'I am no personage.'

'Except,' said Freddy, 'you travelers have such horrendous tales to tell.'

'You know,' said Blaine, 'that we never tell them.'

Freddy clicked his tongue. 'Secrecy,' he said.

'You're wrong,' said Blaine. 'It's rules and regulations.'

'Of course. And that's the reason rumor is a rampant wildfire in this town. Let something happen in the afternoon up here on the hill and by evening it is being told in the finest detail in the lowest dives.'

'But usually not correct.'

'Perhaps not in its more lurid and exact description, but at least in principle.'

Blaine did not answer. He settled back in the seat and turned his head toward the window, watching the lighted streets slide past and above the streets the massive, terraced blocks of buildings that were Fishhook. And marveled at the unfailing wonder of this sight which after all the years never failed to thrill him. Knowing as he thought it that it was not the sight itself, for there were grander in the world, but the fabulous significance which fell like a mantle on the city.

For here, he thought, in fact, if not in name, was the capital of Earth. Here lay the hope and greatness of the future, here was the human link with other worlds deep in outer space.

And he was leaving it.

Incredible as it seemed, with all his love of it and all his devotion to it and all his faith in it, he was running from it like a frightened rabbit.

'What are you guys going to do with all of it?' asked Freddy.

'All of what?'

'All the knowledge, all the secrets, all the concepts that you are raking in.'

'I wouldn't know,' said Blaine.

'Regiments of scientists,' said Freddy, 'working happily away. Corps of technologists doping out new angles. How far ahead of the rest of us are you – a million years or so?'

'You're talking to the wrong man,' said Blaine. 'I don't know a thing. I just do my job. And if you're needling me, you should know that I don't needle.'

'I'm sorry,' said Freddy. 'It's an obsession with me.'

'You and a million other people. Bitching at Fishhook is a worldwide pastime.'

'Look at it my way,' said Freddy, earnestly. 'I'm sitting on the outside. I'm not even looking in. Here I see this great monstrosity, this human paragon, this superhuman project, and I feel an envy of everyone who's in it and a sense of not belonging and distinctly second-rate. Do you wonder the world hates Fishhook's guts?'

'Do they?'

'Shep,' said Freddy, solemnly, 'you should get around.'

'No particular need. I hear enough of it without going anywhere. My question was: Do they hate Fishhook really?'

'I think they do,' said Freddy. 'Maybe not right here. All the talk in this town is mostly fashionable. But get out in the provinces. They really hate it there.'

The streets now were not so closely hemmed nor the lights so bright. There were fewer business places and the residences were thinning out. The traffic had diminished.

'Who'll be at Charline's?' asked Blaine.

'Oh, the usual crowd,' said Freddy. 'Plus the usual zoo. She's the crazy sort. Without any inhibitions, scarcely with a social sense. You might bump into almost anyone.'

'Yes, I know,' said Blaine.

The thing stirred inside his brain, almost a sleepy stir.

It's all right, Blaine told it. *Just settle down and snooze. We have got it made. We are on our way.*

Freddy swung the car off the main road and followed a secondary that went winding up a canyon. The air took on a chill. In the dark outside one could hear the trees talking back and forth and there was the smell of pine.

The car turned an abrupt curve, and the house was shining on a bench above – a modernistic cliff dwelling plastered in the canyon's wall like a swallow's nest.

'Well,' said Freddy, joyously, 'here we finally are.'

5

The party was beginning to get noisy – not boisterous, but noisy. It was beginning to acquire that stale air of futility to which, in the end, all parties must fall victim. And there was something about it – about the sour smell of too many cigarettes, the chill of the canyon breeze through the open windows, the shrill and vacant sound of human chatter – that said it was getting late – late and time to go, although it really wasn't. It wasn't midnight yet.

The man named Herman Dalton stretched his long legs out, slumping in the chair, the big cigar thrust into one corner of his mouth, and his hair like a new-built brush pile from his running hands through it.

'But I tell you, Blaine,' he rumbled, 'there's got to be an end to it. The time will come, if something isn't done, when there'll be no such thing as business. Fishhook, even now, has driven us flat against the wall.'

'Mr Dalton,' Blaine told him wearily, 'if you must argue this, you should find someone else. I know nothing about business and even less of Fishhook despite the fact I work there.'

'Fishhook's absorbing us,' said Dalton, angrily. 'They're taking away our very livelihood. They're destroying a fine system of conventions and of ethics built very painfully through the centuries by men deeply dedicated to the public service. They are breaking down the commercial structure which has been built so carefully. They're ruining us, slowly and inexorably, not all of us at once, but surely, one by one. There is the matter, for example, of this so-called butcher vegetable. You plant a row of seeds, then later you go out and dig up the plants as you would potatoes, but rather than potatoes you have hunks of protein.'

'And so,' said Blaine, 'for the first time in their lives, millions of people are eating meat they couldn't buy before, that your fine, brave system of conventions and of ethics didn't allow them to earn enough to buy.'

'But the farmers!' Dalton yelled. 'And the meat market operators. Not to mention the packing interests . . .'

'I suppose,' suggested Blaine, 'it would have been more cricket if the seeds had been sold exclusively to the farmers or the supermarkets. Or if they were sold at the rate of a dollar or a dollar and a half apiece instead of ten cents a packet. That way we'd keep natural meat competitive and the economy safe and sound. Of course, then, these millions of people—'

'But you do not understand,' protested Dalton. 'Business is the very lifeblood of our society. Destroy it and you destroy Man himself.'

'I doubt that very much,' said Blaine.

'But history proves the position of commercialism. It has built the world as it stands today. It opened up the new lands, it sent out the pioneers, it erected the factories and it—'

'I take it, Mr Dalton, you read a lot of history.'

'Yes, Mr Blaine, I do. I am particulary fond of—'

'Then, perhaps, you've noticed one other thing as well. Ideas and institutions and beliefs in time outlive their usefulness. You'll find it in page after page of all our history – the world evolves and the people and their methods change. Has it ever occurred to you that business as you think of it may have outlived its usefulness? Business has made its contribution and the world moves on. Business is just another dodo . . .'

Dalton came straight out of his slump, his hair standing straight on end, the cigar dangling in his mouth.

'By God,' he cried, 'I believe you actually mean it. Is that what Fishhook thinks?'

Blaine chuckled dryly. 'No, it's what I think. I have no idea what Fishhook may be thinking. I am not in Policy.'

And that was the way it went, Blaine told himself. No matter where you went, that was the way it was. There was always

21

someone who tried to root out a hint, a clue, a tiny secret that might pertain to Fishhook. Like a group of hopping vultures, like a bunch of peeping Toms – athirst to know what was going on, suspecting, perhaps, much more was going on than was actually the case.

The city was a madhouse of intrigue and of whispering and of rumor – filled with representatives and operatives and pseudo-diplomats. And this gent in the chair across from him, Blaine speculated, was here to place a formal protest against some new outrage perpetrated upon some proud commercial unit by some new Fishhook enterprise.

Dalton settled back into his chair. He got a fresh and deadly grip upon the big cigar. His hair fell back again, it seemed, into some semblance of once having known a comb.

'You say you're not in Policy,' he said. 'I believe you told me you are a traveler.'

Blaine nodded.

'That means that you go out in space and visit other stars.'

'I guess that covers it,' said Blaine.

'You're a parry, then.'

'I suppose you'd call me that. Although I'll tell you frankly it is not a name that is regularly employed in polite society.'

The rebuke was lost on Dalton. He was immune to shame.

'What's it like?' he asked.

'Really, Mr Dalton, I cannot begin to tell you.'

'You go out all alone?'

'Well, not alone. I take a taper with me.'

'A taper?'

'A machine. It gets things down on tape. It is full of all sorts of instruments, highly miniaturized, of course, and it keeps a record of everything it sees.'

'And this machine goes out with you—'

'No, damn it. I told you. I take it out with me. When I go out, I take it along with me. Like you'd take along a brief case.'

'Your mind and that machine?'

'That's right. My mind and that machine.'

'Think of it!' said Dalton.

Blaine did not bother with an answer.

Dalton took the cigar out of his mouth and examined it intently. The end that had been in his mouth was very badly chewed. The end of it was shredded, and untidy strips hung down. Grunting with concentration, he tucked it back into his mouth, twirling it a bit to wind up the shreds.

'To get back to what we were talking about before,' he announced pontifically. 'Fishhook has all these alien things and I suppose it is all right. I understand they test them rather thoroughly before they put them on the market. There'd be no hard feelings – no sir, none at all – if they'd only market them through regular retail channels. But they don't do that. They will allow no one to sell any of these items. They've set up their own retail outlets and, to add insult to injury, they call these outlets Trading Posts. As if, mind you, they were dealing with a bunch of savages.'

Blaine chuckled. 'Someone, long ago, in Fishhook must have had a sense of humor. Believe me, Mr Dalton, it is a hard thing to believe.'

'Item after item,' Dalton raged, 'they contrive to ruin us. Year by year they take away or cancel out commodities for which there was demand. It's a process of erosion that wears away at us. There's no vicious threat, there's just the steady chiseling. And I hear now that they may open up their transportation system to the general public. You realize what a blow that would strike at the old commercial setup.'

'I suppose,' said Blaine, 'it would put the truckers out of business and a number of the airlines.'

'You know very well it would. There isn't any transportation system that could compete with a teleportive system.'

Blaine said: 'It seems to me the answer is for you to develop a teleportive system of your own. You could have done it years ago. You've got a lot of people outside of Fishhook who could show you how it's done.'

'Crackpots,' said Dalton viciously.

'No, Dalton. Not crackpots. Just ordinary people who have the paranormal powers that put Fishhook where it is today – the very powers you admire in Fishhook but deplore in your own people.'

'We wouldn't dare,' said Dalton. 'There's the social situation.'

'Yes, I know,' said Blaine. 'The social situation. Are the happy little mobs still crucifying them?'

'The moral climate,' conceded Dalton, 'is at times confusing.'

'I should imagine so,' said Blaine.

Dalton took the cigar from his mouth and regarded it with something like disgust. One end of it was dead and the other badly frayed. After considering for a moment, he tossed it into a potted plant. It caught on the lower part of the greenery and dangled there obscenely.

Dalton leaned back and clamped his hands across his gut. He stared up at the ceiling.

23

'Mr Blaine,' he said.

'Yes?'

'You're a man of great discernment. And of integrity. And of a great impatience with fuddy-duddy thinking. You've brought me up short on a couple of matters and I liked the way you did it.'

'Your servant,' Blaine said, coldly.

'How much do they pay you?'

'Enough,' said Blaine.

'There's no such thing as enough. I never saw a man—'

'If you're trying to buy me, you're out of your ever-loving mind.'

'Not buy you. Hire you. You know the ins and outs of Fishhook. You know a lot of people. In a consultive capacity, you'd be invaluable. We'd be willing to discuss—'

'Excuse me, sir,' said Blaine, 'but I'd be entirely useless to you. Under the present circumstance, I'd be no good at all.'

For he'd been here for an hour and that was much too long. He'd eaten and he'd had a drink and he'd talked with Dalton – he'd wasted a lot of time on Dalton – and he must be getting on. For the word that he was here would filter back to Fishhook and before it did he must be far away.

There was a fabric rustle, and a hand fell on his shoulder.

'Shep,' said Charline Whittier, 'it was nice of you to come.'

He rose and faced her.

'It was good of you to ask me.'

She crinkled impish eyes at him. 'Did I really ask you?'

'No,' he said. 'Leave us be honest. Freddy dragged me in. I hope that you don't mind.'

'You know you're always welcome.' Her hand tightened on his arm. 'There's someone you must meet. You'll forgive us, Mr Dalton.'

'Certainly,' said Dalton.

She led Blaine away.

'You know,' he said, 'that was rather rude of you.'

'I was rescuing you,' she told him. 'The man's a frightful bore. I can't imagine how he got here. I'm sure I didn't ask him.'

'Just who is he?' asked Blaine. 'I'm afraid I never did find out.'

She shrugged bare and dimpled shoulders. 'The head of some business delegation. Down here to cry out their broken hearts to Fishhook.'

'He indicated that much. He's irate and most unhappy.'

'You haven't got a drink,' said Charline.

'I just finished one.'

24

'And you've had something to eat? You're having a good time? I have a new dimensino, the very latest thing . . .'

'Maybe,' said Blaine. 'Maybe later on.'

'Go and get another drink,' said Charline. 'I must say hello to some other of my guests. How about staying after? It's been weeks since I have seen you.'

He shook his head. 'I'm more sorry than I can tell you. It was nice of you to ask.'

'Some other time,' she said.

She moved away, but Blaine reached out and stopped her.

'Charline,' he said, 'did anyone ever tell you you're an awfully good egg?'

'No one,' she told him. 'Absolutely no one.'

She stood on tiptoe to kiss him lightly on the cheek.

'Now run along and play,' she said.

He stood and watched her move away into the crowd.

Inside him the Pinkness stirred, a question mark implicit in its stirring.

Just a while, Blaine told it, watching the crowd. *Let me handle it a little longer. Then we'll talk it over.*

And he felt the gratitude, the sudden tail-wag of appreciation for being recognized.

We'll get along, he said. *We've got to get along. We're stuck with one another.*

It curled up again – he could feel it curling up, leaving things to him.

It had been frightened to start with, it might become frightened again, but at the moment it was accepting the situation – and to it the situation, he knew, must seem particularly horrific, for this place was a far and frightening cry from the detachment and serenity of that blue room on the far-off planet.

He drifted aimlessly across the room, skirting the bar, pausing a moment to peer into the room which contained the newly installed dimensino, then heading for the foyer. For he must be getting on. Before morning light he either must be miles away or be well hidden out.

He skirted little jabbering groups and nodded at a few acquaintances who spoke to him or waved across the room.

It might take some time to find a car in which a forgetful driver had left the key. It might be – and the thought came with brutal force – he would fail to find one. And if that were the case, what was there to do? Take to the hills, perhaps, and hide out there for a day or two while he got things figured out. Charline would be willing to help him, but she was a chatterbox, and he would be a whole lot better off if she knew nothing of the matter. There was no one else he could think of immediately who could give him any help. Some of the boys in Fishhook would, but any help they gave him would compromise themselves, and he was not as desperate as all that. And a lot of others, of course, but each of them with an ax to grind in this mad pattern of intrigue and petition which surrounded Fishhook – and you could never know which of them to trust. There were some of them, he was quite aware, who would sell you out in the hope of gaining some concession or some imagined position of advantage.

He gained the entrance of the foyer and it was like coming out of some deep forest onto a wind-swept plain – for here the surflike chatter was no more than a murmuring, and the air seemed clearer and somehow a great deal cleaner. Gone was the feeling of oppression, of the crowding in of bodies and of minds, of the strange pulse beat and crosscurrent of idle opinion and malicious gossip.

The outer door came open, and a woman stepped into the foyer.

'Harriet,' said Blaine, 'I might have known you'd come. You never miss Charline's parties, I remember now. You pick up a running history of all that's happened of importance and—'

Her telepathic whisper scorched his brain: *Shep, you utter, perfect fool! What are you doing here?* (Picture of an ape with a dunce cap on its head, picture of the south end of a horse, picture of a derisive phallic symbol.)

'But, you—'

Of course. Why not (a row of startled question marks)? *Do you think only in Fishhook? Only in yourself? Secret, sure – but I have a right to secrets. How else would a good newspaperman pick up* (heaps of blowing dirt, endless flutter of statistics, huge ear with a pair of lips flapping loosely at it)?

Harriet Quimby said, sweetly, vocally: 'I wouldn't miss Charline's parties for anything at all. One meets such stunning people.'

Bad manners, said Blaine, reprovingly. For it was bad manners. There were only certain times when it was permissible to use telepathy – and never at a social function.

To hell with that, she said. *Lay bare my soul for you and that is what I get.* (A face remarkably like his with a thin, trim hand laid very smartly on it.) *It is all over town. They even know you're here. They'll be coming soon – if they're not already here. I came as fast as I could immediately I heard. Vocalize, you fool. Someone will catch on. Us just standing here.*

'You're wasting your time,' said Blaine. 'No stunning people here tonight. It's the poorest lot Charline has ever got together.' *Peepers!!!!*

Maybe. We have to take our chance. You are on the lam. Just like Stone. Just like all the others. I am here to help you.

He said: 'I was talking to some business lobbyist. He was an awful bore. I just stepped out to get a breath of air.' *Stone! What do you know of Stone?*

Never mind right now. 'In that case I'll be going. No use to waste my time.' *My car is down the road, but you can't go out with me. I'll go ahead and have the car out in front and running. You wander around awhile, then duck down into the kitchen (map of house with red guideline leading to the kitchen).*

I know where the kitchen is.

Don't muff it. No sudden moves, remember. No grim and awful purpose. Just wander like the average partygoer, almost bored to death. (Cartoon of gent with droopy eyelids and shoulders all bowed down by the weight of a cocktail glass he held limply in his hand, ears puffed out from listening and a frozen smile pasted on his puss.) But wander to the kitchen, then out the side door down the road.

'You don't mean you're leaving – just like that?' said Blaine, 'My judgment, I can assure you, is very often bad.' *But you? Why are you doing this? What do you get out of it? (Perplexed, angry person holding empty sack.)*

Love you. (Board fence with interlocked hearts carved all over it.)

Lie. (Bar of soap energetically washing out a mouth.)

'Don't tell them, Shep,' said Harriet. 'It would break Charline's heart.' *I'm a newspaperman (woman) and I'm working on a story and you are part of it.*

One thing you forgot. Fishhook may be waiting at the mouth of the canyon road.

Shep, don't worry. I've got it all doped out. We'll fool them yet.

'All right, then,' said Blaine. 'I won't say a word. Be seeing you around.' *And thanks.*

She opened the door and was gone, and he could hear the sound of her walking across the patio and clicking down the stairs.

He slowly turned around toward the crowded rooms and as he stepped through the door, the blast of conversation hit him in the face – the jumbled sound of many people talking simultaneously, not caring particularly what they said, not trying to make sense, but simply jabbering for the sake of jabber, seeking for the equivalent of conformity in this sea of noise.

So Harriet was a telly and it was something he would never have suspected. Although, if you were a news hen and you had the talent, it would make only common sense to keep it under cover.

Closemouthed women, he thought, and wondered how any woman could have managed to keep so quiet about it. Although Harriet, he reminded himself, was more newsman than she was woman. You could put her up there with the best of the scribblers.

He stopped at the bar and got a Scotch and ice and stood idly for a moment, sipping at it. He must not appear to hurry, he must never seem to be heading anywhere, and yet he couldn't afford to let himself be sucked into one of the conversational eddies – there wasn't time for that.

He could drop into the dimensino room for a minute or two, but there was danger in that. One got identified with what was going on too quickly. One lost one's sense of time; one lost everything but the situation which dimensino created. And it often was disturbing and confusing to drop into the middle of it.

It would not be, he decided, a very good idea.

He exchanged brief greetings with a couple of acquaintances; he suffered a backslapping reunion with a slightly inebriated gentleman he'd seen no longer than ten days before; he was forced to listen to two off-color stories; he went through a mild flirting routine with a simpering dowager who came charging out of ambush.

And all the time he moved steadily toward the door that led down to the kitchen.

Finally he arrived.

He stepped through the doorway and went casually down the stairs.

The place was empty, a cold, metallic place with the gleam of chrome and the shine of high utility. A clock with a sweep second hand hung upon one wall and its whirring sound hung heavy in the room.

Blaine placed his glass, still half full of Scotch, on the nearest table, and there, six strides away, across the gleaming floor, was the outside door.

He took the first two steps and as he started on the third a silent shout of warning sounded in his brain and he spun around.

Freddy Bates stood beside the huge refrigerator, one hand jammed deep into a jacket pocket.

'Shep,' said Freddy Bates, 'if I were you, I wouldn't try it. Fishhook has the place tied up. You haven't got a chance.'

6

Blaine stood frozen for a second while wonder hammered at him. And it was surprise and bafflement, rather than either fear or anger, that held him frozen there. Surprise that, of all people, it should be Freddy Bates. Freddy, no longer the aimless man-about-town, the inconsequential mystery man in a town that was full of such as he, but an agent of Fishhook and, apparently, a very able one.

And another thing – that Kirby Rand had known and had allowed him to walk out of the office and go down the elevator. But grabbing for a phone as soon as he had reached the corridor to put Freddy on the job.

It had been clever, Blaine admitted to himself – much more clever than he himself had been. There had never been a moment that he had suspected Rand felt anything was wrong, and Freddy, when he picked him up, had been his normal, ineffectual self.

Anger soaked slowly into him, to replace the wonder. Anger that he had been taken in, that he had been trapped by such a jerk as Freddy.

'We'll just walk outside,' said Freddy, 'like the friends we are, and I'll take you back to have a talk with Rand. No fuss, no fight, but very gentlemanly. We would not want to do anything – either one of us – to cause Charline embarrassment.'

'No,' said Blaine. 'No, of course, we wouldn't.'

His mind was racing, seeking for a way, looking for an out, anything at all that would get him out of this. For he was not going back. No matter what might happen, he wasn't going back with Freddy.

He felt the Pinkness stir as if it were coming out.

'No!' yelled Blaine. 'No!'

But it was too late. The Pinkness had crawled out and it filled his brain, and he was still himself but someone else as well. He was two things at once and it was most confusing and something strange had happened.

The room became as still as death except for the groaning of the clock upon the wall. And that was strange, as well, for until this very moment, the clock had done no groaning; it had whirred but never groaned.

Blaine took a swift step forward, and Freddy didn't move. He stayed standing there, with the hand thrust in the pocket.

And another step and still Freddy barely stirred. His eyes stayed stiff and staring and he didn't blink. But his face began to twist, a slow and tortured twist, and the hand in the pocket moved, but so deliberately that one only was aware of a sort of stirring, as if the arm and hand and the thing the hand clutched in the pocket were waking from deep sleep.

And yet another step and Blaine was almost on him, with his fist moving like a piston. Freddy's mouth dropped slowly open, as if the jaw hinge might be rusty, and his eyelids came creeping down in the caricature of a blink.

Then the fist exploded on his jaw. Blaine hit where he was aiming and he hit with everything he had, his torso twisting to follow through the blow. Even as he hit and the pain of contact slashed across his knuckles and tingled in his wrist, he knew it was all wrong. For Freddy had scarcely moved, had not even tried to defend himself.

Freddy was falling, but not as one should fall. He was falling slowly, deliberately, as a tree will topple when the final cut is made. In slow motion, he crumpled toward the floor and as he fell his hand finally cleared the pocket and there was a gun in it. The gun slipped from his flaccid fingers and beat him to the floor.

Blaine bent to scoop it up and he had it in his hand before Freddy hit the floor and he stood there, with the gun in hand, watching Freddy finally strike the floor – not actually striking it, but just sort of settling down on it and relaxing in slow motion on its surface.

The clock still groaned upon the wall, and Blaine swung around to look at it and saw that the second hand was barely crawling across the numbered face. Crawling where it should have galloped, and groaning when it should have whirred, and the clock, Blaine told himself, had gone crazy, too.

There was something wrong with time. The creeping second hand and Freddy's slow reaction was evidence of that.

Time had been slowed down.

And that was impossible.

Time did not slow down; time was a universal constant. But if time, somehow, had slowed down, why had not he been a party to it?

Unless—

Of course, unless time had stayed the way it was and he had been speeded up; had moved so fast that Freddy had not had the time to act, had been unable to defend himself, could under no circumstances have gotten the gun out of his pocket.

Blaine held his fist out in front of him and looked at the gun. It was a squat and ugly thing and it had a deadly bluntness.

Freddy had not been fooling, nor was Fishhook fooling. You do not pack a gun in a little game all filled with lightness and politeness. You do not pack a gun unless you're prepared to use it. And Freddy – there was no doubt of that – had been prepared to use it.

Blaine swung back toward Freddy and he was still upon the floor and he seemed to be most restful. It would be quite a little while before Freddy would be coming round.

Blaine dropped the gun into his pocket and turned toward the door and as he did so he glanced up at the clock and the second hand had barely moved from where he'd seen it last.

He reached the door and opened it and took one last glance back into the room. The room still was bright with chrome, still stark in its utility, and the one untidy thing within it was Freddy sprawled upon the floor.

Blaine stepped out of the door and moved along the flagstone walk that led to the long stone stairway that went slanting down across the great cliff face.

A man was lounging at the head of the stairs and he began to straighten slowly as Blaine raced down the walk toward him.

The light from one of the upstairs windows shone across the face of the straightening man, and Blaine saw the lines of outraged surprise, as if they were sculptured lines in a graven face.

'Sorry, pal,' said Blaine.

He shot his arm out, stiff from the shoulder, with the palm spread flat and caught the graven face.

The man reeled backward slowly, step by cautious step, tilting farther and farther backward with each step. In another little while he'd fall upon his back.

Blaine didn't wait to see. He went running down the stairs. Beyond the dark lines of parked vehicles stood a single car, with its taillights gleaming and its motor humming softly.

It was Harriet's car, Blaine told himself, but it was headed the wrong way – not down the road toward the canyon's mouth, but into the canyon's maw. And that was wrong, he knew, because the road pinched out a mile or two beyond.

He reached the bottom of the steps and threaded his way among the cars out into the road.

Harriet sat waiting in the car, and he walked around it and opened the door. He slid into the seat.

Weariness hit him, a terrible, bone-aching weariness, as if he had been running, as if he'd run too far. He sank into the seat and looked at his hands lying in his lap and saw that they were trembling.

Harriet turned to look at him. 'It didn't take you long,' she said.

'I got a break,' said Blaine. 'I hurried.'

She put the car in gear and it floated up the road, its airjets thrumming and the canyon walls picking up the thrumming to fling it back and forth.

'I hope,' said Blaine, 'you know where you are going. The road ends up here a ways.'

'Don't worry, Shep. I know.'

He was too tired to argue. He was all beaten out.

And he had a right to be, he told himself, for he had been moving ten times (or a hundred times?) faster than he should, than the human body ever had been intended to. He had been using energy at a terrific rate – his heart had beat the faster, his lungs had worked the harder, and his muscles had gone sliding back and forth at an astounding rate.

He lay quietly, his mind agape at what had happened, and wondering, too, what had made it happen. Although the wonder was a formalized and an academic wonder, for he knew what it was.

The Pinkness had faded out of him, and he went hunting it and found it, snug inside its den.

Thanks, he said to it.

Although it seemed a little funny that he should be thanking it, for it was a part of him – it was inside his skull, it sheltered in his brain. And yet not a part of him, not yet a part of him. But a skulker no longer, a fugitive no more.

The car went fleeing up the canyon, and the air was fresh and cool, as if it had been new-washed in some clear mountain stream, and the smell of pine came down between the walls like the smell of a faint and delicate perfume.

Perhaps, he told himself, it had been with no thoughts of helping him that the thing inside his brain had acted as it did. Rather it might have been an almost automatic reflex action for the preservation of itself. But no matter what it was, it had saved him as surely as itself. For the two of them were one. No longer could either of them act independently of the other. They were bound together by the legerdemain of that sprawling Pinkness on that other planet, by the double of the thing that had come to live with him – for the thing within his mind was a shadow of its other self five thousand light years distant.

'Have trouble,' Harriet asked.

'I met up with Freddy.'

'Freddy Bates, you mean.'

'He's the one and only Freddy.'

'The little nincompoop.'

'Your little nincompoop,' said Blaine, 'was packing a gun and he had blood within his eyes.'

'You don't mean—'

'Harriet,' said Blaine, 'this is liable to get rough. Why don't you let me out—'

'Not on your life,' said Harriet. 'I've never had so much fun in all my life.'

'You aren't going anywhere. You haven't much road left.'

'Shep, you may not think it to look at me, but I'm the intellectual type. I do a lot of reading and I like history best of all. Bloody battle history. Especially if there are a lot of campaign maps to follow.'

'So?'

'So I've found out one thing. It is always a good idea to have a line of retreat laid out.'

'But not up this road.'

'Up this road,' she said.

He turned his head and watched her profile and she didn't look the part – not the hard-boiled newspaper gal that she really was. No chatter column writer nor a sob sister nor a society hen, but one of the dozen or so top-notch reporters spelling out the big picture of Fishhook for one of the biggest newspapers in North America.

And yet as chic, he thought, as a fashion model. Chic, without being sleek, and with an air of quiet assurance that would have been arrogance in any other woman.

There was nothing, he was sure, that could be known of Fishhook which she didn't know. She wrote with a strangely objective viewpoint, one might almost say detached, but even in that rare atmosphere of journalistic prose she injected a soft sense of human warmth.

And in the face of all of this, what was she doing here?

She was a friend, of course. He had known her for years, ever since that day shortly after she had arrived at Fishhook and they had gone to dinner at the little place where the old blind woman still sold roses. He had bought her a rose, he remembered, and being far from home and lonesome she had cried a little. But, he told himself, she'd probably not cried since.

Strange, he thought, but it all was strange. Fishhook, itself, was a modern nightmare which the outer world, in a century's time, had not quite accepted.

He wondered what it had been like, that century ago, when the men of science had finally given up, when they had admitted that Man was not for space. And all the years were dead and all the dreams were futile and Man had finally ended up in a little planetary dead-end. For then the gods had toppled, and Man, in his secret mind, had known that after all the years of yearnings, he had achieved nothing more than gadgets.

Hope had fallen on hard times, and the dreams had dwindled, and the trap closed tight – but the urge to space had refused to die. For there was a group of very stubborn men who took another road – a road that Man had missed, or deserted, whichever you might choose, many years ago and ever since that time had sneered at and damned with the name of magic.

For magic was a childish thing; it was an old wives' tale; it was something out of nursery books – and in the hard and brittle world of the road that Man had taken it was intolerable. You were out of your mind if you believed in magic.

But the stubborn men had believed in it, or at least in the principle of this thing which the world called magic, for it was not actually magic if one used the connotation which through the years had been placed upon the word. Rather it was a principle as true as the principles which underlay the physical sciences. But rather than a physical science, it was a mental science; it concerned the using of the mind and the extension of the mind instead of the using of the hands and the extensions of the hands.

Out of this stubbornness and this belief and faith Fishhook had arisen – Fishhook because it was a reaching out, a fishing into space, a going of the mind where the body could not go.

Ahead of the car the road swung to the right, then swiveled to the left, in a tightening curve. This was the turnaround; here the road came to an end.

'Hang on,' said Harriet.

She swung the car off the road and nosed it up a rocky stream bed that ran along one of the canyon walls. The airjets roared and blustered, the engines throbbed and howled. Branches scraped along the bubble top, and the car tilted sharply, then brought itself aright.

'This is not too bad,' said Harriet. 'There is a place or two, later on, where it gets a little rough.'

'This is the line of retreat you were talking about?'

'That's exactly right.'

And why, he wondered, should Harriet Quimby need a line of retreat? He almost asked her but decided not to.

She drove cautiously, traveling in the dry creek bed, clinging close against the wall of rock that came down out of darkness. Birds fled squawking from the bushes, and branches dragged against the car, screeching in their agony of tortured wood.

The headlights showed a sharp bend, with a barn-size boulder hemming in the wall of rock. The car slowed to a crawl, thrust its nose into the space between the boulder and the wall, swiveled its rear around and went inching through the space into the clear again.

Harriet cut down the jets, and the car sank to the ground, grating on the gravel in the creek bed. The jets cut out and the engine stopped and silence closed upon them.

'We walk from here?' asked Blaine.

'No. We only wait awhile. They'll come hunting for us. If they heard the jets, they'd know where we had gone.'

'You go clear to the top?'

'Clear to the top,' she said.

'You have driven it?' he asked.

'Many times,' she told him. 'Because I knew that if the time ever came to use it, I'd have to use it fast. There'd be no time for guessing or for doubling back. I'd have to know the trail.'

'But why, in the name of God—'

'Look, Shep. You are in a jam. I get you out of it. Shall we let it go at that?'

'If that's the way you want it, sure. But you're sticking out your neck. There's no need to stick it out.'

'I've stuck out my neck before. A good newsman sticks out the neck whenever there is need to.'

That might be true, he told himself, but not to this extent. There were a lot of newspapermen in Fishhook and he'd drank with most of them. There were a few he could even call his friends. And yet no one of them – no one but Harriet – would do what she was doing.

So newspapering by itself could not be the answer. Nor could friendship be the entire answer, either. It was something more than either, perhaps a good deal more than either.

The answer might be that Harriet was not a newswoman only.

She must be something else. There must be another interest and a most compelling one.

'One of the other times you stuck your neck out, did you stick it out for Stone?'

'No,' she said. 'I only heard of Stone.'

They sat in the car, listening, and from far down the canyon came the faint muttering of jets. The muttering came swiftly up the road, and Blaine tried to count them and it seemed that there were three, but he could not be sure.

The cars came to the turn-around and stopped, and men got out of them and tramped into the brush. They called to one another.

Harriet put out a hand and her fingers clamped around Blaine's arm.

Shep, what did you do to Freddy? (Picture of a grinning death's-head.)

Knocked him out, is all.

And he had a gun?

Took it away from him.

(Freddy in a coffin, with a tight smile on his painted face, with a monstrous lily stuck between his folded hands.)

No. Not that. (Freddy with a puffed-up eye, with a bloody nose, a cross-hatch of patches on his blotchy face.)

They sat quietly, listening.

The shouts of the men died away, and the cars started up and went down the road.

Now?

We'll wait, said Harriet. *Three came up. Only two went back. There is still one waiting (a row of listening ears, all stretched out of shape with straining for a sound). They're sure we came up the road. They don't know where we are. This is (a gaping trap with jagged rows of teeth). They'll figure we'll think they went away and will betray ourselves.*

They waited. Somewhere in the woods a raccoon whickered, and a bird, disturbed by some nighttime prowler, protested sleepily.

There is a place, said Harriet. *A place where you'll be safe. If you want to go there.*

Anyplace. I haven't any choice.

You know what the outside's like?

I've heard.

They have signs in some towns (a billboard with the words: PARRY, DON'T LET THE SUN SET ON YOU HERE). *They have prejudice and intolerance and there are (bearded, old-time preachers*

36

thumping pulpits; men clad in nightgowns, with masks upon their faces and rope and whip in hand; bewildered, frightened people cowering beneath a symbolic bramblebush).

She said in a vocal whisper: 'It's a dirty, stinking shame.'

Down on the road the car had started up. They listened to it leave.

'They gave up finally,' said Harriet. 'They may still have left a man behind, but we'll have to chance that.'

She started the engine and turned up the jets. With the lights switched on, the car nosed up the stream bed. The way grew steeper and the bed pinched out. The car moved along a hog's back, dodging clumps of bushes. They picked up a wall of rock again, but it was on the left side now. The car dipped into a crevasse no more than a paint-layer distant away from either side and they inched along it. The crevasse pinched sharply out, and they were on a narrow ledge with black rock above and black emptiness below. For an eternity they climbed, and the wind grew chill and bitter and finally before them was a flatness, flooded by a moon dipping toward the west.

Harriet stopped the car and slumped in the seat.

Blaine got out and fumbled in his pocket for a pack of cigarettes. He finally found it and there was only one left in the pack. It was very badly crumpled. He straightened it out carefully and lit it. Then he walked around the car and stuck it between Harriet's lips.

She puffed on it gratefully.

'The border's up ahead,' she said. 'You take the wheel. Another fifty miles across country. Very easy going. There's a little town where we can stop for breakfast.'

7

The crowd had gathered across the street from the restaurant. It was clustered thickly about Harriet's car and it was watching closely and it was deadly silent. Ugly, but not noisy. Angry, and perhaps just slightly apprehensive, perhaps just on the edge of fear. Angry, more than likely, because it was afraid.

Blaine pressed his back against the wall of the restaurant where, a few minutes before, they had finished breakfast. And there had been nothing wrong at breakfast. It had been all right.

No one had said a thing. No one stared at them. Everything had been normal and very commonplace.

'How could they tell?' asked Blaine.

'I don't know,' said Harriet.

'They took down the sign.'

'Or maybe it fell over. Maybe they never had one. There are some that don't. It takes a lot of belligerence to put up a sign.'

'These babies look belligerent enough.'

'They may not be after us.'

'Maybe not,' he said. But there was no one else, there was nothing else against which they would be banded.

Listen closely, Shep. If something happens. If we are separated. Go to South Dakota. Pierre in South Dakota (map of the United States with Piere marked with a star and the name in big red letters and a purple road that led from this tiny border town to the city on the wide Missouri).

I know the place, said Blaine.

Ask for me at this restaurant (the façade of a building, stone-fronted, big plate windows with an ornate, silver-mounted saddle hanging in one window, a magnificent set of elk antlers fixed above the door). It's up on the hill, above the river. Almost anyone will know me. They can tell you where I am.

We won't get separated.

But if we do, you mind what I say.

Of course I will, said Blaine. *You have lugged me this far. I'll trust you all the way.*

The crowd was beginning to seethe a little – not actually moving, but stirring around, beginning to get restless, as if it might be gently frothing. And a murmur rose from it, a sullen, growling murmur without any words.

An old crone pushed through it and shambled out into the street. She was an ancient thing. What could be seen of her – her head, her hands, her bare and muddy feet – were a mass of wrinkles. Her hair was dirty, ragged white and it drooped in wisps all about her head.

She lifted a feeble arm, from which flabby muscles hung like an obscene pouch, and she pointed a crooked, bony, quavering forefinger straight in Blaine's direction.

'That is him,' she screamed. 'He is the one I spotted. There's something queer with him. You can't get into his brain. It's like a shining mirror. It—'

The rest of what she said was drowned out in the rising clamor of the crowd, which began moving forward – not rapidly, but foot by foot – edging along toward the two against the wall, as if it might be fearful and reluctant but pushed along by a civic duty that was greater than its fear.

Blaine put his hand into his jacket pocket and his fingers closed around the gun he'd scooped up in Charline's kitchen. But that was not the way, he knew. That would only make it worse. He pulled his hand out of the pocket and let it dangle at his side.

But there was something wrong – he was standing all alone, just his human self. There was no Pinkness in him, no stir inside his brain. He was a naked human and wondered wildly, for a moment, if he should be glad or not. And then he caught it peeping out of one corner of his brain and he waited for it, but nothing happened and the questioning segment of it pulled out of consciousness again.

There was fury and loathing in the faces that floated atop the mass of human bodies moving in the street. Not the night-shrouded baying of the mob, but the slantwise, daylight slinking of a pack of wolves, and in the forefront of the press, borne along on the edge of this wave of human hatred, was the withered crone who had pointed with her finger to set the pack in motion.

'Stand still,' Blaine said to Harriet. 'That is our only chance.'

Any moment now, he knew, the situation could hit a crisis point. The mob would either lose its nerve and waver, or some slight incident, some smallest motion, some spoken word, would send it forward with a rush.

And if that happened, he knew, he would use the gun. Not that he wanted to, not that he intended to – but it would be the one thing left to do.

But for the moment, in the little interval before violence could erupt, the town stood petrified – a sleepy little town with shabby, two-story business buildings, all in need of paint, fronting on a sun-baked street. Scraggy trees stood at infrequent intervals, and there were faces at the upstairs windows, staring out in astonishment at the potential animal padding in the street.

The mob moved closer, circling, still cautious, and mute; all its murmur quieted, all its hate locked tight behind the savage masks.

A foot clicked sharply on the sidewalk, then another foot, and still another one – the rugged, steady sound of someone's stolid walking.

The footsteps came closer, and Blaine turned his eyes a second to catch out of the corner of them the sight of a tall, angular almost cadaverous man who strode along deliberately, for all the world as if he were out for a morning stroll. The man reached

Blaine and stood to one side of him and then he turned and faced the mob. He never said a word; he just stayed standing there. But the crowd came to a halt and stood there in the street in a dreadful quietness.

Then a man said: 'Good morning to you, Sheriff.'

The sheriff didn't stir; he didn't say a word.

'Them is parries,' said the man.

'Who says so?' asked the sheriff.

'Old Sara, she says so.'

The sheriff looked at the crone: 'How about it, Sara?'

'Tom is right,' Old Sara screeched. 'That one there, he has a funny mind. It bounces back at you.'

'And the woman?' asked the sheriff.

'She is with him, ain't she?'

'I am ashamed of you,' the sheriff said, as if they all were naughty children. 'I have a mind to run you in, every one of you.'

'But them is parries!' yelled a stricken voice. 'You know we don't allow no parries here.'

'Now, I tell you what,' the sheriff said. 'You all get back to business. I'll take care of this.'

'The both of them?' a voice asked.

'Why, I don't know,' the sheriff said. 'The lady ain't no parry. I just kind of figured we'd run her out of town and that would be enough.'

He said to Harriet: 'Are you with this man?'

'And I'm staying with him!'

No! said Blaine. (*A sign for silence, finger to the lips.*)

Fast, hoping that no one would catch it, for in a town like this even a telepath might be in for trouble.

But the warning must be sounded.

'That your car across the street?' the sheriff asked.

Harriet shot a questioning glance at Blaine.

'Yes, it is,' she said.

'Well, I tell you, miss. You just trot over to it and get out of here. The folks will let you through.'

'But I don't intend—'

Blaine said: 'You better do it, Harriet.'

She hesitated.

'Go ahead,' he said.

She stepped slowly off the sidewalk, then turned back.

'I'll be seeing you,' she said to Blaine.

She glanced with contempt at the sheriff. 'Cossack,' she declared.

The sheriff didn't mind. He'd never heard the term.

'Beat it, lady,' he said, and his voice was almost kindly.

The crowd parted to let her through, but buzzed angrily. She reached the car and turned to wave at Blaine. Then she got into the seat and started the motor, gunned the jets and swung the car sharply out into the street. The crowd fled, shrieking, tumbling over one another to get out of the way, blinded by the screaming dust that was spun up by the jets.

The sheriff watched with monumental calm as the car roared down the street.

'You see that, sheriff!' roared an outraged victim. 'Why don't you run her in?'

'Served you right,' the sheriff said. 'You started all of this. Here I was getting ready for a restful day and you got me all stirred up.'

He didn't look stirred up.

The protesting crowd pushed toward the sidewalk, arguing violently.

The sheriff waved his hands, as if he were shooing chickens.

'Get along with you,' he told them. 'You have had your fun. Now I got to get to work. I got this guy to jail.'

He turned to Blaine. 'Come along with me,' he said.

They walked down the street together toward the courthouse.

'You ought to have known better,' said the sheriff. 'This town is hell on parries.'

'No way to tell,' said Blaine. 'There wasn't any sign.'

'Blew down a year or two ago,' the sheriff told him. 'No one had the gumption to set it up again. Really should have a new sign. Old one got pretty rickety. You could hardly read the lettering on it. Sand storms scoured off the paint.'

'What do you intend to do with me?'

The sheriff said: 'Not too much, I reckon. Hold you for a while until the folks cool down. For your own protection. As soon as it is safe, I'll get you out of here.'

He was silent for a moment, considering the situation.

'Can't do it right away,' he said. 'The boys will be watching mighty close.'

They reached the courthouse and climbed the steps. The sheriff opened the door. 'Straight ahead,' he said.

They walked into the sheriff's office, and the sheriff closed the door.

'You know,' said Blaine, 'I don't believe you've got the grounds to hold me. What would happen if I just walked out of here?'

'Nothing much, I guess. Not right away, at least. I certainly wouldn't stop you, although I'd argue some. But you wouldn't get out of town. They'd have you in five minutes.'

'I could have left in the car.'

The sheriff shook his head. 'Son, I know these people. I was raised with them. I am one of them. I know how far I can go with them and when I've got to stop. I could get the lady off, but not the both of you. You ever see a mob in action?'

Blaine shook his head.

'It ain't a pretty sight.'

'How about this Sara? She's a parry, too.'

'Well, I tell you, friend. Sara has good blood behind her. Fell on evil times, but her family's been here for more than a hundred years. The town just tolerates her.'

'And she's handy as a spotter.'

The sheriff shook his head and chuckled. 'There ain't much,' he said, with local pride, 'that filters past our Sara. She has a busy time of it, watching all the strangers that come into town.'

'You catch a lot of parries that way?'

'Tolerable,' said the sheriff. 'Every now and then. A tolerable number, I would say.'

He motioned at the desk. 'Just dump your pockets there. The law says I got to do it. I'll fix up a receipt for you.'

Blaine began digging in his pockets. Billfold, card case, handkerchief, key ring, matches and, finally, the gun.

He lifted it out rather gingerly and laid it with the other stuff.

The sheriff eyed it. 'You had that all the time?'

Blaine nodded.

'And you never reached for it?'

'I was too scared to reach for it.'

'You got a permit for it?'

'I don't even own it.'

The sheriff whistled softly through his teeth.

He picked up the gun and broke it. There was the coppery shine of cartridge cases.

The sheriff opened a desk drawer and tossed it in.

'Now,' he said, as if relieved, 'I've got something legal I can hold you on.'

He picked up the book of matches and handed them to Blaine.

'You'll want these for smoking.'

Blaine put them in his pocket.

'I could get you cigarettes,' the sheriff said.

'No need,' Blaine told him. 'I carry them sometimes, but I don't do much smoking. Usually I wear them out carrying them before I get around to smoking.'

The sheriff lifted a ring of keys off a nail.

'Come along,' he said.

Blaine followed him into a corridor that fronted on a row of cells.

The sheriff unlocked the nearest one, across the corridor from the door.

'You've got it all alone,' he said. 'Ran the last one out last night. Boy who came across the border and got himself tanked up. Figured he was as good as white folks.'

Blaine walked into the cell. The sheriff banged and locked the door.

'Anything you want,' he said, with a fine show of hospitality, 'just yell out and say so. I'll get it for you.'

8

It had gone by many names.

Once it had been known as extrasensory perception. And then there had been a time when it had been psionics, psi for short. But first of all it had been magic.

The medicine man, with the oxides that he used for paint, with his knucklebones to rattle in the skull, with his bag of nauseous content, may have practiced it in a clumsy sort of way before the first word had been written – grasping at a principle he did not understand, more than likely not even knowing that he did not understand, not realizing there was anything he ought to understand. And the knowledge was passed on, from hand to inept hand. The witch doctor of the Congo used it, the priests of Egypt knew it, the wise men of Tibet were acquainted with it. And in all these cases it was not wisely used and it was not understood and it got mixed up with a lot of mumbo jumbo and in the days of reason it became discredited and there was scarcely anyone who believed in it.

Out of the days of reason rose a method and a science, and there was no place for magic in the world that science built – for there was no method in it and there was no system in it and it could not be reduced to a formula or equation. So it was suspect and it was outside the pale and it was all stupid foolishness. No man in his right mind would once consider it.

But they called it PK now for paranormal kinetics, which was too long to say. And the ones who had it they called parries and shut them up in jails and did even worse than that.

It was a queer business, once one thought of it – for despite the strange gulf which lay between PK and science, it had taken the orderly mind which science had drummed into the human race to make PK finally work.

And, strange as it might seem, Blaine told himself, it had been necessary that science should come first. For science had to be developed before Man could understand the forces which had freed his mind from the shackles in which they had been bound, before mental energy could be tapped and put to work by those who quite unsuspectingly had always carried with them that power and energy. For even in the study of PK there had been a need for method, and science had been the training ground in which method had developed.

There were those who said that in some distant past two roads had forked for mankind, one of them marked 'Magic' and the other 'Science', and that Man had taken the 'Science' road and let the 'Magic' go. Many of these people then went on to say that Man had made a great mistake in the choosing of the roads. See how far we'd have gone, they said, if we had taken 'Magic' at the first beginning.

But they were wrong, Blaine said, talking to himself, for there had never been two roads; there'd only been the one. For Man had had to master science before he could master magic.

Although science had almost defeated magic, had almost driven it into limbo with laughter and with scorn.

And would have driven it had there not been stubborn men who had refused to give up the dream of stars. Men who had been willing to do anything at all, to brave the laughter of the world, to accept derision, if they only could lay hands upon the stars.

He wondered how it must have been in those days when Fishhook had been no more than a feeble hope, a glimmer of the mind, an article of faith. For the little band of hopeful, stubborn men had stood entirely by themselves. When they had asked for help, there had been no help, but only scornful chuckling against such errant foolery.

The press had made a field day of it when they had appeared in Washington to ask financial aid. There had, quite naturally, been no such aid forthcoming, for the government would have naught to do with such a wildcat scheme. If science in all its might and glory had failed to reach the stars, how could there be hope that such as these might do it? So the men had worked alone, except for such pittances as they might be given here and there – a small grant from India, another from the Philippines and a little from Columbia – plus dribbles that came in from metaphysical societies and a few sympathetic donors.

Then finally a country with a heart – Mexico – had invited them to come, had provided money, had set up a study center and a laboratory, had lent encouragement rather than guffaws of laughter.

And almost from that day, Fishhook had become reality, had developed into an institution which did credit not to itself alone, but to the country which had opened up its heart.

And I am a part of it, thought Blaine, sitting in his cell; a part of this virtually secret society, although secret through no fault of its own. Made secret, rather, by the envy and intolerance and the surging superstition of the entire world. Even though I am running from it, even though it be hunting me, I am still a part of it.

He got up from the tiny bunk with its dirty blanket and stood at the window, staring out. He could see the sun-baked street and the scraggly trees staggered on the boulevard and across the street the sad, defeated business houses with a few dilapidated cars parked against the curb, some of them so ancient they were equipped with wheels which in turn were driven by internal combustion engines. Men sat on the steps that led up to the store fronts, chewing tobacco and spitting out onto the sidewalks, creating little pools of sticky amber liquid which looked like old bloodstains. They sat there languidly and chewed and occasionally talked among themselves, not looking at the courthouse, looking nowhere in particular, but being very nonchalant about their deadly loafing.

But they were watching the courthouse, Blaine knew. They were watching him – the man with the mirror in his mind. The mind, Old Sara told the sheriff, that bounces back at you.

And that had been what Kirby Rand had seen, that had been what had tipped him off and set Fishhook on the trail. Which meant that Rand, if he were not a peeper, then certainly was a spotter. Although, Blaine thought, it didn't really matter whether Rand was a peeper or a spotter, for a peeper would have little luck in reading a mind that bounced right back at you.

And that meant, Blaine realized, that he carried in his mind the equivalent of a flashing warning light for anyone with the ability to see. There'd be nowhere he'd be safe. There'd be no place he could hide. He'd ring a loud and angry bell for any peeper or any spotter or any hounder that came within his range.

He'd not been that way before. He was quite certain of it. Someone would have mentioned it or it would have been on his psych report.

You, he said to the hider in his mind, *come out of there!*

It wagged its tail. It wriggled like a happy dog. It did not come out.

Blaine went back to the bunk and sat down on the edge of it.

Harriet would be back with some sort of help. Or maybe the sheriff would let him go before then, as soon as it was safe. Although the sheriff didn't have to, for the sheriff had good grounds to hold him – the possession of the gun.

Buster, he said to his boon companion, *it may be up to you again. We may need another trick.*

For the thing inside his mind had come up with a trick before – a very trick in time. Or metabolism? There was no way of knowing which, whether he had moved faster than was customary or whether time had been slowed down for everyone but him.

And when he got away, what then?

Up to South Dakota, as Harriet had said?

He might as well, he told himself, for he had no other plans. There had been no time in which he could make any plans. It had been a bare, bald matter of getting out of Fishhook's clutches. Years ago, he told himself, he should have laid his plans, but it had seemed a far thing then. It had seemed a circumstance that could never happen to him. So here he was, stuck inside a jail cell in a little town of which he did not even know the name, with no more than fifteen dollars and that locked in the sheriff's desk.

He sat and listened to a gasoline car come stuttering down the street, and somewhere a bird was chirping. And he was in a jam, he admitted to himself – he was in an awful jam.

The men were waiting out there, sitting on the steps, trying very hard not to seem to watch the courthouse, and he did not like the looks of it.

The door in the sheriff's office opened and banged again, and there was the sound of feet moving on the floor. Voices came indistinctly, and Blaine didn't try to listen. What was the use of listening? What was the use of anything?

Then the sheriff's deliberate tread moved across the office and out into the corridor. Blaine looked up as the sheriff stopped just outside his cell.

'Blaine,' the sheriff said, 'the Father's here to see you.'

'What father?'

'The priest, you heathen. The pastor of this parish.'

'I can't understand,' said Blaine, 'why he'd be interested.'

'You're a human being, aren't you?' said the sheriff. 'You have got a soul.'

'I will not deny it.'

The sheriff regarded him with a stern and puzzled look. 'Why didn't you tell me that you were from Fishhook?'

Blaine shrugged. 'What difference would it make?'

'Good God, man,' the sheriff said, 'if the folks in this town knew you were from Fishhook, they'd be in to string you up. They might let just a simple parry slip through their fingers, but not a man from Fishhook. They burned down the Trading Post three years ago last month, and the factor got out of town just ahead of them.'

'And what would you do about it,' Blaine demanded, 'if they decided I needed stringing up?'

The sheriff scratched his head. 'Well, naturally, I'd do the best I could.'

'Thanks a lot,' said Blaine. 'I suppose you contacted Fishhook.'

'I told them to come and get you. Take you off my hands.'

'That's a pal,' said Blaine.

The sheriff proceeded to get sore.

'Why did you come blundering into this town?' he demanded, with quite a lot of heat. 'This is a quiet, peaceable, decent place until folks like you show up.'

'We were hungry,' said Blaine, 'and we stopped to get some breakfast.'

'You stuck your head into a noose,' the sheriff told him, sternly. 'I hope to God I can get you out of it.'

He started to turn away and then turned back.

'I'll send the Father in,' he said.

9

The priest came into the cell and stood for a moment, blinking in the dimness.

Blaine stood and said to him: 'I am glad you came. The best I can offer you is a seat here on the bunk.'

'It's all right,' said the priest. 'I thank you. I am Father Flanagan and I hope I'm not intruding.'

'Not in the least,' said Blaine. 'I am glad to see you.'

Father Flanagan eased himself to a seat upon the bunk, groaning a little with the effort. He was an aged man who ran to corpulence, with a kindly face and withered hands that looked as if they might be crippled by arthritis.

'Sit down, my son,' he said. 'I hope I don't disturb you. I warn you at the outset that I'm a horrible busybody. It would come, I would suspect, from being the shepherd to a group of people who are largely children, irrespective of their years. Is there anything you would like to talk about?'

'Anything at all,' said Blaine, 'except possibly religion.'

'You are not a religious man, my son?'

'Not particularly,' said Blaine. 'Whenever I consider it, I tend to become confused.'

The old man shook his head. 'These are ungodly days. There are many like you. It is a worry to me. To Holy Mother Church as well. We have fallen on hard times of the spirit, with many of the people more concerned with fear of evil than contemplation of the good. There is talk of werewolf and incubus and devil, and a hundred years ago all fear of such had been washed out of our minds.'

He turned his body ponderously and sat sidewise the better to face Blaine.

'The sheriff tells me,' he said, 'that you come from Fishhook.'

'There is no use,' said Blaine, 'of my denying it.'

'I have never talked with anyone from Fishhook,' the old priest said, mumbling just a little, as if he might be talking to himself rather than to Blaine. 'I have only heard of Fishhook, and some of the stories I have heard of it are incredible and wild. There was a factor here for a time before the people burned the Post, but I never went to see him. The people would not have understood.'

'From what happened here this morning,' Blaine agreed, 'I rather doubt they would have.'

'They say you are a paranormal . . .'

'Parry is the word,' Blaine told him. 'No need to dress it up.'

'And you are really one?'

'Father, I am at a loss to understand your interest.'

'Just academic,' said Father Flanagan. 'I can assure you, purely academic. Something that is of interest to me personally. You are as safe with me as if you were in confessional.'

'There was a day,' said Blaine, 'when science was deeply suspect as the hidden foes of all religious truth. We have the same thing here.'

'But the people,' said Father Flanagan, 'are afraid again. They close and bar their doors. They do not go out of night. They have hex signs – hex signs, mind you, instead of the blessed crucifix – hanging on their gates and the gables of their houses. They whisper of things which have been dead and dust since the Middle Ages. They tremble in the smoky chimney corners of their minds. They have lost much of their ancient faith. They go through all the rituals, of course, but I see it in their faces, I sense it in their talk, I glimpse it in their minds. They have lost the simple art of faith.'

'No, Father, I don't think they have. They're just very troubled people.'

'The entire world is troubled,' said Father Flanagan.

And that was right, Blaine told himself – the entire world was troubled. For it had lost a cultural hero and had not been able to acquire another for all that it had tried. It had lost an anchor which had held it against the winds of illogic and unreason and it was now adrift upon an ocean for which there was no chart.

At one time science had served as the cultural hero. It had logic and reason and ultimate precision that probed down into the atom and out to the farther edge of space. It spawned gadgets by the millions for the comfort of its worshipers and it placed the hand and eye of Man upon the entire universe, by proxy. It was something you could trust in, for it was the sum of human wisdom among many other things.

But principally it was translated into machines and machine technology, for science was an abstract, but machines were something that anyone could see.

Then there came the day when Man, for all his wondrous machines, for all his famed technology, had been driven back from space, had been whipped howling from the heavens back to the den of Earth. And that day the cultural god of science had shone a bit less brightly, had died a little in the people's minds.

And that other day, when Man had gone to the stars without the benefit of machines, the worship of technology had died for good and all. Machines and technology and science itself still existed, still were in daily use, still were of vast importance, but they no longer formed a cult.

For while Fishhook used machines, they were not machines as such – not machines that could be accepted by the common mass of mankind. For they had no pistons and no wheels, no gears, no shafts, no levers, not a single button – they had nothing of the component parts of a commonplace machine. They were strange and alien and they had no common touch.

So Man had lost his cultural hero and since his nature was so fashioned that he must have some abstract hero-worship, because he must always have an ideal and a goal, a vacuum was created that screamed aloud for filling.

Paranormal kinetics, for all its strangeness, for all its alien concept, filled the bill exactly. For here, finally, were all the crackpot cults completely justified; here, at last, was the promise of ultimate wish-fulfillment; here was something exotic enough, or that could be made exotic, to satisfy the depth of human emotion such as a mere machine never had been able.

Here, so help us God, was magic!

So the world went off on a magic jag.

The pendulum had swung too far, as always, and now was swinging back, and the horror of intolerance had been loosed upon the land.

So Man once again was without a cultural hero, but had acquired instead a neosuperstition that went howling through the dark of a second Middle Ages.

'I have puzzled much upon the matter,' said Father Flanagan. 'It is something which naturally must concern even so unworthy a servant of the Church as I. For whatever may concern the souls and the minds of men is of interest to the Church and to the Holy Father. It has been the historic position of Rome that we must so concern ourselves.'

Blaine bowed slightly in recognition of the sincerity of the man, but there was a fleck of bitterness in his voice when he answered: 'So you've come to study me. You are here to question me.'

There was sadness in the old priest's voice. 'I prayed you would not see it in this light. I have failed, I see. I came to you as to someone who could help me and, through me, the Church. For, my son, the Church at times needs help. It is not too proud to say so, for all that it has been charged, through all its history, with excessive pride. You are a man, an intelligent man, who is a part of this thing which serves to puzzle us. I thought that you might help me.'

Blaine sat silent, and the priest sat looking at him, a humble man who sought a favor, and yet with a sense of inner strength one could not help but feel.

'I would not mind,' said Blaine. 'Not that I think for a moment it would do any good. You're a part of what is in this town.'

'Not so, my son. We neither sanction nor condemn. We do not have facts enough.'

'I'll tell you about myself,' said Blaine, 'if that is what you want to know. I am a traveler. My job is to go out to the stars. I climb into a machine – well, not exactly a machine, rather it's a symbolic contrivance that helps me free my mind, that possibly even gives my mind a kick in the right direction. And it helps with the navigation— Look, Father, this is hard to say in simple, common terms. It sounds like gibberish.'

'I am following you with no difficulty.'

'Well, this navigation. That's another funny thing. There are factors involved that there is no way to put one's tongue to them. In science it would be mathematics, but it's not actually mathematics. It's a way of getting there, of knowing where you're going.'

'Magic?'

'Hell, no – pardon me, Father. No, it isn't magic. Once you understand it, once you get the feel of it, it is clear and simple and it becomes a part of you. It is as natural as breathing and as easy as falling off a log. I would imagine—'

'I would think,' said Father Flanagan, 'that it is unnecessary to go into the mechanics of it. Could you tell me how it feels to be on another star?'

'Why,' Blaine told him, 'no different than sitting here with you. At first – the first few times, that is – you feel obscenely naked, with just your mind and not your body . . .'

'And your mind wanders all about?'

'Well, no. It could, of course, but it doesn't. Usually you stuff yourself inside the machine you took along with you.'

'Machine?'

'A monitoring contraption. It picks up all the data, gets it down on tape. You get the entire picture. Not just what you see yourself – although it's not actually seeing; it's sensing – but you get it all, everything that can possibly be caught. In theory, and largely in practice, the machine picks up the data, and the mind is there for interpretation only.'

'And what do you see?'

Blaine laughed. 'Father, that would take longer than either of us have.'

'Nothing like on Earth?'

'Not often, for there are not too many Earth-like planets. Proportionately, that is. There are, in fact, quite a lot in number. But we're not limited to Earth-like planets. We can go anywhere it is possible for the machine to function, and the way those machines are engineered, that means almost anywhere . . .'

'Even to the heart of another sun?'

'Not the machine. It would be destroyed. I imagine that the mind could. But it's not been done. So far as I know, that is.'

'And your feelings? What do you think?'

'I observe,' said Blaine. 'That is what I go for.'

'You do not get the feeling you're lord of all creation? You do not have the thought that Man holds all the universe in the hollow of his hand?'

'If it's the sin of pride and vanity you're thinking of, no, never. You sometimes get a thrill at knowing where you are. You're often filled with wonder, but more often you are puzzled. You are reminded, again and yet again, of how insignificant you are. And there are times when you forget that you are human. You're just a blob of life – brother to everything that ever existed or ever will exist.'

'And you think of God?'

'No,' said Blaine. 'I can't say I ever do.'

'That is too bad,' said Father Flanagan. 'It is rather frightening. To be out there alone . . .'

'Father, at the very start I made it plain to you that I was not inclined to be a religious sort of man – not in the accepted sense, that is. And I played square with you.'

'So you did,' said Father Flanagan.

'And if your next question is going to be: Could a religious man go out to the stars and still retain his faith; could he go out and come back full of faith; would traveling to the stars take away something of the true belief he held? Then I'd have to ask you to define your terms.'

'My terms?' asked Father Flanagan, amazed.

'Yes, faith, for one thing. What do you mean by faith? Is faith enough for Man? Should he be satisfied with faith alone? Is there no way of finding out the truth? Is the attitude of faith, of believing in something for which there can be no more than philosophic proof, the true mark of a Christian? Or should the Church long since—'

Father Flanagan raised a hand. 'My son!' he said. 'My son!'

'Forget it, Father. I should not have said it.'

They sat for a moment, regarding one another; neither understanding. As if we were two aliens, thought Blaine. With viewpoints that did not come within a million miles of coinciding, and yet they both were men.

'I am truly sorry, Father.'

'No need to be. You said it. There are others who believe it, or think it, but would never say it. You at least are honest.'

He reached out and patted Blaine slowly on the arm.

'You are a telepath?' he asked.

'And a teleporter. But limited. Very limited.'

'And that is all?'

'I don't know. I've never dug around.'

'You mean you may have other abilities you are not aware of?'

'Look, Father, in PK you have a certain mental capacity. First, you are the simple things, the easy things – the telepath, the teleport, the huncher. You go on from there – or there are some who do. You grow. Some stop growing after a time and others keep on growing. Each of these abilities is not a separate ability; the abilities themselves are simply manifestations of a wholeness of the mind. They are, lumped together, the mind working as it always should have worked, even from the very first, if it had had its chance.'

'And it is not evil?'

'Certainly. Wrongly used, it's evil. And it was wrongly used by a lot of people, a lot of amateurs who never took the time to understand or to analyze the power they had. But Man has misused his hands, as well. He killed, he stole—'

'And you are not a warlock?'

Blaine wanted to laugh – the laugh was rising in him – but he could not laugh. There was too much terror for a man to laugh.

'No, Father, I swear to you. I am not a warlock. Nor a were-wolf. Nor a—'

The old man raised his hand and stopped him.

'Now we're even,' he declared. 'I, too, said something I should not have said.'

He rose stiffly from the bunk and held out his hand, the fingers twisted by arthritis or whatever it was that might be wrong with them.

'Thank you,' he said. 'God help you.'

'And you'll be here tonight?'

'Tonight?'

'When the people of this town come to take me out and hang me? Or do they burn them at the stake?'

The old man's face twisted in revulsion. 'You must not think such things. Surely not in this—'

'They burned down the Trading Post. They would have killed the factor.'

'That was wrong,' said Father Flanagan. 'I told them that it was. For I am certain members of my parish participated. Not that they were alone in it, for there were many others. But they should have known better. I have worked for years among them against this very sort of thing.'

Blaine put out his hand and grasped the hand of Father Flanagan. The crippled fingers closed with a warm, hard grip.

'The sheriff is a good man,' said the priest. 'He will do his best. I will talk to some of them myself.'

'Thank you, Father.'

'My son, are you afraid to die?'

'I don't know. I have often thought I wouldn't be. I'll have to wait and see.'

'You must have faith.'

'Perhaps I will. If ever I can find it. You'll say a prayer for me?'

'God watch over you. I'll pray away the blessed afternoon.'

10

Blaine stood at the window and watched them gather in the dusk – not quickly, but slowly; not boisterously, but quietly, almost nonchalantly, as if they might be coming into town for a program at the schoolhouse or a meeting of the grange or some other normal and entirely routine function.

He could hear the sheriff stirring quietly about in the office across the corridor and he wondered if the sheriff knew – although assuredly he did, for he had lived in this town long enough to know what it was apt to do.

Blaine stood at the window and reached up and grasped the metal bars, and out beyond the bars, somewhere in the unkempt trees on the courthouse lawn, a bird was singing his last song of evening before cuddling on a branch and going fast asleep.

And as he stood there watching, the Pinkness crept out of its corner and floated in his mind, expanding until it filled his mind.

I have come to be with you, it seemed to say. *I am done with hiding. I know about you now. I have explored every nook and cranny of you and I know the kind of thing you are. And through you, the kind of world you're in – and the kind of world I'm in, for it is my world now.*

No more foolishness? asked that part of the strange duality that continued to be Blaine.

No more foolishness, said the other. *No more screaming, no more running, no more trying to get out.*

Except there was no death. There was no such thing as death, for the ending of a life was inexplicable. It simply could not happen, although dimly, far back in memory, there seemed there had been others it might have happened to.

Blaine left the window and went back to sit down on the bunk and he was remembering now. But the memories were dim and they came from far away and from very long ago and one could not be sure at once if they were truly memories or if they were no more than quaint imagining.

For there were many planets and many different peoples and a host of strange ideas and there were jumbled bits of cosmic information that lay all helter-skelter like a pile of ten billion heaped-up jackstraws.

'How are you feeling?' asked the sheriff, who had come so quietly across the corridor that Blaine had not heard him coming.

Blaine jerked up his head. 'Why, all right, I suppose. I have just been watching your friends out across the street.'

The sheriff chuckled thinly. 'No need to fear,' he said. 'They haven't got the guts to even cross the street. If they do, I'll go and talk with them.'

'Even if they know that I am Fishhook?'

'That's one thing,' the sheriff said, 'that they wouldn't know.'

'You told the priest.'

'That's different,' said the sheriff. 'I had to tell the father.'

'And he would tell no one?'

'Why should he?' asked the sheriff.

And there was no answer; it was one of those questions which could not be answered.

'And you sent a message.'

'But not to Fishhook. To a friend who'll send it on to Fishhook.'

'It was wasted effort,' Blaine told him. 'You should not have bothered. Fishhook knows where I am.'

For they'd have hounders on the trail by now; they would have picked up the trail many hours ago. There had been but one chance for him to have escaped – to have traveled rapidly and very much alone.

They might be in this very town tonight, he thought, and a surge of hope flowed through him. For Fishhook would scarcely let a posse do him in.

Blaine got up from the bunk and crossed over to the window.

'You better get out there now,' he told the sheriff. 'They're already across the street.'

For they had to hurry, naturally. They must get what they had to do done quickly before the fall of deeper night. When darkness fell in all obscurity, they must be snug inside their homes, with the doors double-locked and barred, with the shutters fastened, with the drapes drawn tight, with the hex signs bravely hanging at every opening. For then, and only then, would they be safe from the hideous forces that prowled the outer darkness, from banshee and werewolf, from vampire, goblin, sprite.

He heard the sheriff turning and going back across the corridor, back into the office. Metal scraped as a gun was taken from a rack, and there was a hollow clicking as the sheriff broke the breech and fed shells into the barrels.

The mob moved like a dark and flowing blanket and it came in utter silence aside from the shuffling of its feet.

Blaine watched it, fascinated, as if it were a thing that stood apart from him, as if it were a circumstance which concerned him not at all. And that was strange, he told himself knowing it was strange, for the mob was coming for him.

But it made no difference, for there was no death. Death was something that made no sense at all and nothing to be thought of. It was a foolish wastefulness and not to be tolerated.

And who was it that said that?

For he knew that there was death – that there must be death if there were evolution, that death was one of the mechanisms that biologically spelled progress and advancement for evolutionary species.

You, he said to the thing within his mind – a thing that was a thing no longer, but was a part of him – *it is your idea. Death is something that you can't accept.*

But something that in all truth must surely be accepted. For it was an actuality, it was an ever-presence, it was something that everything must live with through the shortness of its life.

There was death and it was close – much too close for comfort or denial. It was in the mumble of the mob just outside the building, the mob that now had passed from sight and quit its shuffling, that even now was massed outside the courthouse entrance, arguing with the sheriff. For the sheriff's booming voice came clearly through the outer door, calling upon those outside to break up and go back to their homes.

'All that this will get you,' yelled the sheriff, 'is a belly full of shot.'

But they yelled back at him, and the sheriff yelled again and it went back and forth for quite a little while. Blaine stood at the inner bars and waited, and fear seeped into him, slowly at first, then faster, like an evil tide racing through his blood.

Then the sheriff was coming through the door and there were three men with him – angry men and frightened, but so purposeful and grim their fright was covered up.

The sheriff came across the office and into the corridor, with the shotgun hanging limply from his hand. The other three strode close upon his heels.

The sheriff stopped just outside the bars and looked at Blaine, trying to conceal the sheepishness he wore.

'I am sorry, Blaine,' he said, 'but I just can't do it. These folks are friends of mine. I was raised with a lot of them. I can't bear to shoot them down.'

'Of course you can't,' said Blaine, 'you yellow-bellied coward.'

'Give me them keys,' snarled one of the three. 'Let's get him out of here.'

'They're hanging on the nail beside the door,' the sheriff said.

He glanced at Blaine.

'There's nothing I can do,' he said.

'You can go off and shoot yourself,' said Blaine. 'I'd highly recommend it.'

The man came with the key, and the sheriff stepped aside. The key rattled in the lock.

Blaine said to the man opening the door. 'There is one thing I want understood. I walk out of here alone.'

'Huh!' said the man.

'I said I want to walk alone. I will not be dragged.'

'You'll come the way we want you,' growled the man.

'It's a small thing,' the sheriff urged. 'It wouldn't hurt to let him.'

The man swung the cell door open. 'All right, come on,' he said.

Blaine stepped out into the corridor, and the three men closed in, one on either side of him, the other one behind. They did not raise a hand to touch him. The man with the keys flung them to the floor. They made a clashing sound that filled the corridor, that set Blaine's teeth on edge.

It was happening, thought Blaine. Incredible as it seemed, it was happening to him.

'Get on, you stinking parry,' said the man behind him and punched him in the back.

'You wanted to walk,' said another. 'Leave us see you walk.'

Blaine walked, steadily and straight, concentrating on each step to make sure he did not stumble. For he must not stumble; he must do nothing to disgrace himself.

Hope still lived, he told himself. There still was a chance that someone from Fishhook might be out there, set to snatch him from them. Or that Harriet had gotten help and was coming back or was already here. Although that, he told himself, was quite unlikely. She'd not had time enough and she could not have known the urgency involved.

He marched with steady stride across the sheriff's office and down the hall to the outer door, the three men who were with him pressing close against him.

Someone was holding the outer door, with a gesture of mock politeness, so he could pass through.

He hesitated for an instant, terror sweeping over him. For if he passed that door, if he stood upon the steps outside, if he faced the waiting mob, then all hope was gone.

'Go on, you filthy bastard,' growled the man behind him. 'They are waiting out there for you.'

The man put a hand behind his shoulder blades and shoved. Blaine staggered for a step or two, then was walking straight again.

And now he was across the doorway, now he faced the crowd!

An animal sound came boiling up from it – a sound of intermingled hate and terror, like the howling of a pack of wolves on a bloody trail, like the snarling of the tiger that is tired of waiting, with something in it, too, of the whimper of the cornered animal, hunted to its death.

And these, thought Blaine, with a queer detached corner of his mind, *were* the hunted animals – the people on the run. Here was the terror and the hate and envy of the uninitiate, here the frustration of those who had been left out, here the intolerance and the smuggery of those who refused to understand, the rear guard of an old order holding the narrow pass against the outflankers of the future.

They would kill him as they had killed others, as they would kill many more, but their fate was already settled, the battle already had been won.

Someone pushed him from behind and he went skidding down the smooth stone steps. He slipped and fell and rolled, and the mob closed in upon him. There were many hands upon him, there were fingers grinding into muscles, there was the hot foul breath and the odor of their mouths blowing in his face.

The many hands jerked him to his feet and pushed him back and forth. Someone punched him in the belly and another slapped him hard across the face and out of the bull-roaring of the crowd came one bellowing voice: 'Go on, you stinking parry, teleport yourself! That's all you have to do. Just teleport yourself.'

58

And that was most fitting mockery – for there were very few indeed who could teleport themselves. There were the levitators who could move themselves through the air like birds, and there were many others, like Blaine, who could teleport small objects, and others, also like Blaine, who could teleport their minds over many light years, but with the help of weird machines. But the true self-teleport, who could snap his body from one location to another in the fraction of an instant, was extremely hard to come by.

The crowd took up the mocking chant: 'Teleport yourself! Teleport! Teleport! Teleport yourself, you dirty, stinking parry!' Laughing all the time at their cleverness, smirking all the time at the indignity thus heaped upon their victim. And never for a moment ceasing to use hands and feet upon him.

There was a warmness running down his chin, and one lip felt puffed and swollen, and there was a saltiness in his mouth. His belly ached and his ribs were sore, and the feet and fists still kept punching in.

Then another bellowing voice roared about the din: 'Cut that out! Leave the man alone!'

The crowd fell back, but they still ringed him in, and Blaine, standing in the center of the human circle, looked around it and in the last faint light of dusk saw the rat eyes gleaming, and flaked saliva on the lips, sensed the hate that rose and rolled toward him like a body smell.

The circle parted and two men came through – one a small and fussy man who might have been a bookkeeper or a clerk, and the other a massive bruiser with a face that looked as if it were a place where chickens scratched in their search for grubs and worms. The big man had a rope coiled on one arm and from his hand he dangled one end of the rope fashioned very neatly into a hangman's noose.

The two of them stopped in front of Blaine, and the small man turned slightly to face one segment of the circle.

'Gents,' he said, in a voice that any funeral director would have been proud to own, 'we must conduct ourselves with a certain decency and dignity. We have nothing personal against this man, only against the system and the abomination of which he is a part.'

'You tell 'em, Buster!' yelled an enthusiastic voice from the fringes of the crowd.

The man with the funeral director's voice held up a hand for silence.

'It is a sad and solemn duty,' he said unctuously, 'that we must perform, but it is a duty. Let us proceed with it in a seemly fashion.'

'Yeah,' yelled the enthusiast, 'let us get it done with. Let's hang the dirty bastard!'

The big man came close to Blaine and lifted up the noose. He dropped it almost gently over Blaine's head so that it rested on his shoulders. Then he slowly tightened it until it was snug about the neck.

The rope was new and prickly and it burned like a red-hot iron, and the numbness that had settled into Blaine's body ran out of him like water and left him standing cold and empty and naked before all eternity.

All the time, even while it had been happening, he had clung subconsciously to the firm conviction that it could not happen – that he couldn't die this way; that it could and did happen to many other people, but not to Shepherd Blaine.

And now death was only minutes distant; the instrument of death already put in place. These men – these men he did not know, these men he'd never know – were about to take his life.

He tried to lift his hands to snatch the rope away, but his arms would not stir from where they hung limply from his shoulders. He gulped, for there already was the sense of slow, painful, strangulation.

And they hadn't even begun to hang him yet!

The coldness of his empty self grew colder with the chill of overwhelming fear – fear that took him in its fist and held him stiff and rigid while it froze him solid. The blood, it seemed, stopped running in his veins and he seemed to have no body and the ice piled up and up inside his brain until he thought his skull would burst.

And from some far nether region of that brain came the fleeting realization that he no longer was a man, but mere frightened animal. Too cold, still too proud to whimper, too frozen in his terror to move a single muscle – only kept from screaming because his frozen tongue and throat could no longer function.

But if he could not scream aloud, he screamed inside himself. And the scream built up and up, a mounting tension that could find no way to effect release. And he knew that if no release were found in another instant he would blow apart from the sheer pressure of the tension.

There was a split second – not of blackout, but of unawareness – then he stood alone and he was cold no longer.

He stood on the crumbling brick of the ancient walk that led up to the courthouse entrance, and the rope was still about his neck, but there was no one in the courthouse square.

He was all alone in an empty town!

11

There was less of dusk and more of light and there was a quietness that was unimaginable.

There was no grass.

There were no trees.

There were no men, nor any sign of men.

The courthouse lawn, or what had been the lawn, stretched naked down to the asphalt street. There was no grass upon the lawn. It was soil and pebble. Not dried-out grass or killed-out grass, but not any grass at all. As if there had never been such a thing as grass. As if grass never had existed.

With the rope still trailing from his neck, Blaine slowly pivoted to look in all directions. And in all directions it was the self-same scene. The courthouse still stood starkly against the last light of the day. The street was still and empty, with cars parked at the curb. The store fronts lined the street, their windows staring blindly.

There was one tree – lone and dead – standing at the corner beside the barber shop.

And no men anywhere. No birds or song of birds. No dogs. No cats. Nor an insect humming. Perhaps, thought Blaine, not even a bacteria or a microbe.

Cautiously, almost as if afraid by doing so he might break the spell, Blaine put up his hands and loosened the rope. He slipped it over his head and tossed it to the ground. He massaged his neck carefully with one hand, for the neck still stung. There were little prickles in it, where tiny pieces of the fiber had broken off and still stuck in the skin.

He took a tentative step and found that he could walk, although his body still was sore from the casual beating it had taken. He walked out into the street and stood in the middle of it and looked up and down its length. It was deserted so far as he could see.

The sun had set, and dark was not far off and that meant, he told himself, that he had come back just a little time.

And stood astounded, frozen in the middle of the street, that he should have known.

For he did know! Without a doubt he knew exactly what he had accomplished. Although he thought, he must have done it without a conscious effort, almost instinctively, a sort of conditioned reflex action to escape the danger.

It was something that he had no way of knowing how to do, that a short minute earlier he would have sworn would be impossible that he do. It was something that no human had ever done before, that no human would have ever dreamed of trying.

For he had moved through time. He had gone into the past a half an hour or so.

He stood in the street, attempting to recall how he might have done it, but all he could remember was the mounting terror that had come rolling, wave on wave, to drown him. There was one answer only: He had done it as a matter of deep-seated knowledge which he had not been aware of having and had accomplished it only as a final, desperate, instinctive effort – as one might, without thinking, throw up an arm to ward off an unexpected blow.

As a human it would have been beyond his capability, but it would not, undoubtedly, have been impossible for the alien mind. As a human being he did not have the instinct, did not have even the beginning of the necessary know-how. It was an ability even outside the pale of paranormal action. There was no question of it: the only way he could have snapped himself through time was by the agency and through the courtesy of the alien mind.

But the alien mind, it seemed, had left him; it was no longer with him. He hunted it and called it, and there was no trace and there was no answer.

He turned to face the north and began to walk, keeping to the center of the street, marching through this ghost town of the past.

The graveyard of the past, he thought. No life anywhere. Just the dead, bare stone and brick, the lifeless clay and wood.

And where had gone the life?

Why must the past be dead?

And what had happened to that mind the alien on the distant star had exchanged with him?

He sought for it again and he could not find it, but he did find traces of it; he found the spoor of it, tiny, muddy footprints that went across his brain; he found bits and pieces that it had left behind – strange, chaotic memories and straws of exotic, disconnected information that floated like flecks of jetsam in a frothy tide.

He did not find it, but he found the answer to its going – the instinctive answer that suddenly was there. The mind had not gone and left him. It had, rather, finally, become a part of him. In the forge of fright and terror, in the chemistry of danger, there had been a psychologic factor that had welded the two of them together.

And yet he still was human. Therefore, he told himself, the answer must be false. But it kept on persisting. There was no reason to it and there was no logic – for if he had two minds, if he were half human and half alien, there would be a difference. A difference he would notice.

The business part of the street had dwindled to shabby residences, and up ahead of him he could see where the village ended – this village which half an hour ago (or a half an hour ahead?) had been most intent upon the killing of him.

He halted for a moment and looked back and he could see the courthouse cupola and remembered that he'd left everything he owned back there, locked in the sheriff's desk. He hesitated a moment, wondering if he should go back. It was a terrible thing to be without a dollar to his name, with all his pockets empty.

If he went back, he thought, he could steal a car. If there were none with the keys left in the lock, he could short-circuit the ignition. He should have thought of it before, he told himself. The cars were standing there, waiting to be taken.

He turned and started back. He took two steps, then wheeled about again.

He didn't dare to go back. For he was safely out. There was nothing that could persuade him – money or car or anything – to go back into the village.

The light was waning and he headed northward, settling down to rolling up some distance – not running, but walking fast, with long, loose strides that ate up the very road.

He passed out of the village and came into the country and here there was an even greater loneliness, an even greater barrenness. A few dead cottonwoods lined the stream that ran down the valley, and ghostly fence posts stood in ragged rows – but the land was naked, without a weed, without a blade of grass. And the wind had a crying in it as it swept across the wasteland.

The darkness deepened and the moon came up, a blotch-faced mirror with the silver cracked and blackened, to cast a pallid light upon the arid stretch of earth.

He reached a rough plank bridge that crossed the tiny stream and stopped to rest a second and glance back along his trail. Nothing moved; there was nothing following. The village was some miles behind, and up on the hill above the stream stood the ramshackle bones of some forgotten farm – a barn, what looked like a hog pen, several dilapidated outhouses and the house itself.

Blaine stood and sucked the air into his lungs, and it seemed to him that the very air itself was dead. It had no sparkle in it. There was no smell in it and hardly any taste.

He reached out a hand to rest it on the bridge, and his hand went through the plank. It reached the plank and went into the plank and through it and there was nothing there. There wasn't any plank; there wasn't any bridge.

He tried again. For, he told himself, he might have missed it, he might have reached out for it and fallen short of it and only imagined his hand going through the plank. Moonlight, he reminded himself, is tricky stuff to see by.

So this time he was very careful.

His hand still went through the plank.

He back away from the bridge for a step or two, for it suddenly had become a thing – not of menace, perhaps – but a thing of which one must be very careful. It was nothing to depend on. It was a fantasy and delusion; it was a ghost that stood spraddled on the road. If he had walked out on it, he told himself, or tried to walk upon it, he would have been tumbled down into the stream bed.

And the dead trees and the fence posts – were they delusions, too?

He stood stock-still as the thought came to him: Was it all delusion? For an illogical moment he did not dare to stir, scarcely dared to breathe, for any disturbance he might make might send this frail and unreal place crashing down into the dust of dreary nothingness.

But the ground was solid underneath his feet, or it seemed quite solid. He pressed one foot hard against it, and the ground still held. Cautiously he lowered himself to his knees and felt the ground with spread-out hand, kneading his fingers against it as if to test its consistency, running his fingers through the dust down to the hardness of the earth.

This was foolishness, he told himself, angry with himself – for he had walked this road and it had not shattered beneath the impact of his footsteps; it had held up beneath him.

But even so this was a place where one could not be sure; this was a place where there seemed to be no rules. Or at least a place where you were forced to figure out the rules, like: *Roads are real, but bridges aren't.*

Although it wasn't that, at all. It was something else. It would all basically have to do with the fact there was no life within this world.

This was the past and it was the dead past; there were only corpses in it – and perhaps not even corpses, but the shadows of those corpses. For the dead tree and the fence posts and the bridges and the buildings on the hill all would classify as shadows. There was no life here; the life was up ahead. Life must occupy but a single point in time, and as time moved forward, life moved with it. And so was gone, thought Blaine, any dream that Man might have ever held of visiting the past and living in the action and the thought and viewpoint of men who'd long been dust. For the living past did not exist, nor did the human past except in the records of the past. The present was the only valid point for life – life kept moving on, keeping pace with the present, and once it had passed, all traces of it or its existences were carefully erased.

There were certain basic things, perhaps – the very earth, itself – which existed through every point in time, holding a sort of limited eternity to provide a solid matrix. And the dead – the dead and fabricated – stayed in the past as ghosts. The fence posts and the wire strung on them, the dead trees, the farm buildings and the bridge were shadows of the present persisting in the past. Persisting, perhaps, reluctantly, because since they had no life they could not move along. They were bound in time and stretched through time and they were long, long shadows.

He was, he realized with a shock, the only living thing existing in this moment on this earth. He and nothing else.

He rose from his knees and dusted off his hands. He stood looking at the bridge, and in the brightness of the moonlight there seemed nothing wrong with it. And yet he knew the wrongness of it.

Trapped, he thought. If he did not know how to get out of here, then surely he was trapped – and he did not know.

There was nothing in all of human experience which gave him any chance or any hope to know.

He stood silent in the road, wondering how human he could be, how much humanity there still might be left to him. And if he were not entirely human, if there still were alienness, then he had a chance.

He felt human, he told himself – yet how was he to judge? For he still would be *himself* if he were entirely alien. Human, half human, or not human in the slightest, he still would be himself. He'd scarcely know the difference. There was no other outside point from which he would stand and judge himself with anything like objectivity.

He (or whatever he might be) had known in a time of terror and of panic how to slip into the past, and it stood to reason that, knowing that, he likewise should know how to slide back into the present, or what had been his present – back to that point in time, whatever one might call it, where life was possible.

But the hard, cold fact was there: He had no idea of how it might be done!

He looked about him, at the antiseptic coldness of the moonlight-painted land, and a shudder started at the core of him. He tried to stop the shudder, for he recognized it as the prelude to unreasoned terror, but the shudder would not stop.

He gritted mental teeth, and the shudder kept on growing and suddenly he knew – with one corner of his mind, he knew.

Then there was the sound of wind blowing in the cottonwoods – and there'd been no cottonwoods before. Something, too, had happened to the shudder, for it was there no longer. He was himself again.

There were insects, fiddling stridently somewhere in the grass and bushes, and there were flecks of light moving in the night to betray the lightning bug. And through the shuttered window of the house up on the hill came thin, strangled shafts of light.

He turned off the road and walked down into the stream bed, stepped through the foot-deep water and up the other bank among the cottonwoods.

He was back again, back where he'd started from. He'd come from past to present and he'd done it by himself. For a fleeting moment, at the very end of it, he had caught the method, but it had slipped from him again and he did not know it now.

But that did not matter. He was safely home.

12

He woke before morning light, when the birds first began to chirp, and made his way up the hill to the garden patch just below the house. He got three ears of corn, he dug into a hill of potatoes, he dug up a butcher plant and noted with some satisfaction that it had four steaks upon it.

Back in the grove of cottonwoods, he searched through his pockets until he found the book of matches the sheriff had let him keep of all the stuff he had. He flipped back the cover and saw there were three matches left.

Regarding the three matches gravely, he thought of that day long ago when he had to pass a Boy Scout test by the lighting of a fire with a single match. Was he that good now? he wondered, chuckling at the thought.

He found a dead tree trunk and dug into the heart of it to get punk that was powder-dry. He selected dead, dry twigs. He rustled up some bigger wood, still paying close attention to its dryness, for the fire must be as smokeless as it was possible to make it. There was every reason he should not advertise his presence.

On the road above him the first car of the day went past, and far off a cow was bellowing.

The fire started on the second match, and he nursed it carefully, building it bit by bit with the adding of more twigs and finally larger twigs until there came a time when he could put on some of the bigger wood. The fire burned clear and smokeless, and he sat down beside it to wait for it to burn into a bed of coals.

The sun was not yet up, but the light in the east was growing brighter and there was a coolness on the land. Below him the creek ran chattering across its bed of pebbles. Blaine drew in a deep breath of the morning air and it tasted good.

He was still alive and in the land of other people and he had food to put into his belly – but what did he do next? He had no money – he had nothing but a single match and the clothes he stood in. And he had a mind that would betray him – a mind, the old crone had said, that would bounce back at you. He would be a sitting duck for any peeper, any spotter, that should chance across him.

He could hide by day and walk by night, for it would be safe to be abroad at night when others kept inside. He could raid orchards and gardens for his food. He could keep alive and make a few miles every night, but it would be slow going.

There must, he told himself, be some other way.

He put more wood on the fire and it still burned bright without any smoke. He went down to the stream and lay flat upon his belly and drank from the singing water.

Had he been mistaken, he asked himself, to run away from Fishhook? No matter what had awaited him in Fishhook, the situation in which he now found himself probably was worse. For he was a fugitive now from everyone; there was no one he could trust.

He lay staring down into the stream bed, looking at the pebbles – looking at one pebble, a red one that gleamed like polished ruby. He took the pebble into his mind and he saw what it was made of and the structure of its crystals and he knew where it had come from and he could trace its wanderings through millenia.

Then he tossed it from his mind and took in another pebble, a shiny bit of quartz—

There was something wrong here!

This was something he'd never done before!

And yet he had been doing it as if it were a commonplace performance and nothing at which one should wonder.

He pushed his body up and hunkered by the stream, his human sense aghast, but still not entirely startled – for he was still himself, no matter what he was.

He sought the alienness again and it wasn't there; it did not reveal itself, but he knew that it was there. It still was there, he knew, with its grab bag of senseless memories, with its cockeyed abilities, with its crazy logic and its topsy-turvy values.

In his mind's eye he saw a strange parade of purple geometric figures lurching across a desert of pure gold, with a blood-red sun hanging in a sulfur sky and nothing else in sight. And in the fleetness of that moment he knew the location of the place and the meaning of it and coordinates of a fantastic cosmographic system that could get him there. Then it was gone – the figures and the knowledge.

He got slowly to his feet and went back to the fire and by this time there was a bed of coals. He found a stick and scratched out a hollow in the coals and put in the potatoes and the corn, still wrapped in its husks, and used the stick to scratch the coals back across the hollow. Breaking a green branch off a sapling, he used it as a fork to broil one of the steaks.

Squatted beside the fire, with the warmth of it upon his face and hands, he felt a smug contentment that seemed strangely out of place – the contentment of a man who had reduced his needs to the strictly basic – and with the contentment came a full-bodied confidence that was just as out of place. It seemed almost as if he could look ahead and see that everything would be all right. But it was not prescience. There were hunchers who had prescience or who seemed to have it, but he was not one of them. It was rather as if he could sense ahead of him the pattern of all rightness, but with no specific detail, with no idea of the future's shape, nor of its direction. An assurance only, something that was akin to plain, old-fashioned hunch, a feeling for the future – but nothing more than that.

The steak was sizzling and he could smell the potato baking and he grinned at steak and baked potato as a breakfast menu. Although it was all right. There was nothing at the moment that was not all right.

He remembered Dalton slumped spineless in the chair, with the clenched cigar and the brush-pile hair, raging at the butcher plant as another outrage committed upon the businessman by the maliciousness of Fishhook. And he tried to recall from what planet of which sun the butcher plant had come and the name, it seemed to him, should be at his command, although he could not put it on his tongue.

The butcher plant, he thought, and how many other things? What would be the total score if all of Fishhook's contributions should be totaled up?

There were the drugs, for one thing, an entire new pharmacopoeia brought from other stars to alleviate and to cure the ills of Man. And as a result of this, all of Man's old bugaboos, all of his old killers, were being held at bay. Given another generation – given, at the most, two more generations – and the entire concept of illness would be wiped off the human slate. The human race would then emerge as a people healthful both in body and in mind.

There were new fabrics and new metals and many different foodstuffs. There were new architectural ideas and materials; there were new perfumes, unfamiliar literatures, alien principles in art. And there was dimensino, an entertainment medium that had replaced all the standard human entertainment – the movies, radio and TV.

For in dimensino you did not merely see and hear; you participated. You became a part of the portrayed situation. You identified yourself with one of the characters, or with more than one of them, and you lived out the action and emotion. For a time you ceased to be yourself; you became the person of your choice in the drama dimensino created.

Almost every home had its dimensino room, rigged with the apparatus, which picked up the weird, alien impulses that made you someone else – that lifted you out of the commonplace, out of the humdrum rut of your ordinary life and sent you off on wild adventure or on strange assignments or pitched you headlong into exotic places and fantastic situations.

And all of these, the food, the fabrics, the dimensino, were monopolies of Fishhook.

For all of these, thought Blaine, Fishhook had gained the hatred of the people – the hatred of not understanding, of being left outside, of being helped as no other single agency had ever helped the human race.

The steak was done, and Blaine propped the greenwood stick against a bush while he dug into the coals to hook out the potatoes and the corn.

He sat beside the fire and ate as the sun came up and the breeze died down and the world, on the threshold of another day, appeared to hold its breath. The first sunlight came through the grove of cottonwoods and turned some of the leaves into golden coins, and the brook grew hushed as the daytime sounds took up – the bawling of the cattle on the hill above, the hum of cars passing on the road, the distant drone of a cruising plane far up in the sky.

On the road, down by the bridge, a closed panel truck pulled up and stopped. The driver got out and lifted the hood and crawled halfway under it. Then he crawled out again and went back to the cab. Inside of it he hunted until he found what he was looking for, then got out again. He placed a kit of tools on the fender and unwrapped it, and the clinking of the tools as he unwrapped them came clearly up the hill.

It was an ancient truck – gas engine and with wheels, but it had some jet assistance. There were not many such vehicles left, except, perhaps, in junk yards.

An independent operator, Blaine told himself. Getting along the best he could, competing with the big truck lines by cutting down his rates and keeping down his overhead in any way he could.

The truck's original paint had faded and peeled off in places, but painted over this, in sharp fresh color, were complicated hex signs, guaranteed, no doubt, to fend off the evil of the world.

The truck, Blaine saw, had an Illinois license.

The driver got his tools laid out, then crawled back beneath the hood. The sound of hammering and the screech of stubborn, rusty bolts floated up the hill.

Blaine finished off his breakfast. There were two steaks left and two potatoes and by now the coals were growing black. He stirred up the coals and put on more wood, speared the two steaks on the stick and broiled them carefully.

The pounding and the screeching kept on beneath the hood. A

couple of times the man crept out and rested, then went back to work.

When the steaks were finished, Blaine put the two potatoes in his pocket and went marching down the hill, carrying the two steaks on their stick as another man might take a banner into battle.

At the sound of his footsteps crunching on the road, the driver came out from beneath the hood and turned around to face him.

'Good morning,' said Blaine, being as happy as he could. 'I saw you down here while I was getting breakfast.'

The driver regarded him with considerable suspicion.

'I had some food left over,' Blaine told him, 'so I cooked it up for you. Although, perhaps, you've eaten.'

'No, I haven't,' said the driver, with a show of interest. 'I intended to in the town just down the road, but it was still closed tight.'

'Well, then,' said Blaine and handed him the stick with the two steaks impaled upon it.

The man took the stick and held it as if he feared that it might bite him. Blaine dug in his pockets and pulled out the two potatoes.

'There was some corn,' he said, 'but I ate it all. There were only three ears of it.'

'You mean you're giving this to me?'

'Certainly,' said Blaine. 'Although you can throw it back into my face if that's the way you feel.'

The man grinned uneasily. 'I sure could use it,' he declared. 'The next town is thirty miles and with this,' he gestured at the truck, 'I don't know when I'll get there.'

'There isn't any salt,' said Blaine, 'but it's not so bad without it.'

'Well,' said the man, 'since you've been so kind . . .'

'Sit down,' said Blaine, 'and eat. What's the matter with the engine?'

'I'm not sure. Could be the carburetor.'

Blaine took off his jacket and folded it. He laid it neatly on the fender. He rolled up his sleeves.

The man found a seat on a rock beside the road and began to eat.

Blaine picked up a wrench and climbed up on the fender.

'Say,' said the man, 'where did you get this stuff?'

'Up on the hill,' said Blaine. 'The farmer had a lot of it.'

'You mean you stole it?'

'Well, what would you do if you were out of work and had no money and were trying to get home?'

'Whereabouts is home?'

'Up in South Dakota.'

The man took a big bite of steak, and his mouth became so full he could talk no longer.

Blaine ducked underneath the hood and saw that the driver had all but one bolt loose on the carburetor mounting. He put the wrench on it, and the bolt screeched metallic protest.

'Damn thing rusted tight,' said the driver, watching Blaine.

Blaine finally freed the bolt and lifted out the carburetor. He walked over with it and sat down beside the eating man.

'Rig's about ready to fall apart,' the driver said. 'Wasn't much to start with. Been having trouble with it all the way. My schedule's shot to hell.'

Blaine found a smaller wrench that fitted the bolts on the carburetor assembly and began to wrestle with the threads.

'Tried driving at night,' said the man, 'but not for me. Not after that first time. Too risky!'

'See something?'

'If it hadn't been for those signs I painted on the truck, I would have been a goner. I have a shotgun with me, but it doesn't do no good. Can't drive and handle a gun at the self-same time.'

'Probably wouldn't do you any good even if you could.'

'I tell you, mister,' said the driver. 'I am set for them. I have a pocket full of shells loaded up with silver shot.'

'Expensive, isn't it?'

'Sure. But you have to be prepared.'

'Yeah,' said Blaine. 'I suppose you do.'

'It's getting worse,' declared the man, 'every blessed year. There is this preacher up north.'

'I hear there are a lot of preachers.'

'Yes, a lot of them. But all they do is talk. This one, he is all set to get some action on it.'

'There she is,' said Blaine, loosening the last bolt. He broke open the carburetor and looked at it.

'There it is,' he said.

The man bent over and looked where Blaine was pointing.

'Damned if it ain't,' he said.

'Have it fixed and back in place in another fifteen minutes. You got an oil can we can squirt these threads?'

The driver got up and wiped his hands on the seat of his trousers. 'I'll look it up,' he said.

He started for the truck, then turned back. He held out his hand. 'My name is Buck,' he said. 'Buck Riley.'

'Blaine. You can call me Shep.'

They shook.

Riley stood undecided, shuffling his feet.

'You say you're heading for Dakota.'

Blaine nodded.

'I'm damn near out of my mind,' said Riley. 'I need someone to help me.'

'Anything I can do to help?' asked Blaine.

'Would you drive at night?'

'Hell, yes,' said Blaine.

'You could drive and I could have the shotgun ready.'

'You'll need to get some sleep.'

'We'll manage that, the both of us, somehow or other. We have to keep this wagon rolling. I've lost too much time for comfort.'

'You're going South Dakota way?'

Riley nodded. 'You'll go with me, then?'

'Glad to,' said Blaine. 'It beats walking any time.'

'There'll be some money in it for you. Not much . . .'

'Forget about the money. I just want the ride.'

13

Northeastward out of the southwest they traveled, driving day and night – but not driving all the time; driving, more than likely, not more than half the time. For the truck was no better than a rolling junk heap. They fought with the balky engine, they battled with the old and worn-out tires, they nursed the shaky chassis – and they made some mileage, but not so very much.

The roads were bad, as all roads now were bad. Dead for many years was the old concept of smooth, hard-surfaced, almost polished highways, for they were no longer needed. The traffic in this day was made up almost entirely of cars and trucks that were half planes; there was no need of good roads for vehicles which in their operation never touched the ground.

The old highway surfacing was broken and full of chuckholes. It was rough on tires, and the tires were not too good. Nor were the new ones, even if Riley had been able to afford them, easy to obtain. The demand for tires of the type used by his battered truck had dropped to almost nothing, and it was only by the greatest luck that they could be found.

There also was another ever-present worry – the finding of gasoline to put into the tank. For there were no service stations; there had been no service stations for almost fifty years. There was no need of service stations when highway traffic moved on atomic power. So, at each town they hunted for a farm service store or a co-operative tank farm to obtain their fuel, for the bulk of farm machinery still used gasoline.

They slept as they could, snatching catnaps whenever the chance came up. They ate on the run, usually out of a paper bag of sandwiches or of doughnuts, with coffee in an old tin pail they carried.

Thus the two of them found their way along the ancient highways, used now by the modern traffic only because the engineering of those highways had been good, only because they represented the easiest, shortest distances between two points.

'I never should have took this job,' said Riley, 'but there was good pay in it and I don't mind telling you that I need the money.'

'You'll probably make out all right on it,' Blaine reassured him. 'You may be a few days late, but we'll get through all right.'

'If I have any truck left.'

'You didn't,' Blaine pointed out, 'have very much to start with.'

Riley mopped his face with a faded handkerchief that at one time had been turkey red.

'It's not only the truck and all the work,' he said. 'It's the wear and tear on a man himself.'

For Riley was a frightened man – and the fright, Blaine saw, went down to the bone and core of him.

It was not, Blaine told himself, watching the man, the simple emotional mechanics of a man frightened by the horrific menagerie of mischief and of evil from which, because he had believed in it for his entire life, he could conjure up with no effort whatsoever the terrible fantasies of an age gone past. It was something more than that; it was more immediate than latent night-time fears.

To Blaine the man was an oddity, a human specimen out of some medieval museum; a man who feared the dark and the imagined forms with which he peopled it; a man who placed reliance in a painted hex sign and in a shotgun loaded with a charge of silver buckshot. He had heard of men like this but had never met one. If there had been any such as this among the people that he met in Fishhook, they had kept it closely hidden behind a sophisticated mask.

But if Riley was a curiosity to Blaine, Blaine was likewise one to him.

'You are not afraid?' he'd ask.

Blaine would shake his head.

'You do not believe these things?'

'To me,' Blaine would tell him, 'they have always seemed just a little foolish.'

Riley would protest: 'They are not foolish, friend. I can assure you that. I've known too many people; I've heard too many tales that I know are true. There was an old man when I was a boy back in Indiana. He was found tangled in a fence with his throat ripped out. And there were tracks around the body and the smell of sulfur.'

If it were not this particular story, then it was another, just as gruesome, just as starkly mystic, just as ancient-dark.

And what could one do with that? Blaine wondered. Where would one find an answer? For the belief – the will to believe – was engrained deeply in the human fiber. Not entirely, either, in the matrix of the present situation, but in the blood and bone of Man clear back to the caves. There was in the soul of Man a certain deadly fascination with all things that were macabre. The situation as it stood had been grasped willingly, almost eagerly, by men for whom the world had become a rather tame and vapid place with no terror in it beyond the brute force terror of atomic weapons and the dread uncertainty of unstable men in power.

It had all begun quite innocently as the people grabbed at the new principles of PK for their entertainment and their enjoyment. Almost overnight the fact of mental power had become a fad that had overwhelmed the world. Night clubs had changed their names, there had been startling fashion trends, new teen-age cants had risen, TV had gone overboard with its horror films, and the presses had poured out billions of volumes dealing with the supernatural. There had been new cults, and older cults had flourished. The ouija board came back after two centuries of hiding in the mists of an earlier age which had played with ghosts for kicks but had given up when it had found that you could not play with the spirit world. You either believed in it or you didn't and there was no middle ground.

There had been quacks and there had been earnest men, considerably deluded, who had made names and fortunes from the fad. Manufacturers had turned out carload after carload of novelties and equipment for the pursuance of this new fad, or new hobby, or new study or religion – the specific term would apply in direct proportion to the seriousness with which each individual might consider it.

It all had been wrong, of course – for paranormal kinetics was not supernatural. Nor was it macabre, nor did it deal with ghost or devil or any of the other of the hordes of forgotten things which came charging happily out of the Middle Ages. It was, instead, a new dimension to Man's abilities – but the enamored people, agog at this new toy had adopted it wholeheartedly in all misinterpretation.

As they always did, they had overdone it. They had played so hard at their misinterpretation that they had forgotten, despite warning after warning, that it was misinterpretation. They finally had come to believe in all the weirdness and all the fantasy; they finally regarded it as the gospel truth. Where there had been fun there now were leering fauns; where there had been gags there now were goblins and ghosts.

So the reaction had set in, the inevitable reaction of fanatical reformers, accompanied by the grim, horse-faced cruelty and blindness that goes with all fanatical reform. Now a grim and frightened people hunted down, as a holy mission, their paranormal neighbors.

There were a lot of these, but they were in hiding now or in masquerade. There had always been a lot of them through all the human ages, but mostly unsuspecting, never dreaming that they had powers within themselves fit to reach the stars. They were the people who had been just a little queer, a bit discombobulated and had been regarded tolerantly as harmless by their neighbors. There had been a few, of course, who had been in part effective, but even in their effectiveness they had not believed, or believing, they had used their strange powers poorly, for they could not understand them. And in the later years, when they might have understood it, none of them had dared, for the tribal god of science had called it all damn foolishness.

But when the stubborn men in Mexico had demonstrated that it was not all damn foolishness, then the people dared. Those who had the abilities then felt free to use them, and developed them by use. Others who never suspected that they had them found to their surprise they did and they used them, too. In some cases the abilities were used to good and solid purpose, but in other cases they were wrongly used or used for shallow purpose. And there were those, as well, who practiced this new-found art of theirs for unworthy ends, and a very few, perhaps, who used it in all evil.

Now the good gray moralists and the pulpit-pounding, crag-browed, black-attired reformers were out to quash PK for the evil it had done. They used the psychology of fear; they played upon the natural superstitions; they used the rope and brand and the quick shot in the night and they spread a fear across the land that one could smell in the very air – a thick, foul scent that clogged the nostrils and brought water to the eyes.

'You are lucky,' Riley said to Blaine. 'Not fearing them, you may be safe from them. A dog will bite a man who is afraid of it, but lick the hand of one who is not afraid.'

'The answer's easy, then,' Blaine told him. 'Do not be afraid.'

But it was impossible advice to a man like Riley.

Night after night he sat on the right-hand seat as Blaine drove through the darkness, shivering in terror like a spooky hound, grasping the gun loaded with its silver buckshot.

There were alarms and frights – the swoop of owl, the running of a fox across the road, an imagined roadside shadow, all became an evil out of some darker night, while the howling of coyotes became the wailing of a banshee, hunting for a victim.

But there was more than imagined terror. There was the shadow shaped like a man, but a man no longer, twisting and turning in a lazy dance from a high branch above the thicket; there was the blackened ruins of the roadside farm, with the smoke-streaked chimney standing like an accusing finger pointing up to heaven; there was the smoke from the tiny campfire that Blaine stumbled on as he followed up a creek hunting down a spring while Riley wrestled with the balky spark plugs. Blaine had been moving quietly, and they had heard him just too late to vanish before he caught sight of them, fleeing like wraiths up the timbered slopes of the looming mountain spur.

He had stepped into the tiny, tramped-down circle of the camp site, with its small cooking fire and the skillet on its side, with four half-cooked trout lying in the trampled grass, with the wadded blankets and the comforter that had served as beds, with the rudely built brush shelter as refuge from the rain.

He had knelt beside the fire and righted the skillet. He had picked up the fish and brushed the twigs and grass off them and replaced them in the pan.

And he had thought to call out to the hiders, to try to reassure them, but he knew that it was useless, for they were past all trust.

They were hunted animals. Hunted animals in this great United States which for years had valued freedom, which in its later years had stood as a forthright champion before the entire world for the rights of man.

He knelt there, torn by an anger and a pity, and he felt the smarting of his eyes. He bunched up his fists and rubbed at his eyes, and the moist knuckles smeared streaks of dirt across his face.

He had stayed there for a while, but finally he had risen and gone down the creek again, forgetting that he had hunted for a spring, which no doubt had been only a few feet from the camp.

When he got back to the truck, he did not mention what he'd found to Riley.

They drove across the deserts and labored across the mountains and finally came to the great high plains where the wind came knifing down without a hill to stop it, without a tree to break it, a naked stretch of land that lay flat and hard to a far horizon.

Blaine rode in the seat alongside Riley, slouched and relaxed against the jolting of the truck. The sun beat down, and the wind was dry, and off to the north dust devils rose and spun above a dried-up river bed.

Riley drove hunched tight against the wheel, with his arms braced against the chuckholes and the ruts. His face was tense and at times a nervous tic twitched the muscles of his cheek.

Even in the daytime, Blaine thought, the man is still afraid, still runs his endless race with darkness.

Had it to do, he wondered, with the cargo in the truck? Not once had Riley said what he was hauling, not once had he inspected it. There was a heavy padlock on the rear door of the rig, and the padlock clanged and jangled as the truck lumbered on the road.

There had been a time or two when Blaine had been on the verge of asking, but there had been a certain reticence that had prevented it. Not anything, perhaps, that Riley had said or done or any way he'd acted, but, rather, his studied casualness in all these areas.

And after all, Blaine told himself, it was none of his affair. He did not care what might be in the truck. His only interest was in the truck itself; with every turn of a wheel it was carrying him where he had to go.

Riley said: 'If we get a good run tonight, we'll reach the river in the morning.'

'The Missouri?'

Riley nodded. 'If we don't break down again. If we make good time.'

But that night they met the witches.

14

The first they saw of them was a flicker in the fan of light the headlamps threw out along the road and then they saw them flying in the moonlight. Not flying, actually, for they had no wings, but moving through the air as a fish would move through water, and graceful as only flying things can be.

There was a moment when they might have been moths flying in the lights or night-swooping birds diving in the sky, but once the mind had its instant of utter disbelief and after that, of human rationalization, there was no doubt of what they were.

They were humans flying. They were levitators. They were witches and there was a coven of them.

In the seat beside him, Blaine saw Riley thrust the shotgun out the open window. Blaine slammed on the brakes.

The gun went off, the sound of the report blasting in the cab like a thunderbolt.

The car skidded to a halt, slantwise across the road. Blaine grabbed at Riley's shoulder and jerked him off his balance. With the other hand he jerked the gun away.

He caught a glimpse of Riley's face, and the man was yammering. His jaw went up and down in a devil's tattoo and there were little flecks of foam at each corner of his mouth. His eyes were wild and rolling and his face was stiff, with the muscles bunched and tensed, like a grotesque mask. His hooked fingers made clawing motions to get back the gun.

'Snap out of it!' roared Blaine. 'They're only levitators.'

But the word meant nothing to a man like Riley. All reason and all understanding were lost in the roll of fearful thunder that hammered in his brain.

And even as he spoke to Riley, Blaine became aware of voices in the night – soundless voices reaching out to him, a medley of voices that were talking to him.

Friend – one of us is hit (a line of oozing red across a shapely shoulder) – not bad – he has (a gun with its muzzle limp and drooping and turning suddenly into a rather melancholy and very phallic symbol). Safe – our friend has the gun. Let us get the other (a snarling dog backed into a corner, a skunk with its tail uplifted, a rattler coiled and set to strike).

Wait, yelled Blaine. *Wait! everything's all right. There'll be no more shooting.*

He pressed down with his elbow against the door latch, and the door swung open. He pushed Riley from him and half fell out of the cab, still clutching the gun. He broke the weapon, and the shells jumped out; he threw the gun into the road and backed against the truck.

Suddenly the night was deadly silent except for the sounds of moaning and of wailing that came from Riley in the cab.

Everything is clear, said Blaine. *There is no more danger.*

They came plunging down out of the sky, as if they might be jumping from some hidden platform, but they landed lightly on their feet.

They moved slowly forward, catfooted in the night, and they were silent now.

That was a damn fool thing to do, Blaine told them. *Next time one of you will get your head blown off (a headless human walking casually with the stump of neck frothing furiously).*

He saw that they were young, not out of their teens, and that they wore what appeared to be bathing suits and he caught the sense of fun and the scent of prank.

They moved in cautiously, and he sought for other signs, but there were no other sings.

Who are you? one asked.

Shepherd Blaine of Fishhook.

And you are going?

Up to South Dakota.

In this truck?

And with this man, said Blaine. *I want him left alone.*

He took a shot at us. He hit Marie.

Not bad, said Marie. *Just a scratch is all.*

He's a frightened man, said Blaine. *He's using silver shot.*

He sensed the merriment of them at the thought of silver shot.

And caught the weirdness of the situation, the moonlit night and the deserted road, the car slewed across the highway, the lonely wind that moaned across the prairie, and the two of them, he and Riley, encircled, not by Sioux nor by Comanche nor by Blackfeet, but by a ring of paranormal teen-agers out on a midnight lark.

And who was there to blame or censure them? he asked himself. If in this small action of defiance they found some measure of self-assertion in their hunted lives, if in this manner they snatched at something resembling human dignity, it was then no more than a very human action and not to be condemned.

He studied the faces, the ones that he could see, indistinct in the moon-and-headlamp-light, and there was indecision in them – faces on hair trigger.

From the cab still came the moaning of a man in mental agony.

Then: *Fishhook?* (*The towered buildings on the hill, the acre upon acre of them, massive, majestic, inspiring . . .*)

That is right, said Blaine.

A girl moved out of the huddled group and walked close to Blaine. She held out her hand.

Friend, she said. *We had not expected one. All of us are sorry that we troubled you.*

Blaine put out his hand and felt the firm, strong pressure of young fingers.

We do not often find someone on the road at night, said another one.

Just having fun, another said. *There's little chance for fun.*

I know how little chance, said Blaine. *I've seen how little chance.*

We halloween, still another said.

Halloween? Oh, yes, I see. (*A first banging on a closed shutter, a garden gate hanging in a tree, a hex sign upside down.*)

It's good for them. They've got it coming to them.

I agree, said Blaine. *But it's dangerous.*

Not very. They are all too scared.

But it doesn't help the situation.

Mister, there is nothing that can help.

But Fishhook? asked the girl who stood in front of Blaine.

He studied her and saw that she was beautiful – blue eyes and golden hair and the sort of shape that in the ancient days would have won her beauty contests, one of the old paganisms that had been happily forgotten in the rush to PK fads.

I cannot tell you, said Blaine. *I'm sorry, I can't tell you.*

Trouble? Danger?

Not at the moment, no.

We could help.

No need, making it as casual as he could, as unworried as he could.

We could take you anywhere you wished.

I'm not a levitator.

No need for you to be. We could (*himself flying through the air, dragged along by two levitators, each hanging to an arm*).

Blaine shuddered. *No, thanks. I think I'd rather not.*

Someone opened up the door of the cab, and another one reached in and hurled Riley to the ground.

The trucker crawled along the ground on hands and knees and sobbed.

Leave him alone! yelled Blaine.

The girl turned around. Her thoughts were level, sharp: *Keep away from him! Don't touch him! Don't do a thing to him.*

But, Anita . . .

Not a thing, she said.

He's a dirty reefer. He's using silver shot.

No!

They backed away.

We'll have to go, Anita said to Blaine. *Will you be all right?*

With him, you mean?

She nodded.

I can handle him, he told her.

My name is Anita Andrews. I live in Hamilton. My phone number is 276. Tattoo it.

Tattooed, said Blaine, showing her the words and numbers.

If you need help . . .

I'll call.

Promise?

Promise (cross upon a throbbing heart).

Riley lunged and had the gun, was staggering to his feet, a hand groping in his pocket for a shell.

Blaine flattened in a dive. He caught the man just above the knees, his shoulder slamming hard, one arm about the body, the other slashing at the gun and missing.

And as he leaped, he yelled: *Get out of here! Every one of you!*

He hit the ground and skidded, face down, on the broken pavement. He felt the shattered blacktop scraping on his flesh, tearing at his clothes. But he still kept his grip on Riley and dragged the man down with him.

The skidding stopped, and Blaine groped blindly for the gun, and the gun barrel came lashing down out of the darkness and struck him across the ribs. He swore and grasped for it, but Riley had it raised again for another blow. Blaine punched out desperately in the darkness, and his fist caught yielding flesh that grunted at the blow. The gun thudded down, missing his face by the fraction of an inch.

His hand snaked out and grasped it and jerked, twisting as he jerked, and the gun came free.

Blaine rolled, carrying the gun with him, and scrambled to his feet.

Out at the edge of light, he saw Riley coming in a bull rush, with his arms outspread, with his shoulders bunched, his mouth a snarling slit slashed across his face.

Blaine lifted the gun and flung it out into the darkness with Riley almost on him. He sidestepped, but not quite far enough. One of Riley's hamlike hands caught him on the hip. Blaine spun with the hand and sidestepped again. Riley tried to check his rush but seemed unable to. He twisted his body frantically, but his momentum drove him forward and he slammed with a resounding whack into the front end of the truck.

He folded then and slid into a heap. Blaine stood watching him and there was no motion in the man.

The night was silent. There were just the two of them. All the rest had gone. He and Riley were alone with the battered truck.

Blaine swung around and looked into the sky and there was nothing there but the moon and stars and the lonesome prairie wind.

He turned back to Riley, and the man was alive, he saw. He had hauled himself into a sitting position, braced against the front end of the truck. There was a cut across his forehead where he had struck on metal and there was no fight left in him. He was out of breath and panting and there was a wild glare in his eyes.

Blaine took a pace toward him.

'You damn fool,' he said. 'If you'd fired at them again, they'd have been on top of us. They'd have torn us to pieces.'

Riley stared at him, and his mouth was working but no words came out – just the one word: 'You – you – you.'

Blaine stepped forward and held out a hand to help him to his feet, but Riley shrank away from him, pressing his body tight against the truck as if he would intrude into the very metal.

'You're one of them!' he shouted. 'I guessed it days ago . . .'

'You're crazy!'

'But you are! You are afraid of being seen. You stick close to the truck. I always am the one who goes for the eats and coffee. You won't ever go. I always bargain for the gas. It is never you.'

'It's your truck,' said Blaine. 'You have money and I don't. You know I am dead broke.'

'The way you came to me,' wailed Riley. 'Walking from the woods. You must have spent the night in them there woods! And you never believed in nothing, the way ordinary people do.'

'I'm not a fool,' said Blaine. 'That's the only reason. I'm no more PK than you are. If I were, do you think I'd have ridden this far in your junk heap of a truck?'

He strode forward and seized Riley and jerked him to his feet. He shook him so his head bobbed back and forth.

'Snap out of it!' yelled Blaine. 'We're safe. Let's get out of here.'

'The gun! You threw away the gun!'

'The hell with the gun. Get into that truck.'

'But you talked with them! I heard you talking to them!'

'I never said a word.'

'Not with your mouth,' said Riley. 'Not with your tongue. But I heard you talking with them. Not all of what you said. Just pieces of it. I tell you that I heard you.'

Blaine pushed him back against the truck and held him with one hand while with the other he opened the cab door.

'Get in there and shut up,' Blaine said, bitterly. 'You and your God-damned gun! You and your silver shot! You and your hearing things!'

For it was too late, he told himself. It would be useless telling him. It would be a waste of time to show him or to try to help. Perhaps if he ever guessed the truth, he might lose his last thin fingerhold on reason and finally go insane, wallowing in a morass of guilt associations.

Blaine walked around the truck and got in on the other side. He started the engine and wheeled the vehicle back into a highway lane.

They drove for an hour in silence, with Riley hunched into his corner. Blaine felt his watching eyes.

Finally Riley said: 'I'm sorry, Blaine. I guess that you were right back there.'

'Sure I was,' said Blaine. 'If you had started shooting—'

'That's not what I meant,' said Riley. 'If you'd been one of them, you'd have thrown in with them. They could have whisked you anywhere you wanted quicker than this rig.'

Blaine chuckled. 'Just to prove it to you I'll pick up the eats and coffee in the morning. If you'll trust me with the money, that is.'

15

Blaine sat on the stool in the hamburger joint, waiting for the man to bag a half-dozen sandwiches and fill the pail with coffee. There were only two other customers in the place, and they paid no attention to him. One had finished eating and was reading a paper. The other, poised above his plate, was shoveling in a gooey mess that originally had been eggs and fried potatoes but now looked like some new kind of dog food from being thoroughly mixed together.

Blaine turned from looking at the men and stared out the massive slab of glass which comprised two sides of the building.

The morning street was quiet, with only a few cars moving and only one man walking.

Probably it had been foolish, he told himself, to come out like this in an utterly mad and perhaps rather useless attempt to throw Riley off his guard, to attempt to reassure him. For it was more than likely that no matter what he did and no matter what Riley said, the trucker would continue to carry some suspicion.

But, Blaine thought, it would not be for long, for they must be near the river, and Pierre must be just a few miles to the north. And a funny thing, he thought – Riley had never told him where he had been going. Although it was not queer; it fit in with all the rest of it – the man's evident fright and his secrecy concerning what he carried.

He swung back from the window and watched the man put the hamburgers in the sack and fill the pail with coffee. He paid with the five-dollar bill Riley had given him and pocketed the change.

He went out into the street and headed for the bulk oil station where Riley and the truck were waiting. It was too early yet for anyone to be at the station, and they'd eat their breakfast while waiting for someone to show up. Then they'd fill the tank and be on their way, and this, thought Blaine, might be the last day he'd be with the truck.

For once they hit the river, he'd get off and start heading north for Pierre.

The morning was cool almost to the point of chill, and the air burned in his nose as he breathed it in. It was going to be another good day, he knew – another moment of October with its wine-like air and its smoky sky.

As he came to the street where the bulk station was located, the truck was not in sight.

Perhaps, he told himself, Riley might have moved it. But even as he thought it, he knew it was not right. He knew he had been ditched.

At the cost of a few dollars, at the cost of finding someplace else to get a tank of gas, the trucker had rid himself of Blaine.

It came to Blaine as no great shock, for he realized that he'd been expecting it, although not admitting to himself that he had expected it. After all, from Riley's point of view, it was an astoundingly simple solution to his suspicions of the night before.

To convince himself to make sure there was no mistake, Blaine walked around the block.

The truck was not in sight. And he was on his own.

In just a little while the town would be coming to life, and before that happened he must be out of sight. He must find a place where he could hide out for the day.

He stood for a moment to orient himself.

The nearer edge of town, he was certain, lay to the east, for they had driven through the southern edge of it for a mile or two.

He started out, walking as fast as was possible, but not so fast, he hoped, as would attract attention. A few cars went by along the street, once a man came out of his house to pick up the morning paper, once he met another man with a lunch bucket swinging from his hand. No one paid attention to him.

The houses dwindled out, and he reached the last street in the town. Here the prairie ended and the land began to tumble down, in a jumble of wooded hills and knolls, each one lower than the last, and he knew that the Missouri lay beyond. Somewhere down there where the last hill ended, the mighty stream gurgled on its way with its shifting sand bars and its willow islands.

He made his way across a field and climbed a fence and went down the bank of a steep ravine and at the bottom of it was a tiny creek that chuckled at its banks and just beyond was a pool with a clump of willows growing close beside it.

Blaine got down on his hands and knees and crawled beneath the willows. It was a perfect hideout. It was outside the town and there was nothing to bring anybody here – the stream was too small to fish and it was too late for swimming. He would not be disturbed.

There would be no one to sense the flashing mirror he carried in his mind; there'd be no one to yell 'Parry!'

And come night he could move on.

He ate three of the hamburgers and drank some of the coffee.

The sun came up and filtered through the willows to make a dappled pattern of sunshine and shadow.

From the town came far-off sounds – the rumble of a truck, the purring of an engine, the barking of some dogs, the calling of a mother rounding up the kids.

It had been a long road from that night in Fishhook, Blaine told himself, sitting in the willow shade and poking with a stick into the sandy ground. A long ways from Charline's and from

Freddy Bates. And up until this moment he'd had no time to even think about it.

There had been a question then, and there was still a question now: Whether it had been smart to run away from Fishhook; whether, despite all Godfrey Stone had said, it might not have been the wiser course to stay and take his chances of whatever Fishhook might have had in store.

He sat there and thought about it and he went back to the bright blue room where all had been set in motion. And he saw the room again as if it were only yesterday – better than if it were only yesterday. The alien stars were shining faintly down on this room which had no roof, and the bright blue floor was smooth beneath the rolling of his wheels, and the room was filled with the weird fabricated pieces that might have been furniture or art objects or appliances or almost anything at all.

It all came alive for him as it should not come alive – clear and concise, with no rough edges and nothing blurred, with not a thing put in and not a thing left out.

The Pinkness was sprawling at its ease and it roused and said to him: *So you came back again!*

And he was really there.

Without machine or body, without any outward trappings, with nothing but his naked mind, Shepherd Blaine had come back to the Pinkness.

16

You cannot see a mind.

But the Pinkness saw it, or sensed it – or at least it knew that the mind was there.

And to Shepherd Blaine there was no surprise and no alienness. It seemed almost as if he were coming home, for the bright blue of the room was much more homelike and familiar than it had seemed that first time.

Well, the Pinkness said, looking the mind up and down, *you make a pretty pair!*

And that was it, of course, thought the part of the mind that still was Shepherd Blaine – he, or at least a part of him, perhaps as much as half of him, had come home, indeed. For he was, in some percentage not yet determined, perhaps impossible to determine, a part of the alien he faced. He was Shepherd Blaine, traveler from Earth, and likewise a carbon copy of this thing that dwelt in the bright blue room.

And how are you getting on? the alien asked most affably. As if he didn't know.

There is just one thing, said Blaine, hurrying to get it in against the time when he might be forced to go from here. *There is just one thing. You've made us like a mirror. We bounce back at people.*

Why of course, the alien told him. *That is the only way to do it. On an alien planet you would need some shielding. You don't want intelligences prying round in you. So you bounce back their prying. Here at home, of course, there would be no need . . .*

But you don't understand, protested Blaine. *It doesn't protect us. It attracts attention to us. It almost got us killed.*

There is no such thing, the alien told Blaine, gruffly. *There is no such thing as killed. There is no such thing as death. It is such a horrid waste. Although I may be wrong. It seems to me that there was a planet, very long ago . . .*

One could almost hear him riffling through the dry filing cases of his cluttered memory.

Yes, he said, *there was a planet. There were several planets. And it was a shame. I cannot understand it. It makes no sense at all.*

I can assure you, Blaine told him, *that on my planet there is death for everything. For every single thing . . .*

For everything?

Well, I can't be sure. Perhaps . . .

You see, the creature said. *Even on your planet it is not universal.*

I do not know, said Blaine. *It seems to me that I remember there are deathless things.*

Normal things, you mean.

Death has a purpose, Blaine persisted. *It is a process, a function that has made the development of species and the differentiation of species possible on my planet. It averts the dead end. It is an eraser that wipes out mistakes, that provides for new beginnings.*

The Pinkness settled down. You could sense its settling down – smugly, primly getting set for a long and satisfactory exchange of ideas and, perhaps, an argument.

It may be so, it said, *but it's very primitive. It goes back to the ooze. There are better ways. There even is a point where there is no further need of this improvement that you speak of.*

But, first of all, he asked, *are you satisfied?*

Satisfied?

Well, you're an improved thing yourself. An expanded thing. You are part yourself and you are partly me.

And you are partly me as well.

The Pinkness seemed to chuckle. *But there are just the two of you — yourself and me — and I am so many things I cannot begin to tell you. I have done a lot of visiting and I've picked up a lot of things, including many minds, and some of them, I don't mind telling you, were hardly worth the trading. But do you know, for all the visiting I've done, almost no one ever visits me. I cannot tell you how I appreciate this visit. There was a being once who came to visit me quite often, but it was so long ago it's a bit hard to recall. By the way, you measure time, don't you — surface time, that is?*

Blaine told him how humans measure time.

Hm, now, let's see, the creature said, doing rapid mental calculation, *that would make it about ten thousand of your years ago.*

That this creature came to visit you?

That is right, the Pinkness said. *You are the first since then. And you came visiting me. You didn't wait for me to visit you. And you had that machine . . .*

How come, Blaine asked, *you had to ask me about our count of time? You had it all. You traded minds with me. You have everything I know.*

Of course, the Pinkness mumbled. *Of course I had it. But I hadn't dug it out. You wouldn't believe me if I told you how cluttered up I am.*

And that was true, Blaine thought. Even with just one extra mind, he was cluttered up. He wondered . . .

Yes, of course, the Pinkness told him. *You'll get it straightened out in time. It takes a little while. You'll become one mind, not two. You'll get together. You'll make a team. You like it this way, don't you?*

It's been a little rough, this mirror business.

'*I'm not bent on causing trouble,* said the Pinkness. *I only do the best I can. So I make mistakes. So I fix it up. I take the mirror off, I cancel it. O.K.?*

O.K., said Blaine.

I sit here, said the Pinkness, *and I go visiting. Without stirring from this place, I go anyplace I wish and you'd be surprised how few minds I find that I'd care to trade for.*

In ten thousand years, however, you'd pick up a lot of them.

Ten thousand years, said the creature, startled. *Ten thousand years, my friend, is only yesterday.*

He sat there, mumbling, reaching back and back and not reaching the beginning and he finally gave it up.

And there are so few of them, he complained, that can handle a second mind. I must be careful of them. There are a lot of them that think they are possessed. Some of these would go insane if I traded with them. You perhaps, can understand.

Readily, said Blaine.

Come, said the Pinkness, *and sit down here beside me.*

I'm scarcely, Blaine explained, *in a condition to do much sitting.*

Oh, yes, I see, the creature said. *I should have thought of that. Well, then, move over closer. You came for a visit, I presume.*

Naturally, said Blaine, not knowing what to say.

Then, said the creature grimly, *leave us start to visit.*

Certainly, said Blaine, moving somewhat closer.

Now, where shall I start? the creature asked. *There are so many places and so many times and so many different creatures. It always is a problem. I suppose it comes because of a desire for neatness, an orderliness of mind. The thought persists to plague me that if I could put it all together I might arrive at something of significance. You would not mind, I presume, if I should tell you about those strange creatures that I ran into out at the edge of the galaxy.*

Not at all, said Blaine.

They are rather extraordinary, said the Pinkness, *in that they did not develop machines as your culture did, but became, in effect, machines themselves . . .*

Sitting there in the bright blue room, with the alien stars flaming overhead, with the faint, far-off sound of the raging desert wind a whisper in the room, the Pinkness talked – not only of the machine entities, but of many others. Of the insect tribes that piled up over endless centuries huge reserves of food for which they had no need, slaving on an endless treadmill of a blind economic mania. Of the race that made their art forms the basis of a weird religion. Of the listening posts manned by garrisons of a galactic empire that had long since been forgotten by all except the garrisons themselves. Of the fantastic and complicated sexual arrangements of yet another race of beings who, faced with the massive difficulties of procreation, thought of little else. Of planets that never had known life but rolled along their courses as gaunt and raw and naked as the day they had been formed. And of other planets that were a boiling brew pot of chemical reactions which stretched the mind to think on, let alone to understand, and of how these chemical reactions of themselves gave rise to an unstable, ephemeral sort of sentience that was life one moment and just failed of life another.

This – and yet a great deal more.

Blaine, listening, realized the true fantastic measure of this creature which he had stumbled on – an apparently deathless thing, which had no memory of its beginning, no concept of an end; a creature with a roving mind that had mentally explored, over billions of years, millions of stars and planets for millions of light years, in this present galaxy and in some of the neighbor ones; a mind that had assembled a gigantic grab box of assorted information, but information which it had made no effort to put to any use. That it, more than likely, had no idea of how to put to use, yet troubled by a vague idea that this store of knowledge should not be lying fallow.

The sort of creature that could sit in the sun for endless time and spin eccentric yarns of all that it had seen.

And for the human race, thought Blaine, here squatted an encyclopedia of galactic knowledge, here lounged an atlas that had mapped uncounted cubic light years. Here was the sort of creature that the tribe of Man could use. Here was a running off of mouth that would pay human dividends – dividends from an entity which seemed without emotion, other than a certain sense of friendliness – an entity that, perhaps, in years of armchair observation, had had all emotions, if any had existed, worn away until they were so much dust – who had not used any of the knowledge it had gained, but had not been the loser. For in all its observation, in its galactic window-peeping, it had gained a massive tolerance and an understanding, not of its own nature, not of human nature, but of every nature, an understanding of life itself, of sentience and intelligence. And a sympathy of all motives and all ethics, and of each ambition, no matter how distorted in the eyes of other life.

And all of this, as well, Blaine realized with a start, was likewise stored in the mind of one human being, of one Shepherd Blaine, if he could only separate it and classify and store it and then could dig it out and put it to proper use.

Listening, Blaine lost all sense of time, lost all knowing of what he was or where he was or why he might be there, listening as a boy might listen to some stupendous tale spun by an ancient mariner from far and unknown land.

The room became familiar and the Pinkness was a friend and

the stars were no longer alien and the far-off howling of the desert wind was a cradle song that he had always known.

It was a long time before he realized he was listening only to the wind and that the stories of far away and long ago had ceased.

He stirred, almost sleepily, and the Pinkness said: *That was a nice visit that we had. I think it was the best that I have ever had.*

There is one thing, said Blaine. *One question—*

If it is the shield, the Pinkness said, *you needn't worry. I took it away. There is nothing to betray you.*

It wasn't that, said Blaine. *It was time. I — that is, the two of us — have some control of time. Twice it saved my life...*

It is there, the Pinkness said. *The understanding's in your mind. You only have to find it.*

But, time—

Time, the creature said, *is the simplest thing there is. I'll tell you ...*

17

Blaine lay for a long time, soaking in the feel of body, for now he had a body. He could feel the pressure on it, he could sense the movement of the air as it touched the skin, knew the hot damp of perspiration prickle along his arms and face and chest.

He was no longer in the blue room, for there he had no body and there was no longer the far-off sound of the desert wind. There was, instead, a regular rasping sound that had a slobber in it. And there was a smell, an astringent smell, an aggressively antiseptic odor that filled not only the nostrils, but the entire body.

He let his eyelids come up slowly against possible surprise, set to snap them shut again if there should be a need. But there was only whiteness, plain and unrelieved. There was no more than the whiteness of a ceiling.

His head was on a pillow and there was a sheet beneath him and he was dressed in some sort of garment that had a scratchiness.

He moved his head and he saw the other bed and upon it lay a mummy.

Time, the creature on that other world had said, time is the simplest thing there is. And it had said that it would tell him, but it hadn't told him, for he hadn't stayed to hear.

It was like a dream, he thought – thinking back on it, it had the unreal, flat-planed quality of a dream, but it had not been any dream. He had been in the blue room once again and he'd talked with the creature that was its habitant. He had heard it spin its yarns and he still retained within his mind the details of those yarns. There was no fading of the detail as there would have been if it had been a dream.

The mummy lay upon the bed swathed in bandages. There were holes in the bandages for the nostrils and the mouth but no holes for the eyes. And as it breathed it slobbered.

The walls were of the same whiteness as the ceiling, and the floors were covered with ceramic tile and there was a sterility about the place that shrieked its identity.

He was in a hospital room with a slobbering mummy.

Fear moved in on him, a sudden wash of fear, but he lay there quietly while it washed over him. For even in the fear, he knew that he was safe. There was some reason he was safe. There was some reason if he could think of it.

Where had he been? he wondered; where had he been other than the blue room? His mind went tracking back and he remembered where he'd been – in the willow thicket in the gully beyond the edge of town.

There were footsteps in the hall outside, and a man with a white jacket came into the room.

The man stopped inside the door and stood there looking at him.

'So you've come around at last,' the doctor said. 'Just how do you feel?'

'Not too bad,' said Blaine, and actually he felt fine. There didn't seem to be a thing the matter. 'Where did you pick me up?'

The doctor did not answer. He asked another question. 'Did anything like this ever happen to you before?'

'Like what?'

'Blacking out,' the doctor. 'Falling into coma.'

Blaine rocked his head from side to side upon the pillow. 'Not that I recall.'

'Almost,' the doctor said, 'as if you were the victim of a spell.'

Blaine laughed. 'Witchcraft, doctor?'

The doctor grimaced. 'No, I don't imagine so. But one never knows. The patient sometimes thinks so.'

He crossed the room and sat down on the edge of the bed.

'I'm Dr Wetmore,' he told Blaine. 'You've been here two days.

Some boys were hunting rabbits east of town. They found you. You had crawled underneath some willows. They thought that you were dead.'

'And so you hauled me in.'

'The police did. They went out and got you.'

'And what is wrong with me?'

Wetmore shook his head. 'I don't know.'

'I haven't any money. I can't pay you, Doctor.'

'That,' the doctor told him, 'is not of any moment.'

He sat there, looking at him. 'There is one thing, however. There were no papers on you. Do you remember who you are?'

'Sure. I'm Shepherd Blaine.'

'And you live where?'

'Nowhere,' said Blaine. 'I just wander around.'

'How did you get to this town?'

'I don't somehow recall.'

He sat up in bed. 'Look, Doctor, how about getting out of here? I'm taking up a bed.'

The doctor shook his head. 'I'd like you to stick around. There are several tests—'

'It'll be a lot of trouble.'

'I've never run across a case like yours,' the doctor said. 'You'd be doing me a favor. There was nothing wrong with you. Nothing organically, that is. Your heartbeat was retarded. Your breathing a little shallow. Your temperature off a point or two. But otherwise all right, except that you were out. No way of waking you.'

Blaine jerked his head toward the mummy. 'He's in bad shape, isn't he?'

'Highway accident,' the doctor said.

'That's a bit unusual. Not many any more.'

'Unusual circumstance,' the doctor explained. 'Driving an old truck. Tire blew when he was going fast. One of the curves above the river.'

Blaine looked sharply at the man on the other bed, but there was no way to tell. None of him was showing. His breath went slobbering in and out and there was a rasping to it, but there was no way to tell who he might be.

'I could arrange another room,' the doctor offered.

'No need. I won't be around too long.'

'I wish you'd stay awhile. You might flop over once again. And not be found this time.'

'I'll think on it,' Blaine promised.

He lay back on the bed.

The doctor rose and went to the other bed. He bent over it and listened to the breathing. He found a wad of cotton and dabbed it at the lips. He murmured at the man who lay there, then he straightened up.

'Anything you need?' he inquired of Blaine. 'You must be getting hungry.'

Blaine nodded. Now that he thought of it, he was.

'No hurry, though,' he said.

'I'll speak to the kitchen,' said the doctor. 'They'll find something for you.'

He turned about and walked briskly from the room, and Blaine lay listening to his crisp, quick footsteps going down the hall.

And suddenly he knew – or remembered – why he now was safe. The flashing signal light was gone, for the creature of the far star had taken it from him. Now there was no longer need to skulk, no need of hiding out.

He lay there and thought about it and felt a bit more human – although, to tell the truth, he had never felt anything but human. Although now, for the first time, beneath the humanness, he felt the quick, tense straining of new knowledge of a deep strata of new knowledge that was his to tap.

Across, in the other bed, the mummy wheezed and rasped and slobbered.

'Riley!' whispered Blaine.

There was no break in the breathing, no sign of recognition.

Blaine swung on the bed and thrust out his feet. He sat on the edge of the bed and let his feet down to the floor, and the patterned tile was chill. He stood up, and the scratchy hospital gown hung obscenely around his shanks.

At the other bed, he bent close above the white-swathed thing that lay there.

'Riley! Is it you? Riley, do you hear me?'

The mummy stirred.

The head tried to turn toward him but it couldn't. The lips moved with an effort. The tongue fought to frame a sound.

'Tell . . .' it said, dragging out the word with the effort of its saying.

It tried again. 'Tell Finn,' it said.

There was more to say. Blaine could sense that there was more to say. He waited. The lips moved again, laboriously, and yet again. The tongue writhed heavily inside the slobbering cavern. But there was nothing more.

'Riley!' But there was no answer.

Blaine backed away until the edge of his bed caught him back of the knees and he sat down upon it.

He stayed there, staring at the swathed figure motionless on the bed.

And the fear, he thought, had caught up with the man at last, the fear that he had raced across half a continent. Although, perhaps, not the fear he ran from, but another fear and another danger.

Riley gasped and panted.

And there he lay, thought Blaine, a man who had some piece of information to pass on to a man named Finn. Who was Finn and where? What had he to do with Riley?

Finn?

There had been a Finn.

Once, long ago, he'd known the name of Finn.

Blaine sat stiff and straight upon the bed, remembering what he knew of Finn.

Although it might be a different Finn.

For Lambert Finn had been a Fishhook traveler, too, although he'd disappeared, even as Godfrey Stone had disappeared, but many years before Stone had disappeared, long before Blaine himself had ever come to Fishhook.

And now he was a whispered name, a legend, a chilling character in a chilling story, one of the few Fishhook horror tales.

For, so the story ran, Lambert Finn had come back from the stars one day a screaming maniac!

18

Blaine lay back upon the bed and stared up at the ceiling. A breeze came sniffing through the window, and leaf shadows from a tree outside played fitfully upon the wall. It must be a stubborn tree, Blaine thought, among the last to lose its leaves, for it was late October now.

He listened to the muffled sounds that came from the hushed corridors beyond the room, and the biting antiseptic smell was still hanging in the air.

He must get out of here, he thought; he must be on his way. But on his way to where? On his way to Pierre, of course – to

Pierre and Harriet, if Harriet were there. But Pierre itself was dead end. So far as he might know, there was no purpose in it. So far as he could know, it was just a place to run to.

For he was running still, in blind and desperate flight. He'd been running since that moment when he'd returned from his mission to the stars. And worst of all, running without purpose, running only to be safe, just to get away.

The lack of purpose hurt. It made him an empty thing. It made him a wind-blown striving that had no free will of its own.

He lay there and let the hurt sink in – and the bitterness and wonder, the wonder if it had been wise to run from Fishhook, if it had been the thing to do. Then he remembered Freddy Bates and Freddy's painted smile and the glitter in his eyes and the gun in Freddy's pocket. And he knew there was no doubt about it: it had been the thing to do.

But somewhere there must be something he could lay his fingers on, something he could grasp, some shred of hope or promise he could cling to. He must not go on forever floating without purpose. The time must come when he could stop his running, when he could set his feet, when he could look around.

On the bed Riley gasped and wheezed and gurgled and was silent.

There was no sense in staying, Blaine told himself, as the doctor wished. For there was nothing that the doc could find and nothing Blaine could tell him and there was no profit in it for either one of them.

He got off the bed again and walked across the room to the door that more than likely led into a closet.

He opened the door and it was a closet and his clothes hung there. There was no sign of underwear, but his pants and shirt were hanging there and his shoes sat underneath them. His jacket had fallen off the hook and lay in a crumpled heap upon the floor.

He stripped off the hospital gown and reached for his trousers. He stepped into them and cinched them tight about his middle.

He was reaching for the shirt when the stillness struck him – the peaceful, mellow stillness of an autumn afternoon. The peace of yellow leaf and the mellowness of the haze upon the distant hills and the winelike richness of the season.

But the stillness was all wrong.

There should be a gasping and a bubbling from the man upon the bed.

With his shoulders hunched, as if against a blow, Blaine waited for the sound and there was no sound.

He spun around and took a step toward the bed, then halted. For there was no reason for going near the bed. Riley's swathed body lay still and quiet, and the bubble on the lips was frozen there.

'Doctor!' Blaine yelled, 'Doctor!' running to the door, knowing even as he ran and yelled that he was being foolish, that his reaction was irrational.

He reached the door and stopped. He put his hands against the jambs and leaned forward to thrust his head out into the corridor.

The doctor was coming down the hall, hurrying, but not running.

'Doctor,' whispered Blaine.

The doctor reached the door. He put out a hand and pushed Blaine back into the room. He strode over to the bed.

He stooped with his stethoscope placed against the mummy, then stepped back from the bed.

He looked hard at Blaine.

'And you are going where?' he asked.

'He's dead,' said Blaine. 'His breathing stopped and it was a long time—'

'Yes, he's dead. He never had a chance. Even with gobathian he didn't have a chance.'

'Gobathian? That was what you used? That was why he was all wrapped up?'

'He was broken,' said the doctor. 'Like a toy someone had thrown on the floor and jumped on. He was . . .'

He stopped and for a long, hard moment looked at Blaine.

'What do you know about gobathian?' he asked.

'I've heard of it,' said Blaine.

And he'd heard of it, all right, he thought.

'An alien drug,' the doctor said. 'Used by an insect race. A warring insect race. And it's done miracles. It can patch up a smashed and broken body. It can repair bones and organs. It can grow new tissue.'

He glanced down at the swathed deadness, then looked back at Blaine.

'You've read the literature?' he asked.

'A popularization,' Blaine lied. 'In a magazine.'

And he could see again the seething madness of that jungle planet where he had stumbled on this drug the insects used – although in very truth they were not insects nor was it a drug they used.

Although, he told himself, there was no need to quibble. Terminology, always difficult, had become impossible with the going to the stars. You used approximations and let it go at that. You did the best you could.

'We'll move you to another room,' the doctor told him.

'No need of that,' said Blaine. 'I was just about to leave.'

'You can't,' said the doctor, flatly. 'I will not allow it. I won't have you on my conscience. There's something wrong with you, something very wrong. There's no one to look after you – no friends, no people.'

'I'll get along. I always have before.'

The doctor moved closer.

'I have a feeling,' he said, 'that you're not telling me the truth – not the entire truth.'

Blaine walked away from him. He reached the closet and got his shirt and put it on. He scuffed into his shoes. He picked up his jacket and shut the closet door, then turned around.

'Now,' he said, 'if you'll just move aside, I'll be going out.'

There was someone coming down the corridor. Perhaps, Blaine thought, someone with the food the doctor promised. and maybe he should wait until the food arrived, for he needed it.

But there was more than one person coming down the corridor – there were at least a pair of footsteps. Perhaps someone who had heard him yelling for the doctor, bearing down upon the room to see if help were needed.

'I wish that you would change your mind,' the doctor said. 'Aside from the feeling you need help, there also is the matter of formalities . . .'

Blaine heard no more of what he had to say, for the walkers had reached the door and were standing just outside of it, looking in the room.

Harriet Quimby, cool as ice, was saying: 'Shep, how did you wind up here? We've been looking everywhere for you.'

And the telepathic undertone hit him like a whiplash: *Give! Quick! Fill me in!*

Just claim me, that is all (ferocious woman dragging errant urchin behind her with no ceremony). If you do that, they'll let me go. Found me lying underneath a willow tree . . .

(Drunk who had somehow climbed into a garbage can and can't get out of it, top hat tilted on one ear, nose snapping and flashing like an advertising sign, crossed eyes registering a rather mild surprise.)

No, not that, Blaine pleaded. *Just stretched out underneath the tree, dead to all the world. He thinks there's something wrong with me . . .*

There is . . .

But not what he—

And Godfrey Stone was saying, smoothly, friendly, with a half-relieved, half-worried smile: 'So you've been having the old trouble. Too much liquor, I suppose. You know the doctor told you—'

'Ah, hell,' protested Blaine, 'just a snort or two. Not enough . . .'

'Aunt Edna has been wild,' said Harriet. 'She imagined all sorts of things. You know what an imaginer she is. She was convinced you were gone for good and all this time.'

Godfrey! Godfrey! Oh, my God, three years . . .

Take it easy, Shep. No time now. Get you out of here.

Dr Wetmore said: 'You people know this man? A relative of yours?'

'Not relatives,' said Stone. 'Just friends. His Aunt Edna—'

'Well, let's go,' said Blaine.

Stone glanced questioningly at the doctor, and Wetmore nodded.

'Stop at the desk,' he said, 'and pick up his release. I'll phone it down. They'll want your names.'

'Gladly,' said Stone. 'And thank you very much.'

'It's quite all right.'

Blaine stopped at the door and turned back to the doctor.

'I'm sorry,' he said. 'I didn't tell the truth. I am not proud of it.'

'All of us,' the doctor said, 'have moments in which we can take no pride. You are not alone.'

'Good-by, Doctor.'

'So long,' said the doctor. 'Take care of yourself.'

Then they were going down the corridor, the three of them abreast.

Who was in that other bed? asked Stone.

A man by the name of Riley.

Riley!

A truck driver.

Riley! He was the man we were looking for. We just ran into you.

Stone halted and half turned to go back.

No use, said Blaine. *He's dead.*

And his truck?

Smashed. He ran off the road.

'Oh, Godfrey!' Harriet cried.

He shook his head at her. 'No use,' he said. 'No use.'

Hey, what is going on?

We'll tell you all of it. First, let's get out of here.

Stone seized him by the elbow and hustled him along.

Just one thing. How is Lambert Finn mixed up in all of this?

'Lambert Finn,' Stone said vocally, 'is the most dangerous man in the world today.'

19

'Don't you think we should drive a little farther?' Harriet asked. 'If that doctor should get suspicious . . .'

Stone wheeled the car into the drive.

'Why should he get suspicious?'

'He'll get to thinking. He's puzzled by what happened to Shep and he'll get to wondering. After all, our story had a lot of holes in it.'

'For one thought up on the moment, I thought we did real well.'

'But we're only ten miles out of town.'

'I'll want to go back tonight. I have to do some checking on what became of Riley's truck.'

He braked the car to a halt in front of the unit marked 'Office'.

'Run your head into a noose, you mean,' said Harriet.

The man who had been sweeping off the steps walked over to the car.

'Welcome, folks,' he said, heartily. 'What can the Plainsman do for you?'

'Have you two connecting?'

'It just so happens,' said the man, 'we have. Nice weather we been having.'

'Yes, very splendid weather.'

'Might turn cold, though. Any day. It is getting late. I can remember when we had snow—'

'But not this year,' said Stone.

'No, not this year. You were saying you wanted two connecting.'

'If you don't mind.'

'Drive right on, straight ahead. Numbers ten and eleven. I'll get the keys and be right along.'

Stone lifted the car on gentle jets and slid down the roadway. Other cars were parked cozily against their units. People were unloading trunks. Others were sitting in chairs on the little patios. Down at the far end of the parkway a foursome of old codgers were loudly pitching horseshoes.

The car skidded into the space before No. 10 and settled easily to the ground.

Blaine got out and held the door for Harriet.

And it was good, he thought, it was almost like *home* to be with these two again – with two who had been lost and now were here again. No matter what might happen, he was with his own once more.

The motel sat atop the bluffs above the river, and from where he stood he could see the wide sweep of terrain north and east – the bald, brown bluffs and the erosion of the timbered gullies and ravines that ran down to the river valley, where a tangled expanse of ragged woods hemmed in the chocolate-flowing stream which meandered with an uneasiness of purpose, as if it could not quite make up its mind where it wished to go, leaving behind it, as landmarks of its indecision, isolated ponds and lakes and crazily winding sloughs as erratic in their course as the river ever could be.

There was a cleanness and a roominess that caught one's imagination. There was a breath of freshness and the sense of space.

The manager came trotting down the walk, jangling a couple of keys. He unlocked the doors and flung them open.

'You'll find everything O.K.,' he said. 'We are very careful. There are shutters for all windows, and the locks throughout are the best available. You'll find a supply of hex signs and good luck charms in the supply cabinet. We used to have them installed, but we found our guests have their own ideas on how they are best used.'

'That,' said Stone, 'is very thoughtful of you.'

'It is good,' said the manager, 'to be snug and under cover.'

'You said a mouthful, pal,' said Stone.

'And we have a restaurant up front . . .'

'We'll be using it,' said Harriet. 'I am almost starved.'

'You can stop on your way,' said the manager, 'and sign the register, if you would.'

'Of course,' said Harriet.

He handed her the keys and went jogging up the walk, bobbing and bowing in merry hostship to the occupants of the other units.

'Let's get inside,' said Stone.

He held the door for Harriet and Blaine, then stepped in himself and closed the door behind him.

Harriet tossed the keys down on a dresser and turned around to look about the room.

'And you,' she said to Blaine. 'Whatever happened to you? I went back to that place on the border and the town was in a stew. Something dreadful had happened. I never found out what. I never had a chance to learn. I had to get out fast.'

'I got away,' Blaine told her.

Stone held out his hand. 'You did it better than I did. You got clean away.'

Blaine's hand was engulfed in Stone's great fist and held there – not shaken up and down, but held there.

'It's good to have you here,' said Stone.

'You phoned that night,' said Blaine, 'or I'd have been caught flat-footed. I remembered what you said. I didn't wait around for them to put the finger on me.'

Stone let go of his hand and they stood facing one another and it was a different Stone who stood there than the one that Blaine remembered. Stone had always been a big man and he was still a big man, but now the bigness was not only physical and external – there was a bigness of the spirit and of purpose that one must sense immediately at the sight of him. And a hardness that had not been there before.

'I am not sure,' Blaine told him, 'that I've done you any favor, showing up like this. I traveled slow and awkward. By now Fishhook more than likely has a hounder on me.'

Stone made a motion to dismiss the thought, almost a motion of impatience, as if Fishhook could not matter here, as if Fishhook mattered nowhere any more.

He moved across the room and sat down in a chair.

'What happened to you, Shep?'

'I got contaminated.'

'So did I,' said Stone.

He was silent for a moment, as if he might be thinking back to that time when he had fled from Fishhook.

'I turned from the phone,' he said, 'and they were waiting for me. I went along with them. There was nothing else to do. They took me to a place . . .' (*A great sprawling place set upon a seacoast, with one huge rambling house – white, so white it glistened – with the sky so blue above it that the blueness hurt one's eyes, a blue that picked up and reflected back the brightness of the sun, and yet a blue with depth that one could gaze into so far that he was lost in distance. And around the sprawling building, other buildings that fell short of the sprawling big house only because of their lack of size. A sweep of lawn that one knew instantly could grow so lushly only by virtue of constant watering. Beyond the green of lawn lay a snow-white strip of sandy beach and the green-blue of the ocean with the froth of spray thrown high into the air where the surf came hammering in on the rocks beyond the beach. And upon the beach the gypsy color of many umbrellas . . .)*

'It was, I found out later, in Baja California. A perfect wilderness of a place with this fabulous resort planted in the wilderness . . .' (*The golf course flags flapping in the ocean breeze, the flat white rectangles of the tennis court, the patio with the guests sitting idly and talking, waiting for the liquor carts and the sandwich trays and dressed in vacation costumes that were impeccable.*) 'There was fishing such as you had never dreamed of and hunting in the hills and swimming the entire year around . . .'

'Hard to take,' said Harriet, idly.

'No,' said Stone, 'not hard to take at all. Not for six weeks. Not even for six months. There was everything a man might want. There was food and drink and women. Your slightest wish was filled. Your money was no good. Everything was free.'

'But I can see,' said Blaine, 'how a man might—'

'Of course you can,' said Stone. 'The utter uselessness. As if someone had taken you, a man, and turned you back into a boy, with nothing left but play. And yet Fishhook was being kind. Even as you hated it and resented it and rebelled against it, you could see their point. They had nothing against us, really. There had been no crime, no negligence of duty – that is, with most of us there hadn't. But they couldn't take the chance of continuing to use us and they could not turn us loose, for there must, you understand, be no blot upon the Fishhook name. It never must be said of them that they turned loose upon the world a man with a streak of alienness, with a mind or an emotion that deviated even by a hairsbreadth from the human viewpoint. So they gave us a long vacation – an endless vacation – in the kind of place that millionaires inhabit.

'And it was insidious. You hated it and still you could not leave, for common sense would tell you that you were a fool to leave it. You were living safe and high. There was no question of security. You really had it made. You thought about escaping – although you could scarcely think of it as escape, for there was nothing really holding you. That is, until you tried. Then you found out about the guards and outposts. Only then you learned that every trail and road was covered. This despite the fact that a man afoot would have been committing suicide to go charging out into the land. You found out, by slow degrees, about the men who watched you all the time – the men who posed as guests but were really Fishhook agents who kept an eye on every one of you, waiting for the sign that you were getting set, or even thinking of getting out of there.

'But the bars that held you, the bars that kept you in were the luxury and soft living. It is hard to walk out on a thing like that. And Fishhook knows it is. It is, I tell you, Shep, the tightest, hardest prison man has yet devised.

'But, like any other prison, it made you tough and hard. It made you fight to get tough and hard, to get tough enough to make up your mind, and hard enough, once you'd made it up, to carry out your plan. When you learned about the spies and guards, you got sly and clever, and those very spies and guards were the ones who gave you purpose. Fishhook overplayed its hand by building in any security at all, for none was really needed. Left to yourself, you might have escaped every second week, but come trailing back when you found how rough it was outside. But when you found that there were physical barriers – when you found out about the men and guns and dogs – then you had a challenge and it became a game and it was your life you were shoving out into the pot . . .'

'But,' said Blaine, 'there couldn't have been too many escapes, not even many tries. Otherwise Fishhook would have dreamed up new angles. They'd never let it stand.'

Stone grinned wolfishly. 'You're right. There were not many who ever made it. There were few who even tried.'

'You and Lambert Finn.'

'Lambert,' Stone said, dryly, 'was a daily inspiration for me. He'd escaped some years before I was taken there. And there was one other, years before Lambert. No one knows to this day what ever happened to him.'

'Well, O.K.,' asked Blaine, 'what does happen to a man who escapes from Fishhook, who runs away from Fishhook? Where does he end up? Here I am, with a couple of dollars in my pocket that aren't even mine, but belong to Riley, without identity, without a profession or a trade. How do I—'

'You sound as if you might regret having run away.'

'There are times I have. Momentarily, that is. If I had it to do over, I'd do it differently. I'd have it planned ahead. I'd transfer some funds to some other country. I'd have a new identity all worked out and pat. I'd have boned up on something that would turn me into an economic asset—'

'But you never really believed that you'd have to run. You knew it had happened to me, but you told yourself it couldn't happen to yourself.'

'I guess that is about the size of it.'

'You feel,' said Stone, 'that you've turned into a misfit.'

Blaine nodded.

'Welcome to the club,' said Stone.

'You mean—'

'No, not me. I have a job to do. A most important job.'

'But—'

'I'm speaking,' Stone told him, 'of a vast segment of all mankind. I have no idea how many million people.'

'Well, of course, there always were—'

'Wrong again,' said Stone. 'It's the parries, man, the parries. The parries who are not in Fishhook. You couldn't have traveled almost a thousand miles and—'

'I saw,' said Blaine, a cold shudder building in him, an icelike quality that was neither fear nor hate, but a part of both. 'I saw what was happening.'

'It's a waste,' said Stone. 'A terrible waste, both to the parry and the human race. Here are people who are being hunted down, people who are forced into ghettos, people who are reviled and hated – and all the time, within them lies the hope of humankind.

'And I tell you something else. It is not only these intolerant, bigoted, ignorant savages who think of themselves as normal human beings who are to blame for the situation. It is Fishhook itself; Fishhook which must bear part of the blame. For Fishhook has institutionalized paranormal kinetics for its own selfish and particular purpose. It has taken care, most excellent care, of those parries like you and I, handpicking us to carry on their work. But they've turned their face against the others. They have given not a sign that they might care what might happen to them. All they'd have to do is stretch out their hand and yet they fail to do it and they leave the other parries in the position of wild animals running in the woods.'

'They are afraid—'

'They just don't give a damn,' said Stone. 'The situation as it stands suits them to the ground. Fishhook started as a human crusade. It has turned into one of the greatest monopolies the world has ever known – a monopoly that is unhampered by a single line of regulation or restriction, except as they may choose to impose upon themselves.'

'I am hungry,' Harriet announced.

Stone paid her no attention. He leaned forward in his chair.

'There are millions of these outcasts,' he declared. 'Untrained. Persecuted when they should be given all encouragement. They have abilities at this very moment that mankind, also at this very moment, needs most desperately. They have untrained and latent talents that would prove if exercised, greater than anything that Fishhook ever has attained.

'There was a time when there was a need for Fishhook. No matter what may happen, no matter what event, the world owes Fishhook more than it ever can repay. But the time has come when we no longer have any need of Fishhook. Fishhook today, so long as it ignores the parries who are not within its fold, has become a brake upon the advancement of the human race. The utilization of PK must no longer remain a monopoly of Fishhook.'

'But there is this terrible prejudice,' Blaine pointed out. 'This blind intolerance—'

'Granted,' Stone told him, 'and part of it was earned. PK was abused and used, most shamefully used for selfish and ignoble reasons. It was taken and forced into the pattern of the old world that now is dead. And for that reason the parries have a guilt complex. Under this present persecution and their own deep-rooted sense of guilt they cannot operate effectively, either for their own good or for the benefit of humanity. But there is no question that if they could operate openly and effectively, without the pressure of public censure, they could do far more than Fishhook, as it now is constituted, ever can accomplish. And if they were allowed to do this, if they could only be allowed to show that non-Fishhook PK could operate for human betterment, then they'd become accepted and instead of censure would have support and encouragement, and in that day, Shep, Man would have taken a great step forward.

'But we must show the world that PK is a human ability and not a Fishhook ability. And furthermore – if this could be done, then the entire human race would return to sanity and would regain its old-time self-respect.'

'You're talking in terms,' Blaine told him, 'of cultural evolution. It is a process that will take some time. In the end, of course, it may work out naturally – another hundred years.'

'We can't wait!' cried Stone.

'There were the old religious controversies,' Blaine pointed out. 'War between Protestant and Catholic, between Islam and Christianity. And where is it all now? There was the old battle between the Communist dictatorships and the democracies . . .'

'Fishhook helped with that. Fishhook became a powerful third force.'

'Something always helps,' said Blaine. 'There can be no end to hope. Conditions and events become so ordered that the quarrel of yesterday becomes an academic problem for historians to chew on.'

'A hundred years,' said Stone. 'You'd wait a hundred years?'

'You won't have to,' Harriet told him. 'You have it started now. And Shep will be a help.'

'Me?'

'Yes, you.'

'Shep,' said Stone, 'please listen.'

'I am listening,' said Blaine, and the shudder was growing in him once again, and the sense of alienness, for there was danger here.

'I have made a start,' said Stone. 'I have a group of parries – call them underground, call them cadre, call them committee – a group of parries who are working out preliminary plans and tactics for certain experiments and investigations that will demonstrate the effective action which the free, non-Fishhook parries can contribute to their fellow men . . .'

'Pierre!' exclaimed Blaine, looking at Harriet.

She nodded.

'And this is what you had in mind from the very start. At Charline's party you said old pal, old friend . . .'

'Is it so bad?' she asked.

'No, I don't suppose it is.'

'Would you have gone along,' she asked, 'if you'd known of it?'

'I don't know. Harriet, I honestly don't know.'

Stone rose from his chair and walked the step or two to Blaine. He put out both his hands and dropped them on Blaine's shoulders. His fingers tightened hard.

'Shep,' he said, solemnly. 'Shep, this is important. This is necessary work. Fishhook can't be the only contact Man has with the stars. One part of the human race cannot be free of earth and the rest remain earthbound.'

In the dim light of the room his eyes had lost their hardness. They became mystical, with the shine of unshed tears.

His voice was soft when he spoke again. 'There are certain stars,' he said, almost whispering, as if he might be talking to himself, 'that men must visit. To know what heights the human race can reach. To save their very souls.'

Harriet was busily gathering up her handbag and her gloves.

'I don't care,' she announced. 'I am going out to eat. I am simply starved. You two coming with me?'

'Yes,' said Blaine, 'I'll go.'

Then suddenly remembered.

She caught the thought and laughed softly.

'It'll be on us,' she said. 'Let us say in part payment for the times you fed the both of us.'

'No need to be,' said Stone. 'He's already on the payroll. He's got himself a job. How about it, Shep?'

Blaine said nothing.

'Shep, are you with me? I need you. I can't do without you. You're the difference I need.'

'I am with you,' Blaine said simply.

'Well, now,' said Harriet, 'since that is settled, let us go and eat.'

'You two go along,' said Stone. 'I'll hold the fort.'

'But, Godfrey—'

'I've got some thinking that I have to do. A problem or two . . .'

'Come along,' Harriet said to Blaine. 'He wants to sit and think.'

Puzzled, Blaine went along with her.

20

Harriet settled herself resolutely and comfortably in her chair as they waited for their orders.

'Now tell me all about it,' she demanded. 'What happened in that town? And what has happened since? How did you get in that hospital room?'

'Later,' Blaine objected. 'There'll be time later on to tell you all of that. First tell me what is wrong with Godfrey.'

'You mean him staying back in the room to think?'

'Yes, that. But there is more than that. This strange obsession of his. And the look in his eyes. The way he talks, about men going to the stars to save their souls. He is like an old-time hermit who has seen a vision.'

'He has,' said Harriet. 'That is exactly it.'

Blaine stared.

'It happened on that last exploratory trip,' said Harriet. 'He came back touched. He had seen something that had shaken him.'

'I know,' said Blaine. 'There are things out there. . .'

'Horrible, you mean.'

'Horrible, sure. That is part of it. Incomprehensible is a better word. Processes and motives and mores that are absolutely impossible in the light of human knowledge and morality. Things that make no sense at all, that you can't figure out. A stone wall so far as human understanding is concerned. And it scares you. You have no point of orientation. You stand utterly alone, surrounded by nothing that was ever of your world.'

'And yet you stand up to it?'

'I always did,' said Blaine. 'It takes a certain state of mind – a state of mind that Fishhook drills into you everlastingly.'

'With Godfrey it was different. It was something that he understood and recognized. Perhaps he recognized it just a bit too well. It was goodness.'

'Goodness!'

'A flimsy word,' said Harriet. 'A pantywaist of a word. A sloppy kind of word, but the only word that fits.'

'Goodness,' Blaine said again, as if he were rolling the word about, examining it for texture and for color.

'A place,' said Harriet, 'where there was no greed, no hate, no driving personal ambition to foster either hate or greed. A perfect place with a perfect race. A social paradise.'

'I don't see . . .'

'Think a minute and you will. Have you ever seen a thing, an object, a painting, a piece of statuary, a bit of scenery, so beautiful and so perfect you ached when you looked at it?'

'Yes. A time or two.'

'Well, then – a painting or a piece of statuary is a thing outside the human life, your life. It is an emotional experience only. It actually has nothing at all to do with you yourself. You could live very well the rest of your life if you never saw it again, although you would remember it every now and then and the ache would come again at the memory of it. But imagine a form of life, a culture, a way of life, *a way you, yourself could live*, so beautiful that it made you ache just like the painting, but a thousandfold more so. That's what Godfrey saw, that is what he talked with. That is why he came back touched. Feeling like a dirty little boy from across the tracks looking through the bars into fairyland – a real, actual, living fairyland that he could reach out and touch but never be part of.'

Blaine drew in a long breath and slowly let it out.

'So that is it,' he said. 'That is what he wants.'

'Wouldn't you?'

'I suppose. If I had seen it.'

'Ask Godfrey. He will tell you. Or, come to think of it, don't ask him. He'll tell you anyhow.'

'He told you?'

'Yes.'

'And you are impressed?'

'I am here,' she said.

The waitress came with their orders – great sizzling steaks, with baked potatoes and a salad. She set a coffee bottle in the center of the table.

'That looks good,' said Harriet. 'I am always hungry. Remember, Shep, that first time you took me out?'

Blaine smiled. 'I'll never forget it. You were hungry that time, too.'

'And you bought me a rose.'

'It seems to me I did.'

'You're a sweet guy, Shep.'

'If I recall correctly, you're a newspaper gal. How come—'

'I'm still working on a story.'

'Fishhook,' said Blaine. 'Fishhook is your story.'

'Part of it,' she said, returning to her steak.

They ate for a while with very little talk.

'There is one other thing,' Blaine finally said. 'Just what gives with Finn? Godfrey said he was dangerous.'

'What do you know of Finn?'

'Not much of anything. He was out of Fishhook before I tied up with it. But the story went around. He came back screaming. Something happened to him.'

'Something did,' said Harriet. 'And he's been preaching it up and down the land.'

'Preaching?'

'Hell and brimstone preaching. Bible-pounding preaching, except there is no Bible. The evil of the stars. Man must stay on Earth. It's the only safe place for him. There is evil out there. And it has been the parries who have opened up the gates to this spawn of evil . . .'

'And the people swallow that?'

'They swallow it,' said Harriet. 'They wallow in it clear up to their middles. They absolutely love it. They can't have the stars, you see. So there's satisfaction to them that the stars are evil.'

'And the parries, I suspect, are evil, too. They are ghouls and werewolves . . .'

'And goblins,' said Harriet. 'And witches. And harpies. You name it and they're it.'

'The man's a mountebank.'

Harriet shook her head. 'Not a mountebank. He's as serious as Godfrey. He believes the evil. Because, you see, he saw the evil.'

'And Godfrey saw the good.'

'That's it. It's as simple as all that. Finn is just as convinced Man has no business among the stars as Godfrey is convinced he'll find salvation there.'

'And both of them are fighting Fishhook.'

'Godfrey wants to end the monopoly but retain the structure. Finn goes farther. Fishhook's incidental to him. PK is his target. He wants to wipe it out.'

'And Finn's been fighting Stone.'

'Harassing him,' said Harriet. 'There's no way to fight him, really. Godfrey shows little for anyone to hit at. But Finn found out about him and sees him as the one key figure who can prop the parries on their feet. If he can, he'll knock him out.'

'You don't seem too worried.'

'Godfrey's not worried. Finn's just another problem, another obstacle.'

They left the restaurant and walked down the strip of pavement that fronted on the units.

The river valley lay in black and purple shadow with the river a murky bronze in the dying light of day. The tops of the bluffs across the valley still were flecked with sunlight, and far up in the sky a hawk still wheeled, wings a silver flash as he tilted in the blue.

They reached the door of the unit, and Blaine pushed it open and stood aside for Harriet, then followed. He had just crossed the threshold when she bumped into him as she took a backward step.

He heard the sharp gasp in her throat, and her body, pressed against his, went hard and tense.

Looking over her shoulder, he saw Godfrey Stone, face downward, stretched upon the floor.

21

Even as he bent above him, Blaine knew that Stone was dead. There was a smallness to him, a sort of essential withering of the human form, as if life had been a basic dimension that had helped to fill him out. Now he was something less than six feet of limp body clothed in crumpled cloth, and the stillness of him was somehow very dreadful.

Behind him, he heard Harriet pulling shut the door and shooting home the bolts. And in the clatter of the bolts he thought he heard a sob.

He bent down for a closer look and in the dimness could make out the darker shine of hair where the blood had oozed out of the skull.

The window shutters creaked and groaned, sliding home with a clatter as Harriet shoved the lever that controlled them.

'Maybe, now,' he said, 'we can have a little light.'

'Just a minute, Shep.'

The lighting toggle clicked and light sprang from the ceiling, and in the glare of it Blaine could see how a heavy blow had crushed in the skull.

There was no need to hunt for pulse, no need to listen for a heartbeat. No man could live with a skull so out of shape.

Blaine rocked back and teetered, crouched upon his toes, marveling at the ferocity and, perhaps, the desperation, which must have driven the arm that had delivered such a blow.

He looked at Harriet and nodded quietly, wondering at her calmness, then remembering, even as he wondered, that in her reporting days violent death could have been no stranger to her.

'It was Finn,' she said, her voice quiet and low, so quiet that one could sense the checkrein she'd put upon herself. 'Not Finn, himself, of course. Someone that he hired. Or someone that volunteered. One of his wide-eyed followers. There are a lot of people who'd do anything for him.'

She came across the room and squatted across the corpse from Blaine. Her mouth was set in a straight, grim line. Her face was pinched and stern. And there was a streak down her face where a single tear had run.

'What do we do now?' he asked. 'The police, I would imagine.'

She made a restraining motion with her arm.

'Not the police,' she said. 'We can't afford to get tangled up in this. That would be exactly what Finn and his crew would want. What do you bet that someone has phoned the police already?'

'You mean the killer?'

'Certainly. Why not? Just a voice saying that a man has been killed in unit number ten out at The Plainsman. Then hang up real quick.'

'To put us on the spot?'

'To put whoever was with Godfrey on the spot. They maybe even know exactly who we are. That doctor—'

'I don't know,' said Blaine. 'He may have.'

'Listen, Shep, I'm positive from all that's happened that Finn is in Belmont.'

'Belmont?'

'That town we found you in.'

'So that's the name of it.'

'There's something happening,' she said. 'Something happening right here. Something important going on. There was Riley and the truck and—'

'But what are we to do?'

'We can't let them find Godfrey here.'

'We could pull the car out back and take him out the back door.'

'There's probably someone watching. Then they'd have us cold.'

She beat her hands together in exasperation.

'If Finn has a free hand now,' she said, 'he probably can pull off whatever he is planning. We can't let him put us out of action. We have got to stop him.'

'We?'

'You and I. You step into Godfrey's shoes. Now it's up to you.'

'But I—'

Her eyes blazed suddenly. 'You were his friend. You heard his story. You told him you were with him.'

'Sure I did,' said Blaine. 'But I am starting cold. I don't know the score.'

'Stop Finn,' she said. 'Find out what he's doing and stop him in his tracks. Fight a delaying action . . .'

'You and your military thinking. Your delaying actions and your lines of retreat laid out.' (*A very female general with enormous jackboots and a flock of medals pendant from very spearlike breasts.*)

Cut that out!

A newspaper gal. And you are objective.

'Shep,' she said, 'shut up. How can I be objective? I believed in Godfrey. I believed in what he was doing.'

'I suppose that I do, too. But it is all so new, so quick . . .'

'Maybe we should just cut and run.'

'No! Wait a minute. If we cut and run, we'd be out of it as surely as if they caught us here.'

'But, Shep, there is no way.'

'There just might be,' he told her. 'Is there a town around here by the name of Hamilton?'

'Why, yes, just a mile or two away. Down by the river.'

He sprang to his feet and glanced about the room.

The phone sat on the night table between the single beds.

'What—'

'A friend,' said Blaine. 'Someone that I met. Someone who might help us. A mile or two away?'

'Yes, Hamilton is. If that is whàt—'

'It is,' said Blaine.

He stepped swiftly across the room and picked the handpiece out of the cradle. He dialed for operator.

'I want to get a number in Hamilton. How do I go about it?'

'What is the number, sir?'

'276.'

'I will ring it for you.'

He turned his head toward Harriet. 'Is it getting dark outside?'

'It was getting dark when I closed the shutters.'

He heard the purring of the signal on the wire.

'They'll need some darkness,' he said. 'They couldn't come in—'

'I don't know,' said Harriet, 'what you could be up to.'

'Hello,' said a voice in the phone.

'Is Anita there?'

'Right here,' said the voice. 'Just a moment.' *Anita, for you. A man.*

And that was impossible, Blaine thought wildly: You simply couldn't do it. Perhaps he'd imagined it.

'Hello,' said Anita Andrews. 'Who is this?'

Blaine. Shepherd Blaine. Remember? I was with the man who had the shotgun. With the silver shot.

Yes, I remember you.

And it was true, he thought. He had not imagined it. You *could* use telepathy on the telephone!

You said that if I ever needed help.

Yes, I told you that.

I need help now. (*A body on the floor; police car coming down*

115

*the road, red light flashing, siren howling; a speedometer and
clock that had sprouted legs and were racing for a tape; the sign
that said The Plainsman, the unit number on the door.) I swear
to you, Anita. This is on the level. I can't explain right now. But
this is on the level. I can't let them find him here.*

We'll take him off your hands.

On faith?

On faith alone. You were square with us that night.

Hurry!

Right away. I'll bring some others.

Thanks, Anita. But she was already gone.

He stood there, holding the receiver out from his face, staring
at it, then slowly put it in the cradle.

'I caught part of that,' said Harriet. 'It isn't possible.'

'Of course it's not,' said Blaine. 'Telly transmission on a wire.
You don't have to tell me.'

He stared down at the man lying on the floor. 'It's one of the
things he talked about. Greater than Fishhook could ever be, he
said.'

Harriet didn't answer.

'I wonder how much else they have?' said Blaine.

'She said they'd come for Godfrey. How will they come for
him? How soon?'

There was a hint of hysteria in her voice.

'They fly,' he told her. 'They are levitators. Witches.'

He made a bitter laugh.

'But you—'

'How did I know them? They ambushed us one night. Just out
to raise some hell. Riley had a shotgun . . .'

'Riley!'

'The man in the hospital room, remember? The man who died.
He was in an accident.'

'But, Shep, were you with Riley? How did you come to be with
him?'

'I hitched a ride. He was scared at night. He wanted someone
with him. We nursed that ramshackle truck . . .'

She was staring at him, a startled look about her.

'Wait a minute,' he said. 'You said something back there in the
hospital. You said you were—'

'Looking for him. Godfrey had hired him and he was late
and—'

'But . . .'

'What is it, Shep?'

'I talked to him just before he died. He tried to give me a

message, but he couldn't get it out. The message was for Finn. That was the first I heard of Finn.'

'Everything went wrong,' said Harriet. 'Every blessed thing. There was the star machine . . .'

She stopped what she was saying and came across the room to stand beside him. 'But you don't know about the star machine. Or do you?'

He shook his head. 'Like the ones in Fishhook? The ones that helped us to the stars?'

She nodded. 'That's what Riley was hauling in his truck. Godfrey had arranged to get it and he had to get it moved to Pierre somehow. So he hired Riley . . .'

'A bootleg star machine!' said Blaine, a little awed. 'You know that every nation in the world has laws against possessing them. They're only legal if they are in Fishhook.'

'Godfrey knew all that. But he needed one. He tried to build one, but he couldn't. There aren't any blueprints.'

'You bet your life there aren't.'

'Shep, what is wrong with you?'

'I don't know. There's really nothing wrong. A bit confused, perhaps. At how, all along the line, I was pitchforked into this.'

'You can always run.'

'Harriet, you know better. I am through with running. There's no place for me to go.'

'You could always approach some business group. They'd be glad to have you. They'd give you a job, pay you plenty for what you know of Fishhook.'

He shook his head, thinking back to Charline's party, with Dalton sitting there, long legs outstretched, his hair a rumpled mouse nest, his mouth mangling the cigar. And Dalton saying: 'In a consultive capacity you'd be worth a lot of money.'

'Well, you could,' said Harriet.

'I couldn't stomach it Besides, I made a promise. I told Godfrey I was with him. And I don't like the way that things are going. I don't like the people taking me out to hang me because I am a parry. I don't like some of the things I saw along the road and—'

'You're bitter,' she said. 'You have a right to be.'

'And you?'

'Not bitter. Just scared. Scared down to the marrow.'

You scared! A tough newspaper gal . . .

He turned toward her, remembering something – the place where the old blind woman sold the roses. That night, he had seen the mask slip from Harriet Quimby and this was the second time.

Her face told him the truth – the tough newspaper gal also, at times, could be a frightened woman.

He half lifted his arms, and she crossed the little space between them. He held her close against him, and she was soft and pliant, not hard, not made of steely purpose, but very human flesh.

It'll be all right, he said. *Everything will be all right.*

And wondered at the sudden tenderness and protectiveness he felt, which certainly was alien in any relation he might have with this girl within his arms.

But the truck is wrecked and the trucker's dead and the police, or maybe even Finn, have the star machine. And now Godfrey's lying dead and the police are coming . . .

We'll lick them all, he told her. *There's nothing that can stop us . . .*

A siren sounded from far off, a wail torn by the prairie wind.

She sprang away from him. 'Shep, they're coming!'

'The back door!' Blaine said, quickly. 'Run toward the river. We'll get down into the breaks.'

He sprang toward the door, and as his fingers found the bolt, there was a tapping on it.

He threw back the bolt and jerked open the door and standing in the fan of light that came pouring from the room was Anita Andrews and back of her other youthful faces.

'Just in time,' said Blaine.

'This body?'

'Over there,' he said.

They came in with a rush.

The siren was much closer.

'He was a friend of ours,' said Harriet, uncertainly. 'This seems a dreadful way—'

'Miss,' Anita said, 'we'll take care of him. We'll give him every honor . . .'

The siren was a steady howl that seemed to fill the room.

Quick! Anita said. *Fly low. You don't want to silhouette against the sky.*

Even as she spoke the room was emptying and there was no body on the floor.

She hesitated for a moment, looking at the two of them.

Someday you'll tell me what this is all about?

Someday, said Blaine. *And thanks.*

Any time, she said. *We parries stick together. We have to stick together. They'll smash us if we don't.*

She swung toward Blaine, and he felt the touch of her, mind against mind, and there was suddenly the sense of fireflies in the evening dusk and the smell of lilacs drifting in the softness of a river fog.

Then she was gone and the front door was closing and someone was hammering at the front.

Sit down, Blaine said to Harriet. *Act as naturally as you can. Unconcerned. Relaxed. We were just sitting here and talking. Godfrey had been with us, but he went into town. Someone came and he rode into town with them. We don't know who it was. He should be back in an hour or two.*

Check, said Harriet.

She sat down in a chair and folded her hands in her lap sedately.

Blaine went to the door to let in the law.

22

Belmont was beginning to close up. All the houses, as they drove past, had been tightly shuttered, and in the business district, as they drove into it, the shop lights were going out.

Up the street a block or two, the marquee of the hotel still gleamed brightly in the dusk and just this side of it was a flashing sign that proclaimed the Wild West Bar still was willing to take on a customer.

'I don't think,' said Harriet, 'that we fooled those police too much.'

Blaine agreed. 'Maybe not. But we had them stopped. There was nothing they could find.'

'I thought for a while they would pull us in.'

'So did I. But you sat there making gentle fun of them. That was hard to take. They were glad to get away. They must have felt like fools.'

He motioned at the flashing bar sign. 'Maybe we should start with that.'

'As good a place as any. Likewise, about the only place there is.'

The bar was empty when they came into the place. The bartender had an elbow propped and was idly dabbing with a cloth at imaginary wet spots.

Blaine and Harriet hoisted themselves onto stools opposite the man.

'What'll it be?' he demanded of them.

They told him.

He got glasses and reached for bottles.

'Little slow tonight,' said Blaine.

'Almost closing time,' said the man. 'They don't stick around. Soon as it gets dark folks get under cover. Everyone in this town.'

'Bad town?'

'No, not especially. It's the curfew law. This place has got a tough one. Patrols all over the place and them cops are tough. They really make it stick.'

'How about yourself?' asked Harriet.

'Oh, I am all right, miss. The boys, they know me. They know the circumstances. They know I got to stick around just in case a late customer, like you, drops in. From the hotel mostly. They know I got to get the place tucked in and turn out the lights. They give me extra minutes.'

'Sounds tough, all right,' said Blaine.

The barkeep wagged his head. 'For your own protection, mister. Folks ain't got no sense. If it wasn't for the curfew, they'd stay out to all hours where anything could get them.'

He stopped what he was doing.

'I just happened to think,' he announced. 'I got something new. You might like to try it.'

'Like what?' asked Harriet.

He reached back and got the bottle, held it up to show them.

'Something new,' he said. 'Straight out of Fishhook. They picked it up some outlandish place. Sap of a tree or something. Probably loaded with a lot of hydrocarbons. I got a couple of bottles off the factor at the Trading Post. Just to try, you know. Thought there might be some folks who might like it.'

Blaine shook his head. 'Not for me. God knows what is in it.'

'Me, neither,' said Harriet.

The barkeep set the bottle back regretfully.

'I don't blame you folks,' he said, giving them the drinks he'd made. 'I took a nip of it myself. Just to test it out, you see, because I'm no drinking man.

'Not,' he added, quickly and parenthetically, 'that I have anything against it.'

'Of course not,' Harriet sympathized.

'It was funny tasting stuff,' he said. 'Not bad, you know. Not good, either. Had a musty tang. You might get to like it if you had a drink or two.'

He stood in silence for a moment, with his hands planted solidly on the bar.

'You know what I been thinking?' he demanded.

'Not the least,' said Harriet.

'I been wondering all this afternoon if that factor down at the Trading Post concocted that stuff up himself. Just as a sort of stinking joke, you see.'

'Oh, he wouldn't dare.'

'Well, I imagine you are right, miss. But all of them factors are funny sorts of jerks. Folks don't have much to do with them — socially, at least – but even so they manage to know more of what is going on than anyone in town. They must be listening all the time, for they have all the latest gossip.

'And,' said the barkeep, laying emphasis upon this horrid crime and this social failing, 'they don't never tell you nothing.'

Ain't it a fact,' Harriet agreed, enthusiastically.

The barkeep subsided into brooding silence.

Blaine took a wild shot in the dark. 'Lots of folks in town,' he said. 'Big doings?'

The barkeeper settled down into solid conversational stance and his voice dropped to a confidential level.

'You mean you ain't heard about it?'

'No. Just got in town a couple of hours ago.'

'Well, mister, you won't believe this – but we got a star machine.'

'A what?'

'A star machine. It's one of them contraptions that parries use to travel to the stars.'

'Never heard of them.'

'No reason that you should. The only place they're legal is in Fishhook.'

'You mean this one is illegal?'

'Couldn't be no more illegal. The state police, they've got it down in the old highway shed. You know, the one on the west edge of town. Maybe you drove by it coming in tonight.'

'I don't remember it.'

'Well, anyhow, it's there. And then, on top of that, who should show up but Lambert Finn.'

'You don't mean *the* Lambert Finn?'

'No one else. He's up there, in the hotel right now. He's going to have a big mass meeting out by the highway shed tomorrow. I hear the police have agreed to haul out the star machine so he can preach about it, with it standing there, right out in plain sight of all the people. I tell you, mister, that will be something worth your while to listen. He'll spout more brimstone than you ever heard before. He'll lay it on them parries. He'll take the hide clean off them. They won't dare to show their faces.'

'Not many of them around, most likely, in a town like this.'

'Well,' the bartender said, drawing out the word, 'not many in the town itself. But there's a place just a ways from here, down by the river. A place called Hamilton. It's all parry. It's a new town the parries built. Parries from all over. There's a name for a place like that – I should know the name, but I can't remember it. Like the place they used to keep the Jews in Europe.'

'Ghetto.'

The bartender smote the bar with a disgusted hand. 'Now, why couldn't I think of that? Yes, mister, that's the word. Ghetto. Except in the old days it was in the poor part of a city and now its out in the country, in the poor part of the country. That land down by the river don't amount to shucks. No place to build a town. But them parries like it down there. Long as they don't bother no one, no one bothers them. Long as they stay in line, we leave them alone. And we know where they are, and they know we know. Any time things start going wrong, we know right where to look.'

He glanced at the clock. 'If you folks want me to start another round, you'll have time to gulp it down.'

'No, thanks,' said Blaine. He laid two bills on the bar. 'Let it ride,' he said.

'Why, thank you, sir. I thank you very much.'

As they slid off the stools, he said: 'If I were you, I'd get under cover as soon as possible. The cops will be down on top of you if they catch you out.'

'We will,' said Harriet. 'And thanks for the conversation.'

'Pleasure,' said the barkeep. 'Pleasure any time.'

Outside the bar, Blaine held the car door for Harriet, then walked around it to get in on the other side.

'The highway shed?' he asked.

'Shep, what would you do there? We'd just get into trouble.'

'I'll figure out a way. We simply can't leave that machine there for Finn to preach a sermon over.'

'So I suppose you figure you'll just haul it off.'

'No, I guess not. It's too big and clumsy. But there has to be a way. We have to put a crimp in Finn. Somehow, we've got to manage.'

'They'll have a guard.'

'I don't think so, Harriet. Locked and bolted, but no guard.

There isn't anyone who would stand on guard. This town is plenty scared.'

'You're just like Godfrey,' she said. 'Both of you go around sticking out your necks.'

'You thought a lot of Godfrey.'

'Yes, a lot,' she said.

He started up the engine and swung the car out into the street.

The old highway shed was black and silent and there was nothing to indicate there was anyone around. They rode past it twice to look it over, moving slowly, and it was the same each time – just the big shed standing there, a relic of the days when there were highways to maintain, when there was need of road machinery to keep their surfaces in shape.

Blaine pulled the car off the road and threaded it easily through a willow thicket, set it down and turned off the lights.

Silence closed down on them; the darkness pulsed with quietness.

'Harriet,' said Blaine.

'Yes, Shep.'

'You stay here. Don't move. I am going up there.'

'You won't be long? There's nothing you can do.'

'I won't be long,' he said. 'Have we got a flashlight?'

'There's one in the glove compartment.'

He heard her fumbling in the dark. The catch on the door of the compartment clicked and the tiny light inside came on. The flashlight lay amid a clutter of road maps, of sunglasses, of other odds and ends.

She handed it to him. He snapped it on to test it, and it worked. He shut it off again and got out of the car.

'Sit tight,' he told her.

'And you,' she warned, 'be careful.'

23

The shed was larger than it had appeared to be when seen from the highway. It was surrounded by a high, rank growth of dead, dried weeds that rustled with stealthy sound in the slightest movement of the air. It was built of the corrugated metal sheets which had been much in use for buildings of this sort before the introduction some three-score years before the putty-plastic from

Aldebaran VII. Occasional windows, begrimed with dirt and ancient spider webs, broke the smooth expanse of metal. Two great upward-folding doors filled almost the entire front exposure.

To the east lay the dark outline of the town, silhouetted against the faint flush in the sky which told of a moon about to rise.

Cautiously, Blaine made a circuit of the building, looking for a way that might allow him to get in. He found nothing that was easy. The two folding doors were locked. There were a few sheets of metal that had loosened at the bottom, but the material was too heavy to allow one to bend it upward and thus create a rathole for a man to sneak inside.

There was, he realized, only one way to get in.

He went to the corner of the building nearest to the road and stood listening. Except for the harsh whispering of the weeds there was nothing to be heard. The highway was deserted and, he knew, most likely would remain so. There was no sign of light – no lamp, no glitter through a distant window. It was as if he and the shed stood in a world where there was no life at all.

He stared for a time at the willow thicket by the road, but there was no glint, no shine, nothing to indicate that a car was hidden there.

He stepped quickly from the corner and moved along the wall of metal until he came to a window. He took off his tattered jacket and wrapped it about his fist and forearm.

Then he struck a blow, and the window shattered. He struck other blows to remove the glass that was still hanging in the frame. Carefully he picked out the remaining splinters that would slash a man trying to crawl in.

Then he went back to the corner and stood there for a moment. The night still was motionless and silent.

Back at the window, he crawled into the shed, let himself down carefully, felt the floor beneath his feet. He took the flashlight from his pocket and turned it on. He swept a swath of light across the empty cavern of the shed's interior.

And there, close to the door, was the battered, broken truck which had found its rest at last, and the gleaming star machine that it had carried.

Walking as softly as he could, Blaine moved across the floor and stood beside the machine, shining his light upon it. And it was something that he knew well, it was a machine that back in Fishhook he had known intimately. There was a strange beauty in it, he told himself as he stood and looked at it, almost as if one could see, reflected in its surface, the far reaches of the universe to which it could help a man to go.

But it was old – one of the older models that Fishhook had replaced some ten years or so ago, and there was little doubt, he knew that it had somehow come from Fishhook. There must be many of the older models such as this stacked away in some almost forgotten storehouse, stored there more than likely because it was easier to store them than it was to break them up. For something such as this must either be stored under lock and key or it must be broken up, for they could not be simply thrown away. In this machine lay the key to Fishhook's monopoly and there must be no possibility that one of them should fall into any other hands.

But one of them had fallen into other hands and here it lay tonight, mute evidence of one of the smartest, slickest bits of intrigue to which Fishhook, intrigue-ridden as it was, had ever been unwitting party.

Blaine tried to imagine how Stone had ever managed, and thinking of it, his admiration for the man rose a notch or two. It had taken money, surely, and it had taken trusted agents and it had required a plan of operation which would countenance no slip-up.

He wondered vaguely, as he stood there, how much Harriet might have had to do with it. Certainly, he told himself, she had had no qualms, in the process of smuggling him from Fishhook, of getting out herself. She was, he thought, just the kind of woman who could engineer a thing like this – selfpossessed and calm and with a sure and certain knowledge of all those inner workings which made Fishhook keep on ticking. And with a mind that operated with the fine precision of a good Swiss watch.

Stone had had great hopes of this machine and now the hopes were gone. Now Stone was dead and the star machine lay here in this abandoned shed, a showpiece bit of evidence for a man so filled with hate that he would destroy paranormal kinetics, root and branch and leaf.

And Finn could make much of this machine, for while it might be called machine, it was not the kind of machine to which the human mind for centuries has become accustomed. It had no moving parts and it had no function that was discernible. It was designed to work upon nothing more material than the human mind and senses. It worked with symbolism rather than with energy – and yet it worked. Just as a rosary in the hands of the devout had worked for centuries before there had ever been a thought of such a thing as a paranormal human.

If the hope were gone, thought Blaine, then the machine could not remain. If he owed Stone nothing else, he owed him that much at least. He owed him, he reminded himself, some slight repayment for that night he'd phoned.

There was a way – there was a way, he knew, if out of the frothing sea of alien knowledge which surged inside of him he could only pull it forth.

He sought for it and found it and in the finding of it he touched on other knowledge, all neatly docketed and primly pigeonholed, as if some filing clerk had been busily at work within his cluttered mind.

He stood weak and trembling at the discovery of this pigeon-holing, for he had not known, had had no inkling that it was going on. But it was the human way, he told himself – it was an evidence of human rebellion against the piecemeal disorderliness of the mass of data which had been dumped into his mind by the creature on that distant planet.

The creature still was with him, or the essence of the creature, and he hunted for it among the pigeonholes, but it was not there; there was no sign of it as such, but there was something else; there was something very wrong.

Startled, he went scrambling on the trail of wrongness and he caught and held it, muzzling it with a nose of horror – for it was simply this: His mind no longer was an entirely human mind. And in the edge of terror was the terrible wonder of how he still retained enough pure humanity to know this was the case.

He put out his hand in a blind and groping way and caught a corner of the star machine and held tightly onto it.

It all spelled out, he suspected, to the simple fact that he remained human, or mostly human, on the surface, while beneath that surface was a fusion of two individuals, of the knowledge and perhaps the ethics and the motives of two different forms of life. And that made sense when one thought of it, for the Pinkness had not changed, it had stayed its sprawling, slobby self; there had been no trace of human in it, although inside of it was a certain portion of humanity and God knew what else besides.

He released the grip he had upon the star machine and ran his hand against the glasslike smoothness of its metal structure.

There was a way – if he could only do it. He had the knowledge now, but did he have the technique?

Time, the Pinkness had told him – time is the simplest thing there is. But still, Blaine told himself, not as easily handled as the creature had made out.

He stood there thinking, and the thing that he must do became very clear indeed.

The past was a worthless path to follow, for the machine was in the past already. It had left a long and nebulous trail clear across the past.

But the future was a different matter. If it could be moved into the future, this present moment and all succeeding present moments would then become its past and all that would remain would be the ghostly track of it – and a laughter and a mocking and a thing of magic which would make no proper subject for a rabble-rousing sermon by a man named Lambert Finn.

And more than that, thought Blaine, it would, more than likely, scare the hell right out of him.

He reached out with his mind to encircle the machine and it was no use. His mind would open up and reach, but there was a lack of stretch in it and he could not take in all of the machine. So he rested and then he tried again.

There was a strangeness and an alienness in the shed he had not noticed, and there was an unknown menace in the scraping of the weeds outside the broken window, and the air held a sharpness and a tang that raised bristles on his neck. It was most confusing, for suddenly it seemed that he had lost all rapport with this world in which he found himself and that nothing, not the earth he stood on nor the air he breathed or even the body that he wore was anything he'd ever known before and there was a horror in this lack of familiarity, in this shift from the known which he no longer could remember into this unknown for which he had no focal points. But it would be all right, it all would come aright if he could move this strange artifact he held within his mind, for it had been for this purpose that he had been called forth from the darkness and the warmness and the snug security and if he got the job done he could go back again, back to his memories of other days and his slow assimilation of new data and the miser-satisfaction of counting up the new facts, one by one, as he piled them in neat stacks.

The artifact, for all its strangeness, was an easy thing to handle. Its roots did not run back too far and the co-ordinates were falling very satisfactorily into place and he almost had it made. But he must not hurry despite his screaming need to hurry; he must somewhere snare some patience. So he waited for the co-ordinates to go clicking into place and he made exact and unhurried measurement of the temporal strain and he gave the thing a twitch at just the right degree of twist and it was exactly where he had wanted it.

Then he dived back home again, back into the dark and

warmness, and Blaine stood shorn of all but his human self in a place of foggy nothingness.

There was nothing there – nothing but himself and the star machine. He reached out his hand and touched the star machine and it was very solid. It was, so far as he could see, the only solid thing there was.

For the fog itself, if fog were what it was, had an unreal quality, as if it were striving to camouflage its very fact of being.

Blaine stood quietly, afraid to move – afraid that any movement might plunge him into some pit of black foreverness.

For this, he realized, was the future. It was a place without a single feature of the space-time matrix that he knew. It was a place where nothing yet had happened – an utter emptiness. There was neither light nor dark; there was nothing here but emptiness. There had never been anything in this place, nor was anything ever intended to occupy this place – until this very moment when he and his machine had been thrust upon it, intruders who have overstepped their time.

He let his breath out slowly and breathed in again – and there was nothing to breathe in!

Blackness rushed in upon him, and the throbbing of his heartbeat was loud within his head, and he reached out desperately to grab at something – at anything – in this place where there was not a thing to grab.

Even as he did, the alienness came back, a startled, frightened alienness, and a hodgepodge of queer symbolic figures, which even in his agony of mind, he took to be some *outré* mathematics, went flooding through his brain.

There was air again to breathe and there was solid floor beneath his feet and he smelled the mustiness of the inside of the highway shed.

He was back home again and so was the alienness, for it was gone from him. Back, he told himself, to the darkness and the warmth inside his very brain.

He stood erect and mentally checked himself and he was all right. He opened his eyes slowly, for they somehow had been closed, and there was only darkness until he remembered the flashlight still clutched in his hand. And yet not as dark as it had been before. Now light from a newly risen moon poured through the broken window.

He lifted the flashlight and shoved the contact button, and the light sprang out and the machine was there before him, but strange and unsubstantial – the ghost of a machine, the trail that it had left behind it when it had moved into the future.

He lifted his free arm and used his jacket sleeve to wipe his forehead dry. For it was over now. He had done what he had come to do. He'd struck the blow for Stone? he'd stopped Finn in his tracks.

There was here no object lesson; there was no longer any text for Finn to preach upon. There was, instead, a mocking jeer from the very magic that Finn had fought for years.

Behind him he sensed a movement and he swung around so hurriedly that his fingers loosened on the flashlight and it fell upon the floor and rolled.

Out of the darkness a voice spoke.

'Shep,' it said, with full heartiness, 'that was very neatly done.'

Blaine froze and hopelessness flooded in.

For this was the end, he knew. He had come as far as he was going to. He had finally run his race.

He knew that hearty voice. He never could forget it.

The man standing in the darkness of the shed was his old friend, Kirby Rand!

24

Rand was a blacker blob in the darkness as he stepped forward and picked the flashlight off the floor. He pivoted to turn the light full upon the star machine and in the flood of brightness tiny little dust motes could be seen dancing in the heart of the machine.

'Yes,' said Rand, 'very neatly done. I don't know how you did it and I don't know why you did it, but you most certainly have taken care of it.'

He turned the flashlight off and for a moment they stood silent in the darkness, relieved by the streaks of moonlight that came through the windows.

Then Rand said: 'I suppose you know that Fishhook owes you a vote of thanks for this.'

'Come off of it,' Blaine told him, roughly. 'You know very well it was not done for Fishhook.'

'Nevertheless,' said Kirby, 'it happens that in this particular area our interests coincide. We could not let this machine stay lost. We could not allow it to remain in improper hands. You understand, of course.'

'Perfectly,' said Blaine.

Rand sighed. 'I had expected trouble and if there is anything Fishhook doesn't want, it's trouble. Particularly when that trouble is out in the hinterlands.'

'There's not been any trouble,' Blaine told him, 'that needs to worry Fishhook.'

'I am glad to hear it. And you, Shep? How are you getting on,'

'Not too badly, Kirby.'

'That is nice,' said Kirby. 'That is very nice. It makes me feel so good. And now, I would imagine, we should get out of here.'

He led the way across the floor back to the broken window and stood aside.

'You first,' he said to Blaine, 'and I'll be right behind you. I would ask, as one friend to another, that you not try to run away.'

'No need to fear,' Blaine told him dryly, then climbed quickly through the window.

He could run, of course, he told himself, but that would be extremely foolish, for there was no doubt Rand would have a gun and he would be quite efficient with it, even in the moonlight. And more than that, if there were any shooting, Harriet might come running to be of what help she could and if she got involved in this, then he'd be truly friendless. Otherwise, he told himself, almost prayerfully, Harriet would stay hidden in the willow clump. She would see what happened and in just a little while she'd have an angle figured out.

Harriet was, he told himself, the only hope he had.

He dropped out of the window and stood to one side for Rand to clamber through.

Rand hit the ground and turned toward him, just a bit too quickly, too much like a hunter, then he relaxed and chuckled.

'It was a slick trick, Shep,' he said. 'Efficiently engineered. Someday you'll have to tell me exactly how you did it. To steal a star machine is not an easy thing.'

Blaine gulped down his astonishment and hoped the moonlight hid the look he knew must be upon his face.

Rand reached out a hand and took him companionably by the elbow.

'The car's down here,' he said. 'Right down by the road.'

They walked together across the patch of rustling weeds, and the land lay different now, no longer dark and fearsome, but a place of painted magic stretched out in the moonlight. To their right lay the town, a mass of darkened houses that looked more like mounds than houses, with the faint tracery of nude trees standing up like ragged paintbrushes reared against the eastern sky. To the west and north lay the silver prairie land, flat and featureless and made immense by its very lack of features.

And just down the road was the clump of willows.

Blaine shot a quick glance at the clump and there were only willows. There was no glint of moonlight bouncing off metal. He walked a pace or two, then took another look and this time, he knew, there could be no mistake. There was no car in that clump of willows. Harriet was gone.

Good girl, he thought. She had a lot of sense. She'd probably gotten out of there as soon as Rand showed up. She'd figure, more than likely, that the one way she'd be most valuable would be to make a getaway against another day.

'I don't suppose,' said Rand, 'that you have a place to stay.'

'No,' said Blaine, 'I haven't.'

'Bad town,' Rand told him. 'They take this witchcraft-werewolf business seriously indeed. Cops stopped me twice. Warned me under cover. Told me very sternly it was for my own protection.'

'They're all wrought up,' said Blaine. 'Lambert Finn is here.'

'Oh, yes,' Rand said carelessly. 'An old friend of ours.'

'Not of mine. I never met the man.'

'A charming soul,' said Rand. 'A very charming one.'

Blaine said: 'I know very little of him. Just what I have heard.'

Rand grunted.

'I would suggest,' he said, 'that you spend the night at the Post. The factor will be able to find some place to bed you down. I wouldn't be surprised if he could dig up a bottle, too. I suddenly feel the need of a monstrous slug of booze.'

'I could stand one myself,' Blaine told him.

For there was no sense of fighting now, no more sense than running. You went along with them and waited for your chance. They tried to throw you off your balance and you tried to throw them off theirs. And all along you knew, both of you might know, that it was a most polite but very deadly game.

Although he wondered why he bothered. After the last few weeks, he told himself, Fishhook would seem an engaging place. Even if they sent him to the detention resort in Baja California, it would be better than the prospect he faced in this Missouri river town.

They reached the car that sat beside the road, and Blaine waited for Rand to get underneath the wheel, then crawled in himself.

Rand started the engine but did not switch on the lights. He pulled the machine out into the roadway and went drifting down it.

'The police can't really do much more,' he said, 'than run you under cover, but there seems to me no point in getting tangled up with them if you can avoid it.'

'None at all,' said Blaine.

Rand avoided the center of the town, went sneaking down the side streets. Finally he cut back and went sliding up an alley, swung into a parking lot and stopped.

'Here we are,' he said. 'Let's go get that drink.'

The back door opened to his knock and they walked into the back room of the Trading Post. Most of the place, Blaine saw, was used as storage space, but one corner of it served as a living room. There was a bed and stove and table. There was a massive stone fireplace with a wood fire burning in it and comfortable chairs ranged in front of it.

Up near the door that went into the front part of the store stood a massive boxlike structure, and Blaine, although he'd never seen one, recognized it immediately as a transo – the matter transference machine which made the vast network of Trading Posts stretched around the globe and economic possibility. Through that box could come, with a moment's notice, any of the merchandise for which any of the thousands of retail outlets might find itself in need.

This was the machine that Dalton had talked about that night at Charline's party – the machine which he had said could wipe out the world's transportation interests if Fishhook ever chose to put it in public use.

Rand waved a hand at one of the chairs. 'Make yourself comfortable,' he said to Blaine. 'Grant will rustle up a bottle. You have one, don't you, Grant?'

The factor grinned. 'You know I do. How else could I live in a place like this?'

Blaine sat down in one of the chairs before the fire, and Rand took one facing him. He rubbed his hands together.

'We parted over a bottle,' he reminded Blaine. 'I'd say it was only fitting to renew our acquaintance over one.'

Blaine felt a tenseness growing in him, the sense of being trapped, but he grinned at Rand.

'You know the margin that I had that night?' he asked. 'Eight lousy little minutes. That was all I had.'

'You miscalculated, Shep. You had exactly twelve. The boys were a little slow in getting out the tape.'

'And Freddy. Who'd ever thought that Freddy worked for you?'

'You'd be surprised,' Rand told him blandly, 'at some of the people I have working for me.'

They sat easily before the blazing fire of apple wood, measuring one another.

Finally Rand said: 'Why don't you tell me, Shep? I haven't all the answers. I can't get it figured out. You ran into that situation out beyond the Pleiades and you got it buttoned up ...'

'Buttoned up?'

'Sure. Buttoned up. Exclusive. We knew that you had something and we sent some others out there and your creature sits and stares at them and that is all it does. They try to talk with it and it's absolutely dumb. It pretends it doesn't hear them. It makes out not to understand ...'

'Brotherhood,' said Blaine. 'We went through the rites. You wouldn't understand.'

'I think I do,' said Rand. 'How alien are you, Shep?'

'Try me out and see.'

Rand shuddered. 'No, thanks. You see, I've followed up your trail. It began with Freddy and got weirder as it went along.'

'And what do you intend to do about it?'

'Damned if I know,' said Rand.

The factor brought a bottle and two glasses.

'None for yourself?' asked Rand.

Grant shook his head. 'I've got some stock arranging up front. If you don't mind ...'

'Of course not,' Rand told him. 'Go on with your work. One thing ...'

'What, sir?'

'I wonder if Mr Blaine could spend the night here.'

'Certainly. Although it's pretty crude.'

'I don't mind,' said Blaine.

'I'd offer you my bed, sir, but frankly it's no bargain. Once you get used to it, you can live with it, but to start out with—'

'I wouldn't think of taking it.'

'I could get some blankets and you could bed down on the floor. Believe me, it would be better than the bed.'

'Anything,' said Blaine. 'I'll be thankful for anything at all.'

Rand picked up the bottle and uncorked it.

'I'll bring out the blankets in a little while,' the factor told them.

'Thank you, Grant,' said Rand.

The man left. The door that led into the front part of the store sighed softly shut behind him.

Rand poured out the liquor.

'Actually,' he said, 'unless you want to, you don't have to stay here.'

'No?'

'I'm going back to Fishhook. Through the transo. You could come along.'

Blaine was silent. Rand handed him the drink.

'Well, what do you say?' he asked.

Blaine laughed. 'You're making it too easy.'

'Perhaps I am,' said Rand.

He took a drink and settled back into the chair.

'The alien part I can understand,' he said. 'That is an occupational hazard faced by every traveler. But how does the star machine tie up? You were in cahoots with Stone, of course.'

'You know that Stone is dead.'

'No, I haven't heard that.' But he was unconvincing.

And suddenly, from the quality of Rand's voice, from some intuition, Blaine knew that Rand did not care that Stone was dead or that Finn might be in town. It was all one with him. Or it might be even more than that. It might be that Rand was quite satisfied to know that Stone was dead, that he might approve in good part with what Finn was doing. For Fishhook's monopoly rested upon a nonparry world, upon all the millions of people in the world being forced to look to Fishhook for the commerce with stars. And so Fishhook and Rand, Blaine realized with something of a shock, might even be quite willing to see Finn's crusade go rolling ahead to its inevitable conclusion.

And if that was true, could it have been Fishhook instead of Finn which had struck the lethal blow at Stone?

He recoiled at the thought, but it clung inside his brain – for the situation was revealing itself as more than just a simple struggle between Finn and Stone.

It might be best, he told himself, to disclaim immediately any connection whatsoever with the star machine. Perhaps he should have made the disclaimer back there at the shed when Rand first had mentioned it. But if he told the truth, if he told Rand now that he had not known of the star machine until just hours ago, he conceivably might lose a bargaining point of uncertain value. And even if he told him, Rand more than likely would refuse to believe him, for he, after all, had helped Riley nurse the truck which had carried it almost all the way from Mexico.

'It took you plenty long,' said Blaine, 'to catch up with me. Are you, maybe, losing your grip? Or were you just amused?'

Rand frowned. 'We almost lost you, Shep. We had you pegged in that town where they were about to hang you.'

'You were even there that night?'

'Well, not personally,' said Rand, 'but I had some men there.'

'And you were about to let me hang?'

'Well, I tell you honestly, we were of divided mind. But you took the decision right out of our hands.'

'But if not . . .'

'I think most likely we would have let you hang. There was the possibility, of course, that if we grabbed you off, you could have led us to the star machine. But we were fairly confident, at that point, we could spot it for ourselves.'

He crashed his glass down on the table. 'Of all the crazy things!' he yelled. 'Hauling a machine like that in the rattletrap you used. Whatever—'

'Simple,' said Blaine, answering for Stone. 'And you know the answer just as well as I do. No one would be that crazy. If you had stolen something very valuable, you'd get it as far away and as fast as possible . . .'

'Anybody would,' said Rand.

He saw Blaine grinning at him and grinned back.

'Shep,' he said, 'come clean with me. We were good friends once. Maybe, for all I know, we're still the best of friends.'

'What do you want to know?'

'You took that machine someplace just now.'

Blaine nodded.

'And you can get it back again.'

'No,' Blaine told him. 'I'm pretty sure I can't. I was – well, just sort of playing a joke on someone.'

'On me, perhaps?'

'Not you. On Lambert Finn.'

'You don't like Finn, do you?'

'I've never met the man.'

Rand picked up the bottle and filled the glasses once again. He drank half of the liquor in his glass and then stood up.

'I have to leave,' he said, looking at his watch. 'One of Charline's parties. Wouldn't miss it for the world. You're sure that you won't come? Charline would be glad to have you.'

'No, thanks. I'll stay right here. Give Freddy my regards.'

'Freddy,' said Rand, 'isn't with us any more.'

Blaine got up and walked with Rand over to the transo. Rand opened the door. The inside of it looked something like a freight elevator.

'Too bad,' said Rand, 'we can't use these out in space. It would free a lot of manpower.'

'I suppose,' Blaine said, 'that you are working on it.'

135

'Oh, certainly,' Rand told him. 'It's just a matter of refining the controls.'

He held out his hand. 'So long, Shep. I'll be seeing you.'

'Good-by, Kirby,' said Blaine. 'Not if I can help it.'

Rand grinned and stepped into the machine and closed the door. There was no flashing light – nothing to show the machine had operated.

And yet by now, Blaine knew, Kirby Rand was back in Fishhook.

He turned from the transo and started back for the chair beside the fire.

The door from the store up front swung open, and Grant came into the room. He had a striped robe folded on his arm.

'I've got just the thing,' he announced. 'I had forgotten that I had it.'

He lifted the robe off his arm and shook it out.

'Isn't it a beauty?' he demanded.

It was all of that. It was a fur of some sort and there was something about the fur itself that made it glitter in the firelight, as if someone had dusted it with tiny diamond fragments. It was a golden yellow with black stripes that ran diagonally and it had the look of silk rather than of fur.

'It's been around for years,' said Grant. 'There was this man camping on the river and he came in and ordered it. Fishhook had a bit of trouble locating one immediately, but they finally delivered. As you know, sir, they always do.'

'Yes, I know,' said Blaine.

'Then the man never did show up. But the fur was so beautiful I could never send it back. I kept it on inventory, pretending that someday I'd have a chance to sell it. I never will, of course. It costs too much money for a one-horse town like this.'

'What is it?'

'The warmest, lightest, softest fur in the universe. Campers carry it. Better than a sleeping bag.'

'I couldn't use it,' protested Blaine. 'Just an ordinary blanket—'

'But you must,' Grant told him. 'As a favor to me, sir. My accommodations are so poor, I feel deeply shamed. But if I knew you were sleeping in a luxury item . . .'

Blaine laughed and held out his hand.

'All right,' he said. 'And thanks.'

Grant gave him the robe, and Blaine weighed it in his hand, not quite believing it could be so light.

'I've still got a little work,' the factor told him. 'If you don't mind, I'll go back and finish it. You can bed down anywhere.'

'Go ahead,' said Blaine. 'I'll finish up my drink and then turn in. Would you have one with me?'

'Later on,' the factor said. 'I always have a snort before I go to bed.'

'I'll leave the bottle for you.'

'Good night, sir,' the factor said. 'See you in the morning.'

Blaine went back to the chair and sat down in it, with the robe lying in his lap. He stroked it with his hand and it was so soft and warm that it gave the illusion of being still alive.

He picked up the glass and worked leisurely on the liquor and puzzled over Rand.

The man was probably the most dangerous man on earth, despite what Stone had said of Finn – the most dangerous personally, a silky, bulldog danger, a bloodhound of a man who carried out the policies of Fishhook as if they had been holy orders. No enemy of Fishhook was ever safe from Rand.

And yet he had not insisted that Blaine go back with him. He had been almost casual in his invitation, as if it had been no more than a minor social matter, and he had displayed no resentment nor no apparent disappointment upon Blaine's refusal. Nor had he made a move toward force, although that, Blaine told himself, was more than likely due to his lack of knowledge with what he might be dealing. Along the trail, apparently, he had happened on enough to put him on his guard, to know that the man he followed had some secret abilities entirely new to Fishhook.

So he'd move slowly and cautiously, and he'd cover up with a nonchalance that fooled no one at all. For Rand, Blaine knew, was a man who would not give up.

He had something up his sleeve, Blaine knew – something so well hidden that no corner of it showed.

There was a trap all set and baited. There was no doubt of it.

Blaine sat quietly in his chair and finished off the liquor in his glass.

Perhaps it was foolish of him to remain here in the Post. Perhaps it would be better if he just got up and left. And yet that might be the very thing Rand would have figured him to do. Perhaps the trap was outside the door and not in the Post at all. It could be very likely that this room was the one safe place in all the world for him to spend the night.

He needed shelter, but he did not need the sleep. Perhaps the thing to do was stay here, but not to go to sleep. He could lie on the floor, with the robe wrapped tight about him and pretend to sleep, but keeping watch on Grant. For if there were a trap in this room, Grant was the one to spring it.

He put his glass back on the table beside the one that Rand had used, still a quarter full of liquor. He moved the bottle over to make a set piece out of the bottle and the glasses, the three of them together. He bundled the robe underneath his arm and walked over to the fire. He picked up the poker and pushed the burning logs together to revive their dying flame.

He'd bed down here, he decided, just before the fire, so that the light of it would be back of him, out into the room.

He spread the robe carefully on the floor, took off his jacket and folded it for a pillow. He kicked off his shoes and lay down on the robe. It was soft and yielding, almost like a mattress despite its lack of thickness. He pulled it over him and it fell together smoothly, like a sleeping bag. There was a comfort in it that he had not felt since those days when he had been a boy and had snuggled down into his bed, underneath the blankets, in his room on the coldest winter nights.

He lay there, staring out into the darkness of the storeroom beyond the living quarters. He could see the faint outlines of barrels and bales and boxes. And lying there in the silence, unbroken except by the occasional crackle of the fire behind him, he became aware of the faint scent which perfumed the room – the indescribable odor of things alien to the Earth. Not an offensive scent, nor exotic, not in any way startling at all, but a smell such as was not upon the Earth, the compounded smell of spice and fabric, of wood and food, of all the many other things which were gathered from the stars. And only a small stock of it here, he knew, only the staples considered necessary for one of the smaller Posts. But a Post with the entire resources of the massive Fishhook warehouses available within a moment's notice, thanks to the transo standing in its corner.

And this was only a small part of that traffic with the stars – this was only the part that you could put your hands upon, the one small part of it that one could buy or own.

There was also that greater unseen, almost unrealized part of the Fishhook operation – the securing and collecting (and the hoarding, as well) of ideas and of knowledge snared from the depths of space. In the universities of Fishhook, scholars from all parts of the world sifted through this knowledge and sought to correlate and study it, and in some cases to apply it, and in the years to come it would be this knowledge and these ideas which would shape the course and the eventual destiny of all humanity.

But there was more to it than that. There was, first of all, the revealed knowledge and ideas, and secondly, the secret files of learning and the facts kept under lock and key or at the very best reviewed by most confidential boards and panels.

For Fishhook could not, in the name of humanity as well as its own self-interest, release everything it found.

There were certain new approaches, philosophies, ideas, call them what you might, which, while valid in their own particular social structures, were not human in any sense whatever, nor by any stretch of imagination adaptable to the human race and the human sense of value. And there were those others which, while applicable, must be studied closely for possible side effects on human thinking and the human viewpoint before they could be introduced, no matter how obliquely, into the human cultural pattern. And there still were others, wholly applicable, which could not be released for perhaps another hundred years – ideas so far ahead, so revolutionary that they must wait for the human race to catch up with them.

And in this must have lain something of what Stone had been thinking when he had started his crusade to break the monopoly of Fishhook, to bring to the paranormal people of the world outside of Fishhook some measure of the heritage which was rightly theirs by the very virtue of their abilities.

In that Blaine could find agreement with him, for it was not right, he told himself, that all the results of PK should be forever funneled through the tight controls of a monopoly that in the course of a century of existence had somehow lost the fervor of its belief and its strength of human purpose in a welter of commercialism such as no human being, nor any age, had ever known before.

By every rule of decency, parakinetics belonged to Man himself, not to a band of men, not to a corporation, not even to its discoverers nor the inheritors of its discoverers – for the discovery of it, or the realization of it, no matter by what term one might choose to call it, could not in any case be the work of one man or one group of men alone. It was something that must lay within the public domain. It was a truly natural phenomena – more peculiarly a natural resource than wind or wood or water.

Behind Blaine the logs, burning to the point of collapse, fell apart in a fiery crash. He turned to look at them—

Or tried to turn.

But he could not turn.

There was something wrong.

Somehow or other, the robe had become wrapped too tightly.

He pushed his hands out from his side to pull it loose, but he could not push his hands and it would not loosen.

Rather, it tightened. He could feel it tighten.

Terrified, he tried to thrust his body upward, trying to sit up. He could not do it.

The robe held him in a gentle but unyielding grasp.

He was as effectively trussed as if he'd been tied with rope. The robe, without his knowing it, had become a strait jacket that held him close and snug.

He lay quietly on his back and while a chill went through his body, sweat poured down his forehead and ran into his eyes.

For there had been a trap.

He had been afraid of one.

He had been on guard against it.

And yet, of his own free will and unsuspecting, he had wrapped the trap about him.

25

Rand had said 'I'll be seeing you,' when he had shaken hands and stepped into the transo. He had sounded cheerful and very confident. And he'd had a right to sound that way, Blaine thought ruefully, for he'd had it all planned out. He had known exactly what would happen and he'd planned it letter perfect – the one way to apprehend a man you happened to be just a little scared of, not knowing exactly what to expect from him.

Blaine lay on the floor, stretched out, held stretched out and motionless by the encircling robe – except, of course, it was not a robe. It was, more than likely, one of those weird discoveries which Fishhook, for purposes of its own, had found expedient to keep under very careful cover. Foreseeing, no doubt, that certain unique uses might be found for it.

Blaine searched his memory and there was nothing there – nothing that even hinted of a thing like this, some parasitic life, perhaps, which for time on end could lie quiet and easy, making like a robe, but which came to deadly life once it was exposed to something warm and living.

It had him now and within a little while it might start feeding on him, or whatever else it might plan to do with him. There was no use, he knew, to struggle, for at every movement of his body the thing would only close the tighter.

He searched his mind again for a clue to this thing and all at once he found a place – he could see a place – a murky, tumbled planet with tangled forestation and weird residents that flapped and crawled and shambled. It was a place of horror, seen only mistily through the fogs of memory, but the most startling thing about it was that he was fairly certain, even as he dredged it up, he had no such memory. He had never been there and he'd never talked to one who had, although it might have been something he'd picked up from dimensino – from some idle hour of many years before, buried deep within his mind and unsuspected until this very moment.

The picture grew the brighter and the clearer, as if somewhere in his brain someone might be screwing at a lens to get a better picture, and now he could see in remarkable and mind-chilling detail the sort of life that lived within the welter of chaotic jungle. It was horrendous and obscene and it crawled and crept and there was about it a studied, cold ferociousness, the cruelty of the uncaring and unknowing, driven only by a primal hunger and a primal hate.

Blaine lay frozen by the pitlike horror of the place, for it was almost as if he actually were there, as if a part of him lay on the floor before the fireplace while the other half was standing, in all reality, within the loathsome jungle.

He seemed to hear a noise, or this other half of him seemed to hear a noise, and this other half of him looked upward into what might have been a tree, although it was too gnarled, too thorned and too obnoxious to be any proper tree, and looked up, he saw the robe, hanging from a branch, with the shattered diamond dust sparkling in its fur, about to drop upon him.

He screamed, or seemed to scream, and the planet and its denizens faded out, as if the hand within his brain had turned the viewing lens out of proper focus.

He was back, entire, in the land of fireplace and of storeroom, with the transo machine standing in its corner. The door that went into the store was opening, and Grant was coming through.

Grant moved out into the room and eased the door behind him to its closed position. Then he swung around and stood silently, huge and stolid, staring at the man upon the floor.

'Mr Blaine,' he said, speaking softly. 'Mr Blaine, are you awake?'

Blaine did not answer.

'Your eyes are open, Mr Blaine. Is there something wrong with you?'

'Not a thing,' said Blaine. 'I was just lying here and thinking.'

'Good thoughts, Mr Blaine?'

'Very good, indeed.'

Grant moved forward slowly, catfooted, as if he might be stalking something. He reached the table and picked up the bottle. He put it to his mouth and let it gurgle.

He put the bottle down.

'Mr Blaine, why don't you get up? We could sit around and talk and have a drink or two. I don't get to talk to people much. They come here and buy, of course, but they don't talk to me no more than they just have to.'

'No, thanks,' said Blaine. 'I'm quite comfortable.'

Grant moved from the table and sat down in one of the chairs before the fireplace.

'It was a shame,' he said, 'you didn't go back to Fishhook with Mr Rand. Fishhook is an exciting place to be.'

'You're quite right,' Blaine told him, replying automatically, not paying much attention.

For now he knew — he knew where he'd got that memory, where he'd picked up the mental picture of that other planet. He had gotten it from the neat stacks of information he'd picked up from the Pinkness. He, himself, of course, had never visited the planet, but the Pinkness had.

And there was more to the memory than just the magic-lantern picture of the place. There was, as well, a file of data about the planet and its life. But disorderly, not yet sorted out, and very hard to get at.

Grant leaned back into his chair, smirking just a little.

Grant reached out a hand and tapped his fingers on the robe. It gave forth a sound like a muted drum.

'Well,' he demanded, 'How do you like it, Mr Blaine?'

'I'll let you know,' Blaine told him, 'when I get my hands on you.'

Grant got up from the chair and walked back to the table, following an exaggerated, mocking path around the stretched-out Blaine. He picked up the bottle and had another slug.

'You won't get your hands on me,' he said, 'because in just another minute I'm going to shove you into the transo over there and back you go to Fishhook.'

He took another drink and set the bottle back.

'I don't know what you done,' he said. 'I don't know why they want you. But I got my orders.'

He half lifted the bottle, then thought better of it. He shoved it back to the center of the table. He walked forward and stood towering over Blaine.

There was another picture, of another planet, and there was a thing that walked along what might have been a road. The thing was nothing such as Blaine had ever seen before. It looked something like a walking cactus, but it was not a cactus and there was every doubt that it was vegetable. But neither the creature nor the road were too significant. What was significant was that following at the creature's heels, gamboling awkwardly along the could-be road, were a half dozen of the robes.

Hunting dogs, thought Blaine. The cactus was a hunter and these were his hunting dogs. Or he was a trapper and these things were his traps. Robes, domesticated from that other jungle planet, perhaps picked up by some space-going trader, tough enough to survive stellar radiation, and brought to this planet to be bartered for something else of value.

Perhaps, Blaine thought wildly, it was from this very planet that the robe now wrapped about him had been found and taken back to Fishhook.

There was something else pounding in his brain – some sort of phrase, a very alien phrase, perhaps a phrase from the cactus language. It was barbarous in its twisting of the tongue and it made no sense, but as Grant stooped with his hands outstretched to lift him, Blaine shouted out the phrase with all his strength.

And as he shouted, the robe came loose. It no longer held him. Blaine rolled, with a powerful twist of body, against the legs of the man who was bending over him.

Grant went over, face forward on the floor, with a roar of rage. Blaine, clawing his way to his hands and knees, broke free and lunged to his feet out beyond the table.

Grant swarmed off the floor. Blood dripped slowly from his nose where it had struck against the boards. One hand was raw with blood oozing from the knuckles where his hand had scraped.

He took a quick step forward and his face was twisted with a double fear – the fear of a man who could free himself from the clutches of the robe, the fear of having failed his job.

Then he lunged, head lowered, arms outthrust, fingers spread, driving straight for Blaine. He was big and powerful and he was driven by an utter desperation that made him doubly dangerous since he would be careless of any danger to himself.

Blaine pivoted to one side – not quite far enough. One of Grant's outstretched hands caught at his shoulder, slipped off it,

143

the fingers dragging, clawing wildly, and closing on Blaine's shirt. The cloth held momentarily throwing Blaine off balance, then the fabric parted and ripped loose with a low-pitched screeching.

Grant swung around, then flung forward once again, a snarl rising in his throat. Blaine, his heels dug into the floor, brought his fist up fast, felt the jolt of it hitting bone and flesh, sensed the shiver that went through Grant's body as the big man staggered back.

Blaine swung again and yet again, following Grant, blows that started from his knees and landed with an impact that made his arm a dead thing from the elbow down – blows that shook and staggered Grant and drove him back, ruthlessly and relentlessly.

It was not anger that drove Blaine, although there was anger in him, nor fear, nor confidence, but a plain and simple logic that this was his only chance, that he had to finish the man in front of him or himself be finished.

He had gotten in one lucky blow and he must never stop. No rough-and-tumble fighter, he would lose everything he'd gained if he let Grant regain his balance, if he ever gave him a chance to rush him again or land a solid blow.

Grant tottered blindly, hands clawing frantically at the air, groggy with the blows. Deliberately, mercilessly, Blaine aimed at the chin.

The blow smacked hollowly, and Grant's head snapped back, pivoting to one side. His body became a limp thing without any bone or muscle that folded in upon itself. Grant slumped and hit the floor, lying like a rag doll robbed of its inner strength of sawdust.

Blaine let his arms fall to his side. He felt the stinging of the cuts across his knuckles and the dead, dull ache that went through his punished muscles.

A faint surprise ran through him – that he should have been able to do a thing like this; that he, with his own two fists, should have beaten this big brute of a man into a bloody pulp.

He'd got in the first good blow and that had been nothing but pure and simple luck. And he had found the key that unlocked the robe and had that been a piece of luck as well?

He thought about it and he knew that it had not been luck, that it had been good and solid information plucked from the file of facts dumped into his brain when the creature on that planet five thousand lights years distant had traded minds with him. The phrase had been a command to the robe to get its clutches off whatever it had trapped. Sometime in its mental wanderings across unimagined space, the Pinkness had soaked up a wondrous amount of information about the cactus people. And out of this incredible junk heap of miscellaneous facts the terribly discerning brain that belonged to humankind had been able to select the one undistinguished fact which at a given moment had high survival value.

Blaine stood and stared at Grant and there was still no movement in the man.

And what did he do now? Blaine wondered.

He got out of here, of course, as quickly as he could. For in just a little while someone from Fishhook would be stepping from the transo, wondering why he had not been delivered, all neatly trussed and gentle.

He would run again, of course, Blaine told himself with bitterness. Running was the one thing he could do really well. He'd been running now for weeks on end and there seemed no end to it.

Someday, he knew, he would have to stop the running. Somewhere he'd have to make a stand, for the salvation of his self-respect if for no other reason.

But that time had not yet come. Tonight he'd run again, but this time he'd run with purpose. This night he'd gain something for the running.

He turned to get the bottle off the table and as he moved, he bumped into the robe, which was humping slowly on the floor. He kicked it savagely and it skidded weakly, almost wetly, into a lump in the fireplace corner.

Blaine grabbed the bottle in his fist and went across the room to the pile of goods stacked in the warehouse section.

He found a bale of goods and prodded it and it was soft and dry. He poured the contents of the bottle over it, then threw the bottle back into the corner of the room.

Back at the fireplace, he lifted the screen away, found the shovel and scooped up flaming coals. He dumped the coals on top the liquor-wetted goods, then flung the shovel from him and stepped back.

Little blue flames licked along the bale. They spread and grew. They crackled.

It was all right, Blaine knew.

Given five good minutes and the place would be in flames. The warehouse would be an inferno and there'd be nothing that could stop it. The transo would buckle and melt down, and the trail to Fishhook would be closed.

He bent and grasped the collar of Grant's shirt and tugged

him to the door. He opened the door and hauled the man out into the yard, some thirty feet distant from the building.

Grant groaned and tried to get to hands and knees, then collapsed upon the ground again. Blaine bent and tugged him another ten feet along the ground and let loose of him. Grant muttered and thrashed, but he was too beaten to get up.

Blaine walked to the alley and stood for a minute, watching. The windows of the Post were filling very satisfactorily with the red of roaring flames.

Blaine turned and padded softly down the alley.

Now, he told himself, would be a splendid time to make a call on Finn. In just a little while the town would be agog with the burning of the Post and the police much too busy and officious to bother with a man out on the street in violation of the curfew.

26

A group of people were standing on the hotel steps, looking at the fire, which roared into the nighttime sky just two blocks away. They paid Blaine no notice. There was no sign of police.

'Some more reefer business,' said one man to another.

The other nodded. 'You wonder how their minds work,' he said. 'They'll go and trade there in the daytime, then sneak back and burn the place at night.'

'I swear to God,' said the first man, 'I don't see why Fishhook puts up with it. They needn't simply stand and take it.'

'Fishhook doesn't care,' the other told him. 'I spent five years in Fishhook. I tell you, the place is weird.'

Newsmen, Blaine told himself. A hotel crammed full of newsmen come to cover what Finn would say tomorrow. He looked at the man who had spent five years in Fishhook, but he did not recognize him.

Blaine went up the steps and into the empty lobby. He jammed his fists into his jacket pockets so that no one could spot the bruised and bloody knuckles.

The hotel was an old one and its lobby furnishings, he judged, had not been changed for years. The place was faded and old-fashioned and it had the faint, sour smell of many people who had lived short hours beneath its roof.

A few people sat here and there, reading papers or simply

sitting and staring into space, with the bored look of waiting imprinted on their faces.

Blaine glanced at the clock above the desk and it was 11:30.

He went on past the desk, heading for the elevator and the stairs beyond.

'Shep!'

Blaine spun around.

A man had heaved himself out of a huge leather chair and was lumbering across the lobby toward him.

Blaine waited until the man came up and all the time there were little insect feet running on his spine.

The man stuck out his hand.

Blaine took his right hand from his pocket and showed it to him.

'Fell down,' he said. 'Stumbled in the dark.'

The man looked at the hand. 'You better get that washed up,' he said.

'That's what I intend to do.'

'You know me, don't you?' the man demanded. 'Bob Collins. Met you a couple of times in Fishhook. Down at the Red Ghost Bar.'

'Yes, of course,' Blaine said, uncomfortably. 'I know you now. You slipped my mind at first. How are you?'

'Getting along all right. Sore that they pulled me out of Fishhook, but you get all sorts of breaks, mostly lousy, in this newspaper racket.'

'You're out here to cover Finn?'

'Collins nodded. 'How about yourself?'

'I'm going up to see him.'

'You'll be lucky if you get to see him. He up in 210. Got a big tough bruiser sitting just outside his door.'

'I think he'll see me.'

Collins cocked his head. 'Heard you took it on the lam. Just grapevine stuff.'

'You heard it right,' said Blaine.

'You don't look so good,' said Collins. 'Don't be offended, but I got an extra buck or two . . .'

Blaine laughed.

'A drink, perhaps?'

'No. I must hurry and see Finn.'

'You with him?'

'Well, not exactly . . .'

'Look, Shep, we were good pals back there in Fishhook. Can you give me what you know? Anything at all. Do a good job on this one, they might send me back to Fishhook. There's nothing I want worse.'

Blaine shook his head.

'Look, Shep, there are all sorts of rumors. There was a truck went off the road down by the river. There was something in that truck, something that was terribly important to Finn. He leaked it to the press. He'd have a sensational announcement to the press. He had something he wanted us to see. There's a rumor it's a star machine. Tell me, Shep, could it be a star machine? No one knows for sure.'

'I don't know a thing.'

Collins moved closer, his voice dropping to a husky whisper. 'This is big, Shep. If Finn can nail it down. He thinks he has hold of something that will blow the parries – every single parry, the whole concept of PK – clear out of the water. You know he's worked for that for years. In a rather hateful way, of course, but he has worked for it for years. He's preached hate up and down the land. He's a first-class rabble-rouser. He needs just this one to cinch his case. Give him a good one now and the entire world tips to him. Give him that clincher and the world will shut its eyes to the way he did it. They'll be out howling, out after parry blood.'

'You forgot that I'm a parry.'

'So was Lambert Finn – at one time.'

'There's too much hate,' Blaine said wearily. 'There are too many derogatory labels. The reformers call the paranormal people parries, and the parries call the reformers reefers. And you don't give a damn. You don't care which way it goes. You wouldn't go out and hunt someone to his death. But you'll write about it. You'll spread the blood across the page. And you don't care where it comes from, just so it is blood.'

'For the love of God, Shep . . .'

'So I will give you something. You can say that Finn hasn't anything to show, not a word to say. You can say that he is scared. You can say he stubbed his toe . . .'

'Shep, you're kidding me!'

'He won't dare show you what he's got.'

'What is it that he's got?'

'Something that, if he showed it, would make him out a fool. I tell you, he won't dare to show it. Tomorrow morning Lambert Finn will be the most frightened man the world has ever known.'

'I can't write that. You know I can't . . .'

'Tomorrow noon,' Blaine told him, 'everyone will be writing it,

If you start right now, you can catch the last morning editions. You'll scoop the world – if you've got the guts to do it.'

'You're giving me straight dope? You're—'

'Make up your mind,' said Blaine. 'It's true, every word of it. It is up to you. Now I've got to get along.'

Collins hesitated. 'Thanks, Shep,' he said. 'Thanks an awful lot.'

Blaine left him standing there, went past the elevator and turned up the stairs.

He came to the second floor and there, at the end of the left-hand corridor a man sat in a chair tilted back against the wall.

Blaine paced purposefully down the corridor. As he came closer, the guard tilted forward in his chair and came to his feet.

He put his hand out against Blaine's chest.

'Just a minute, mister.'

'It's urgent I see Finn.'

'He ain't seeing no one, mister.'

'You'll give him a message?'

'Not at this hour, I won't.'

'Tell him I'm from Stone.'

'But Stone—'

'Just tell him I'm from Stone.'

The man stood undecided. Then he let his arm drop.

'You wait right here,' he said. 'I'll go in and ask him. Don't try no funny stuff.'

'That's all right. I'll wait.'

He waited. wondering just how smart he was to wait. In the half-dark, rancid corridor he felt the ancient doubt. Maybe, he told himself, he should simply turn around and walk rapidly away.

The man came out.

'Stand still,' he commanded. 'I've got to run you down.'

Expert hands went over Blaine, seeking knife or gun.

The man nodded, satisfied. 'You're clean,' he said. 'You can go on in. I'll be right outside the door.'

'I understand,' Blaine told him.

The guard opened the door, and Blaine went through it.

The room was furnished as a living room. Beyond it was a bedroom.

There was a desk across the room, and a man stood behind the desk. He was clad in funeral block with a white scarf at this throat and he was tall. His face was long and bony and made one think of a winter-gaunted horse, but there was a hard, stern purpose to him that was somehow frightening.

Blaine walked steadily forward until he reached the desk.

'You are Finn,' he said.

'Lambert Finn,' said the man in a hollow voice, the tone of an accomplished orator who never can quite stop being an orator even when at rest.

Blaine brought his hands out of his pockets and rested his knuckles on the desk. He saw Finn looking at the blood and dirt.

'Your name,' said Finn, 'is Shepherd Blaine and I know all about you.'

'Including that someday I intend to kill you?'

'Including that,' said Finn. 'Or at least a suspicion of it.'

'But not tonight,' said Blaine, 'because I want to see your face tomorrow. I want to see if you can take it as well as dish it out.'

'And that's why you came to see me? That's what you have to tell me?'

'It's a funny thing,' Blaine told him, 'But at this particular moment, I can think of no other reason. I actually can't tell why I bothered to come up.'

'To make a bargain, maybe?'

'I hadn't thought of that. There's nothing that I want that you can give me.'

'Perhaps not, Mr Blaine, but you have something that I want. Something for which I'd pay most handsomely.'

Blaine stared at him, not answering.

'You were in on the deal with the star machine,' said Finn. 'You could provide the aims and motives. You could connect up the pieces. You could tell the story. It would be good evidence.'

Blaine chuckled at him. 'You had me once,' he said. 'You let me get away.'

'It was that sniveling doctor,' Finn said ferociously. 'He was concerned there would be a rumpus and his hospital would somehow get bad publicity.'

'You should pick your people better, Finn.'

Finn growled. 'You haven't answered me.'

'About the deal, you mean? It would come high. It would come awfully high.'

'I am prepared to pay,' said Finn. 'And you need the money. You are running naked with Fishhook at your heels.'

'Just an hour ago,' Blaine told him, 'Fishhook had me trussed up for the kill.'

'So you got away,' Finn said, nodding. 'Maybe the next time, too. And the time after that as well. But Fishhook never quits. As the situation stands, you haven't got a chance.'

'Me especially, you mean? Or just anyone? How about your-self?'

'You especially,' said Finn. 'You know a Harriet Quimby?'

'Very well,' said Blaine.

'She,' Finn said, levelly, 'is a Fishhook spy.'

'You're staring mad!' yelled Blaine.

'Stop and think of it,' said Finn. 'I think you will agree.'

They stood looking at one another across the space of desk, and the silence was a live thing, a third presence in the room.

The red thought rose up inside Blaine's brain: why not kill him now?

For the killing would come easy. He was an easy man to hate. Not on principle alone, but personally, clear down to his guts.

All one had to do was think of the hate that rode throughout the land. All one had to do was close one's eyes and see the slowly turning body, half masked by the leaves; the deserted camp with the propped-up quilts for shelters and the fish for dinner laid out in the pan; the flame-scarred chimney stark against the sky.

He half lifted his hands off the table, then put them down again.

Then he did a thing quite involuntarily, without thinking of it, without a second's planning or an instant's thought. And even as he did it, he knew it was not he who did it, but the other one, the lurker in the skull.

For he could not have done it. He could not have thought of doing it. No human being could.

Blaine said, very calmly: 'I trade with you my mind.'

27

The moon rode high above the knobby bluffs that hemmed in the river valley, and down in the valley a dismal owl was hooting and chuckling to himself in between the hoots. The chuckling of the owl carried clearly in the sharp night air that held the hint of frost.

Blaine halted at the edge of the clump of scraggly cedars that hugged the ground like gnarled and bent old men, and stood tense and listening. But there was nothing except the chuckling of the owl and the faint sound of the stubborn leaves still clinging to a cottonwood downhill from him, and another sound so faint that one wondered if one really heard it – the remote and faery murmur which was the voice of the mighty river flowing stolidly below the face of the moonlit bluffs.

Blaine lowered himself and squatted close against the ground, huddling against the tumbled darkness of the cowering cedars and told himself again that there was no follower, that no one hunted him. Not Fishhook, for with the burning of the Post the way to Fishhook was temporarily closed. And not Lambert Finn. Right at this moment, Finn would be the last to hunt him.

Blaine squatted there, remembering, without a trace of pity in him, the look that had come into Finn's eyes when he'd traded minds with him – the glassy stare of terror at this impertinent defilement, at this deliberate befoulment of the mighty preacher and great prophet who had cloaked his hate with a mantle that was not quite religion, but as close to it as Finn had dared to push it.

'What have you done!' he'd cried in cold and stony horror. 'What have you done to me!'

For he had felt the biting chill of alienness and the great inhumanity and he'd tasted of the hatred that came from Blaine himself.

'Thing!' Blaine had told him. 'You're nothing but a thing! You're no longer Finn. You're only partly human. You are a part of me and a part of something that I found five thousand light-years out. And I hope you choke on it.'

Finn had opened up his mouth, then had closed it like a trap.

'Now I must leave,' Blaine had said to him, 'and just so there's no misunderstanding, perhaps you should come along. With an arm about my shoulder as if we were long-lost brothers. You'll talk to me like a valued and an ancient friend, for if you fail to do this, I'll manage to make it known exactly what you are.'

Finn had hesitated.

'Exactly what you are,' said Blaine again. 'With all of those reporters hearing every word I say.'

That had been enough for Finn – more than enough for him.

For here was a man, thought Blaine, who could not afford to be attainted with any magic mumbo jumbo even if it worked. Here was the strait-laced, ruthless, stone-jawed reformer who thought of himself as the guardian of the moral values of the entire human race and there must be no hint of scandal, no whisper of suspicion.

So the two of them had gone down the corridor and down the stairs and across the lobby, arm in arm, and talking, with the reporters watching them as they walked along.

They'd gone down into the street, with the burning Post still red against the sky, and had walked along the sidewalk, as if they moved aside for some final word.

Then Blaine had slipped into an alley and had run, heading toward the east, toward the river bluffs.

And here he was, he thought, on the lam again, and without a single plan – just running once again. Although, in between his runnings, he'd struck a blow or two – he'd stopped Finn in his tracks. He'd robbed him of his horrible example of the perfidy of the parries and of the danger in them; he had diluted a mind that never again, no matter what Finn did, could be as narrow and as egomaniac as it had been before.

He squatted listening, and the night was empty except for the river and the owl and the leaves on the cottonwood.

He came slowly to his feet and as he did there was another sound, a howling that had the sound of teeth in it, and for an instant he stood paralyzed and cold. Out of the centuries the sound struck a chord of involuntary fear – out of the caves and beyond the caves to that other day when man had lived in terror of the night.

It was a dog, he told himself, or perhaps a prairie wolf. For there were no werewolves. He knew there were no werewolves.

And yet there was an instinct he barely could fight down – the instinct to run, madly and without reason, seeking for a shelter, for any kind of shelter, against the slavering danger that loped across the moonlight.

He stood, tensed, waiting for the howl again, but it did not come again. His body loosened up, knotted muscle and tangled nerve, and he was almost himself again.

He would have run, he realized, if he had believed, if he'd even half-believed. It was an easy thing – first to believe and then to run. And that was what made men like Finn so dangerous. They were working on a human instinct that lay just beneath the skin – the instinct of fear, and after fear, of hate.

He left the clump of cedar and walked carefully along the bluff. The footing, he had learned, was tricky in the moonlight. There were rocks, half-hidden, that rolled beneath the foot, shadow-hidden holes and humps that were ankle traps.

He thought again of the one thing that bothered him – that had bothered him ever since that moment he had talked with Finn.

Harriet Quimby, Finn had said, was a Fishhook spy.

And that was wrong, of course, for it had been Harriet who had helped him escape from Fishhook.

And yet — she had been with him in that town where he had been nearly hanged. She had been with him while Stone was being killed. She had been with him when he'd gone into the highway shed and there been trapped by Rand.

He thrust the catalog of thoughts back into his mind, but they would not stay there. They kept creeping out to plague him.

It was ridiculous. Harriet was no spy. She was a top-notch news hen and a damn good pal to have and she was capable and cool and hard. She could be, Blaine admitted to himself, a good spy if she only wanted to — but it was alien to her nature. There was no subterfuge in her.

The bluff broke into a steep ravine that went plunging down toward the river and on the lip of it was a small clump of twisted trees.

Blaine walked around to the lower side of the clump and sat down on the ground.

Below him the river surged along, the blackness of its waters flecked with silver, and the frost of the river valley blacker than the river, while the bluffs marched up on either side like silver, humpbacked ghosts.

The owl had fallen silent, but the murmur of the river had grown louder now and if one listened closely he could hear the gurgle of the water as it swept around the sand and forced its liquid way through the tree that had toppled from the bank and hung there, its roots still anchored, its topknot in the water.

This would not, thought Blaine, be a bad place to stop the night. He'd have no quilt or blanket, but the tree would shelter him and hide him. And he'd be safer than he'd been anyplace this day.

He crawled back into the thicket that grew underneath the trees and rooted out a nest. There was a stone or two to move, there was a broken branch to be pushed out of the way. Feeling in the darkness, he scraped a pile of leaves together and it was not until he'd done all this that he thought of rattlesnakes. Although, he told himself, the season was a bit too late for many rattlesnakes.

He curled himself into a ball atop the pile of leaves and it was not as comfortable as he had hoped it might be. But it was passable and he'd spend not too many hours here. The sun would soon be up.

He lay quietly in the dark, and the happenings of the day began their remorseless march across his screen of consciousness — a mental summing up that he tried to put a stop to, but with no success.

Relentlessly, the endless reels ran on, snatches and impressions of a day that had been full, and charged with the unrealism of all post-mortem mental reviews.

If he could only stop them somehow, if he could think of something else.

And there was something else – the mind of Lambert Finn.

Gingerly he dug down into it and it hit him in the face, a cold, unrelenting tangle of hate and fear and plotting that writhed like a pail of worms. And in the center of the mass, stark horror – the horror of that other planet which had turned its human viewer into a screaming maniac who had come surging up out of his star machine with drooling mouth and staring eyes and fingers hooked like claws.

It was repulsive and obscene. It was bleak and raw. It was everything that was the opposite of humanity. It gibbered and it squawked and howled. It leered with an alien death's-head. was nothing clear or clean; there was no detail, but an overriding sense of abysmal evil.

Blaine jerked away with a scream exploding in his brain, and the scream wiped out the central core of horror.

But there was another thought – an incongruous, fleeting thought.

The thought of Halloween.

Blaine grabbed tight hold of it, fighting to keep the core of alien horror from being added to the footage of the endless film.

Halloween – the soft October night with the thin layers of leaf smoke floating in the street, lighted by the street lamps or the great full moon which hung just above the naked tree tops, larger than one ever had remembered it, as if it might have drawn a little closer to the Earth to spy on all the fun. The high, shrill, childish voices rang along the street and there was the continual patter of little racing feet as the goblin bands made their merry round, shrieking with delight or calling back and forth. The lights above the doors were all turned on in genial invitation to the trick-or-treaters, and the shrouded figures came and went, clutching bags which bulged the bigger and the heavier as the evening passed.

Blaine could remember it in detail – almost as if it were only yesterday and he was a happy child running in the town. But it was, in actuality, he thought, very long ago.

It was before the terror had grown foul and thick – when the magic still was a fading fad and there still was fun in it and Halloween was happy. And parents had no fear of their children being out at night.

Today such a Halloween would be unthinkable. Now Halloween was a time for the double-barring of the doors, of the tight-stuffed chimney, of the extra-potent hex sign nailed above the lintel.

It was too bad, he thought. It had been such a lot of fun. There had been that night he and Charlie Jones had rigged up the tick-tack beside Old Man Chandler's window and the old man had come roaring out in simulated anger with a shotgun in his hand and they had got out of there so fast they'd fell into the ditch back of the Lewis house.

And there had been that other time — and that other time — hanging to it hard so he could think of nothing else.

28

He woke cramped and cold and confused, not remembering where he was. For the branches interwined above him and were like nothing he'd ever seen before. He lay with his body aching from rough ground and the cold, staring at the branches, and slowly the knowledge soaked into him — who he was and where.

And why.

And the thought of Halloween.

He sat bolt upright and bumped his head upon the branches.

For now there was more than just the thought of Halloween.

There was the plot of Halloween!

He sat cold and frozen, while the fury and the fear raged inside of him.

It was diabolic and so simple — it was the very kind of gambit a man like Lambert Finn would plan.

It was something that could not be allowed to happen. For if it did, a new onslaught of public animosity would be roused against the parries and once the fierce reaction had worn off, there'd be new restrictive laws. Although the laws might not be needed, for it might set off a pogrom that would wipe out thousands of the parries. Such a plan of Halloween would result in a storm of public outrage such as the world had seldom known.

There was just one chance, he knew. He had to get to Hamilton, for it was the nearest place where he could find some help. Surely the folks of Hamilton would help him, for Hamilton was a parry village that lived by suffrance alone. If a thing like this should happen, then Hamilton would die.

And Halloween, unless he had lost count, was the day after tomorrow. No, that was wrong, for this was tomorrow. Starting now, there were just two days to stop it.

He crawled out of the thicket and saw that the sun was no more than a handsbreadth above the eastern hills. There was a sharp, clean tang in the morning air, and the sloping bluff ran smooth, with the blond of sun-cured grass, down to the brown flood of the river. He shivered in the chill and beat his hands together to try to get them warm.

Hamilton would be north along the river, for The Plainsman motel had been on the road that ran north from Belmont, and Hamilton, from there, had been only a mile or two away.

He went angling down the slope, and the movement of his body drove away the chill. The climbing sun seemed to gather strength and there was more warmth in it.

He reached a sand bar that ran out into the river and walked out on it. The water was brown with sand and clay and it rumbled angrily as it swirled around the sand bar's end.

Blaine walked to the edge of the bar and squatted down. He put down cupped hands and dipped, and the trapped water came up roiled with sand. He raised the cupped hands to his face and drank and the water had a dark brown taste – the taste of silted clay and of ancient vegetation. When he closed his mouth, his teeth gritted on the sand.

But it was water. It was wet. He dipped and drank again, the water running through his fingers, no matter how tightly pressed together, leaving little for his throat.

He squatted in the stillness and sensed the loneliness and peace, as if this moment might be no later than the next day after the world had first been made – as if the earth lay new and clean and there'd been as yet no time to build up the historic backlog of worry and of greed and of all the other things which plagued the race of Man.

A splash broke the silence and he rose swiftly to his feet. There was nothing to be seen, either on the shore or on the river itself or the willow island which lay just beyond the sand bar. An animal, he thought. A mink or muskrat, an otter or a beaver, or perhaps a fish.

The splash came again, and a boat nosed around the island and came toward the bar. In its stern sat a man muffled in a cloak, swinging the paddle with an awkwardness that was embarrassing to watch. The bow was raised out of the water by the weight of the man and the canted outboard motor fastened to the stern.

The boat came lumbering around and there was something hauntingly familiar in the man who swung the paddle. Somewhere, sometime, Blaine knew, he had met this man; somehow their lives had touched.

He walked out into the shallows and grabbed the bow as the craft drew close and dragged it onto the sand.

'God be with you,' said the boatman. 'And how are you this morning?'

'Father Flanagan!' cried Blaine.

The old priest grinned, a very human, almost sunny grin.

'You,' Blaine told him, 'are very far from home.'

'I go,' said Father Flanagan, 'where the good Lord sends me.'

He reached forward and patted the seat in front of him.

'Why don't you come and sit awhile?' he invited. 'God forgive me, but I'm all beat up and weary.'

Blaine pulled the boat up harder on the sand and got into it. He took the seat the priest had patted and held out his hand. Father Flanagan took it in both his arthritis-crippled but very gentle paws.

'It's good to see you, Father.'

'And I,' the Father told him, 'am covered with confusion. For I must confess that I've been following you.'

'It would seem to me,' Blaine said, half amused, half frightened, 'that a man of your persuasion might find better things to do.'

The priest put Blaine's hand away, not forgetting to give it a placid pat.'

'Ah, my son,' he said, 'but that is it. There can be, for me, no better occupation than keeping on your trail.'

'I'm sorry, Father. I don't quite understand.'

Father Flanagan leaned forward, capping each of his knees with a crippled fist.

'It is important,' he said, 'that you understand. You will listen carefully. You will not get angry. You'll let me have my time.'

'Most certainly,' said Blaine.

'You have heard, perhaps,' said Father Flanagan, 'that Holy Mother Church is inflexible and rigid, that she clings to old custom and to ancient thought, that she changes slowly if she changes at all. That the Church is stern and dogmatized and—'

'I've heard all that,' said Blaine.

'But it is not true. The church is modern and it changes. If it had been opposed to change, God save us, it would not have endured in all its greatness and its glory. It is not swayed by the winds of public utterance, it can stand against the groundswell of changing human mores. But it does, adapt, although it does so slowly. But that slowness is because it must be very sure.'

'Father, you can't mean—'

'But I do. I asked you, if you will remember, if you were a warlock and you thought it very funny . . .'

'Of course I did.'

'It was a basic question,' said Father Flanagan, 'a much too simple question, purposely made simple so it could be answered with a yes or no.'

'I'll answer once again, then. I am not a warlock.'

The old priest sighed. 'You persist,' he complained, 'in making the telling of what I have to tell you very difficult.'

'Go ahead,' said Blaine. 'I'll restrain myself.'

'The Church must know,' said Father Flanagan, 'whether parakinetics is a true human ability or if it may be magic. One day, perhaps many years from now, it must make a ruling. It must take a stand as it historically has taken positions on all moral values through the centuries. It is no secret that a committee of theologians have had the matter under study . . .'

'And you?' asked Blaine.

'I am only one of many who has been assigned an investigatory role. We simply gather evidence which in due time will come under the scrutiny of the theologians.'

'And I am part of your evidence.'

Father Flanagan nodded solemnly.

'There's one thing I fail to understand,' said Blaine, 'and that is why your faith should have any doubts at all. You have your miracles, completely documented. And what, I ask you, are miracles if they don't involve PK? Somewhere in the universe human power and divine power must link. Here may be your bridge.'

'You really believe this, son?'

'I'm not a religico . . .'

'I know you're not. You told me you were not. But answer me: Is this what you believe?'

'I rather think it is.'

'I do not know,' said Father Flanagan, 'if I can quite agree with you. The idea has the smell of heresy. But that's neither here nor there. The point is that there's a certain strangeness in you, a strangeness I've not found in any of the others.'

'I'm half alien,' Blaine told him bitterly. 'No other man has ever been given that distinction. You talk not only with me, but with a being not remotely human – a being that sits on a planet five thousand light years distant. He has lived a million years or more. He'll live another million or maybe more than that. He sends out his mind to visit other planets and he is a very lonely being for all his visiting. Time is no mystery to him. I doubt there's very much that is. And all he knows I know and can put to better use than he – when I get the time, if I ever get the time, to get it all dug out and leveled and stacked along the shelves inside my brain.'

The priest drew his breath in slowly. 'I thought it might be something of that sort.'

'So do your job,' said Blaine. 'Get out the holy water. Sprinkle me with it and I'll go up in a puff of dirty smoke.'

'You mistake me,' said Father Flanagain. 'You mistake my purpose. And my attitude. If there is no evil in the power that sent you to the stars, then there can be no more than incidental evil in what you may absorb there.'

One cripple hand reached out and grasped Blaine's arm in a crushing grip which one would have sworn was not within its strength.

'You have a great power,' said the priest, 'and great knowledge. You have an obligation to use it for the glory of God and the good of all mankind. I, a feeble voice, charge you with that burden and that responsibility. It is not often that such a load is put upon one man. You must not waste it, son. You must not use it wrongly. Nor can you simply let it lie on fallow ground. It was given to you – perhaps by the intervention of some divine power neither of us can understand for a purpose neither of us know. Such things, I am certain, do not come about by pure happenstance.'

'The finger of God,' said Blaine, meaning to jest, but not quite able to make a proper jest, sorry that he'd said it as soon as the words were out.

'The finger of God,' said Father Flanagan, 'laid upon your heart.'

'I did not ask for it,' said Blaine. 'If anyone had asked me, I would have told them no.'

'Tell me about it,' said Father Flanagan. 'From the very start. As a favor to me.'

'In return for a favor of your own.'

'And what is that?' asked Father Flanagan.

'You say you followed me. How could you follow me?'

'Why, bless your soul,' said Father Flanagan. 'I thought you might have guessed. You see, I am one of you. I'm a quite efficient hounder.'

29

Hamilton dreamed beside the river. It had a certain hazy quality and the mellowness of old river towns, for all that it was new. Above it rose the tawny hills and below the hills the checked fields that came up to the town. Lazy morning smoke rose from the chimneys, and each picketed fence had in its corner a clump of hollyhocks.

'It looks a peaceful place,' said Father Flanagan. 'You know what you are doing?'

Blaine nodded. 'And you, Father? What about yourself?'

'There is an abbey down the river. I will be welcome there.'

'And I'll see you again.'

'Perhaps. I'll be going back to my border town. I'll be a lonely picket on the borderland of Fishhook.'

'Watching for others who may be coming through?'

The priest nodded. He cut the motor's speed and turned the boat for shore. It grated gently on the sand and pebbles, and Blaine jumped out of it.

Father Flanagan raised his face toward the western sky and sniffed. 'There is weather making,' he declared, looking like a hound-dog snuffling a cold trail. 'I can smell the edge of it.'

Blaine walked back through water that came up to his ankles and held out his hand.

'Thanks for the lift,' he said. 'It would have been tough walking. And it saved a lot of time.'

'Good-by, my son. God go with you.'

Blaine pushed the boat out into the water. The priest speeded up the motor and swept the boat around. Blaine stood watching as he headed down the stream. Father Flanagan lifted his hand in a last farewell, and Blaine waved back.

Then he waded from the water and took the path up to the village.

He came up to the street and he knew it to be home.

Not his home, not the home he once had known, no home he'd ever dreamed of, but home for all the world. It had the peace and surety, the calmness of the spirit, the feel of mental comfort – the sort of place a man could settle down and live in, merely counting off the days, taking each day as it came and the fullness of it, without a thought of future.

There was no one on the street, which was flanked by trim,

neat houses, but he could feel them looking at him from out the windows of each house – not spying on him or suspicious of him, but watching with a kindly interest.

A dog came from one of the yards – a sad and lovely hound – and went along with him, walking by his side in good companionship.

He came to a cross-street and to the left was a small group of business houses. A group of men were sitting on the steps of what he took to be a general store.

He and the hound turned up the street and walked until they came up to the group. The men sat silently and looked at him.

'Good morning, gentlemen,' he said. 'Can any of you tell me where I can find a man named Andrews?'

They were silent for another heartbeat, then one of them said: 'I'm Andrews.'

'I want to talk with you,' said Blaine.

'Sit down,' said Andrews, 'and talk to all of us.'

'My name is Shepherd Blaine.'

'We know who you are,' said Andrews. 'We knew when that boat pulled into shore.'

'Yes, of course,' said Blaine. 'I should have realized.'

'This man,' Andrews said, 'is Thomas Jackson and over there is Johnson Carter and the other one of us is Ernie Ellis.'

'I am glad,' said Blaine, 'to know each one of you.'

'Sit down,' said Thomas Jackson. 'You have come to tell us something.'

Jackson moved over to make room for him, and Blaine sat down between him and Andrews.

'First of all,' said Blaine, 'Maybe I should tell you that I'm a fugitive from Fishhook.'

'We know a little of you,' Andrews told him. 'My daughter met you several nights ago. You were with a man named Riley. Then only last night we brought a dead friend of yours here—'

'He's buried on the hill,' said Jackson. 'We held a rather hasty funeral for him, but at least a funeral. You see, he was not unknown to us.'

'Thank you, sir,' said Blaine.

'Last night, also,' said Andrews, 'there was some sort of ruckus going on in Belmont—'

'We're not too happy with such goings-on,' said Carter, interrupting. 'We're too apt to become involved.'

'I'm sorry if that's the case,' Blaine told them. 'I'm afraid I'm bringing you more trouble. You know of a man named Finn.

They nodded.

'I talked with Finn last night. I found out something from him. Something he had no intention, I might add, of ever telling me.'

They waited.

'Tomorrow night is Halloween,' said Blaine. 'It's set to happen then.'

He saw them stiffen and went quickly on: 'Somehow or other – I'm not just sure how he managed to achieve it – Finn has set up a sort of feeble underground among the paranormal people. None of them, naturally, know that he's behind it. They view it as a sort of pseudopatriotic movement, a sort of cultural protest movement. Not too successful or extensive, but it would not have to be extensive. All that he needs is to create a few incidents – a few horrible examples. For that is how he works, using horrible examples to whip up the public frenzy.

'And this underground of his, working through the teen-age paranormals, has arranged a series of PK demonstrations on the night of Halloween. A chance, they've been told, to demonstrate paranormal powers. A chance, perhaps, to pay off some old scores. God knows, there must be old scores a-plenty that need some paying off.'

He stopped and looked around at their stricken faces. 'You realize what a dozen of these demonstrations – a dozen in the entire world, given the kind of publicity Finn intends to give them – would do to the imagination of the normal population.'

'It would not be a dozen,' Andrews said, quietly. 'Worldwide, it might be a hundred or even several hundreds. The morning after they'd sweep us off the earth.'

Carter leaned forward, intently. 'How did you find this out?' he asked. 'Finn would not have told you unless you were in with him.'

'I traded minds with him,' said Blaine. 'It's a technique I picked up among the stars. I gave him a pattern of my mind and took in exchange a duplicate of his. A sort of carbon copy business. I can't explain it to you, but it can be done.'

'Finn,' said Andrews, 'won't thank you for this. Yours must be a most disturbing mind to have inside his head.'

'He was quite upset,' said Blaine.

'These kids,' said Carter. 'They would make like witches. They would burst open doors. They would whisk cars to another place. Small buildings would be upset and demolished. Voices and wailings would be heard.'

'That's the idea,' Blaine told him. 'Just like an old-fashioned, hell-raising Halloween. But to the victims it would not be merely mischief. It would be all the forces of the ancient darkness let loose upon the world. It would be goblins and ghosts and werewolves. On its surface it would be bad enough, but in the imagination of the victims it would grow out of all proportion. There would be, by morning, guts strung along the fence and men with their throats slashed ragged and girl children carried off. Not here, not where it was being told, but always somewhere else. And the people would believe. They'd believe everything they heard.'

'But still,' said Jackson, 'you can't criticize the teen-age parries too harshly if they should want to do this. I tell you, mister, you can't imagine what they have been through. Snubbed and ostracized. Here, at the beginning of their lives, they find bars raised against them, fingers leveled at them—'

'I know,' Blaine said, 'but even so you have got to stop it. There must be a way to stop it. You can use telepathy on the telephone. Somehow or other—'

'A simple device,' said Andrews. 'Although ingenious. Developed about two years ago.'

'Use it then,' said Blaine. 'Call everyone you can. Urge the people you talk with to pass the warning on and the ones they talk with to pass the warning on. Set up a chain of communication—'

Andrews shook his head. 'We couldn't reach them all.'

'You can try,' Blaine shouted.

'We will try, of course,' said Andrews. 'We'll do everything we can. Don't think that we're ungrateful. Very far from that. We thank you. We never can repay you. But—'

'But what?'

'You can't stay here,' said Jackson. 'Finn is hunting you. Fishhook, too, perhaps. And they'll all come here to look. They'll figure you'd run to cover here.'

'My God,' yelled Blaine, 'I came here—'

'We are sorry,' Andrews told him. 'We know how you must feel. We could try to hide you out, but if you were found—'

'All right, then. You'll let me have a car.'

Andrews shook his head. 'Too dangerous. Finn would watch the roads. And they could trace the registration . . .'

'What then? The hills?'

'Andrews nodded.

'You'll give me food?'

Jackson got up. 'I'll get you grub,' he said.

'And you can come back,' said Andrews. 'When this all blows over, we'll be glad to have you back.'

'Thanks a lot,' said Blaine.

30

He sat beneath a lone tree that stood on a lesser spur of one of the great bluffs and stared out across the river. A flock of mallards came winging down the valley, a black line against the sky above the eastern hills.

There had been a day, he thought, when this season of the year the sky had been blackened by the flights that came down from the north, scooting before the first boisterous outriders of the winter storms. But today there were few of them – shot out, starved out by the drying up of areas which had been their nesting places.

And once this very land had teemed with buffalo and there had been beaver for the taking in almost every stream. Now the buffalo were gone and almost all the beaver.

Man had wiped them out, all three of them, the wild fowl, the buffalo, the beaver. And many other things besides.

He sat there thinking of Man's capacity for the wiping out of species – sometimes in hate or fear, at other times for the simple love of gain.

And this, he knew, was what was about to happen in large measure to the parries if Finn's plan were carried out. Back there in Hamilton they would do their best, of course, but would it be enough? They had thirty-six hours in which to put together a vast network of warning. They could cut down the incidents, but could they call them off entirely? It seemed impossible.

Although, he told himself, he should be the last to worry, for they had thrown him out; they had run him off. His own people, in a town that felt like home, and they had run him off.

He leaned over and fastened the straps of the knapsack in which Jackson had packed the food. He lifted and set it and the canteen close beside him.

To the south he could see the distant chimney smoke of Hamilton and even in his half-anger at being thrown out, he seemed to feel again that strange sense of home which he had encountered as he walked its streets. Over the world there must be many such villages as that – ghettos of this latter-day, where paranormal people lived as quietly and as inconspicuously as was possible. They were the ones who huddled in the corners of the earth, waiting for the day, if it ever came, when their children or their children's children might be free to walk abroad, equals of the people who still were only normal.

In those villages, he wondered, how much ability and genius might be lying barren, ability and genius that the world could use but would never know because of the intolerance and hate which was held against the very people who were least qualified as the targets of it.

And the pity of it was that such hate and such intolerance would never have been born, could never have existed, had it not been for men like Finn – the bigots and the egomaniacs; the harsh, stern Puritans; the little men who felt the need of power to lift them from their smallness.

There was little moderation in humanity, he thought. It either was for you or it was against you. There was little middle ground.

Take science, for example. Science had failed in the dream of space, and science was a bum. And yet, men of science still worked as they had always worked, for the benefit of all humanity. So long, as Man might exist, there would be need of science. In Fishhook there were corps of scientists working on the discoveries and the problems that stemmed from the galaxy – and yet science, in the minds of the masses, was a has-been and a heel.

But it was time to go, he told himself. There was no use staying on. There was no use thinking. He must be moving on, for there was nothing else to do. He had sounded the warning and that was all the men of Hamilton had allowed.

He'd go up to Pierre and he'd ask for Harriet at the café with the elk horns nailed above the door. Perhaps he'd find some of Stone's men and they might find a place for him.

He rose and slung the knapsack and canteen from one shoulder. He stepped out from the tree.

Behind him there was a sudden rustle and he swung around short hairs rising on his neck.

The girl was settling to earth, feet just above the grass, graceful as a bird, beautiful as morning.

Blaine stood watching, caught up in her beauty, for this was the first time that he'd really seen her. Once before he'd seen her in the pale slash of light from the headlamps of the truck, and once again last night, but for no more than a minute, in a dimly lighted room.

Her feet touched ground and she came toward him.

'I just found out,' she said. 'I think that it is shameful. After all, you came to help us . . .'

'It's O.K.,' Blaine told her. 'I don't deny it hurts, but I can see their reasoning.'

'They've worked so hard,' she said, 'to keep us quiet, away from all attention. They have tried to make a decent life. They can't take any chances.'

'I know,' said Blaine. 'I've seen some who weren't able to make a decent life.'

'Us young folks are a worry to them. We shouldn't go out halloweening, but there's nothing we can do. We have to stay at home so much. And we don't do it often.'

'I'm glad you came out that night,' Blaine told her. 'If I hadn't known of you, Harriet and I would have been trapped with Stone dead upon the floor . . .'

'We did what we could for Mr Stone. We had to hurry and we couldn't be too formal. But everyone turned out. He's buried on the hill.'

'Your father told me.'

'We couldn't put up a marker and we couldn't make a mound. We cut the sod and put it back exactly as it was before. No one would ever know. But all of us have the place tattooed on our minds.'

'Stone and I were friends from long ago.'

'In Fishhook?'

Blaine nodded.

'Tell me about Fishhook, Mr Blaine.'

'The name is Shep.'

'Shep, then. Tell me.'

'It is a big place and a tall place (*the towers on the hill, the plazas and the walks, the trees and mighty buildings, the stores and shops and dives, the people . . .*)

Shep, why don't they let us come?

Let you come?

There were some of us who wrote them and they sent application blanks. Just application blanks, that's all. But we filled them out and mailed them. And we never heard.

There are thousands who want to get into Fishhook.

Then why don't they let us come? Why not take all of us? A Fishhook reservation. Where all the little frightened people can have some peace at last:

He didn't answer. He closed his mind to her.

Shep! Shep, what's wrong? Something that I said?

167

Listen, Anita. Fishhook doesn't want you people. Fishhook isn't what you think it is. It has changed. It's become a corporation.

But, we have always . . .

I know. I KNOW. I KNOW. It has been the promised land. It has been the ultimate solution. The never-never land. But it's not like that at all. It is a counting house. It figures loss and profit. Oh, sure, it will help the world; it will advance mankind. It's theoretically, and even actually, the greatest thing that ever happened. But it has no kindness in it, no kinship with the other paranormals. If we want that promised land, we'll have to work it out ourselves. We have to fight our own fight, like stopping Finn and his Project Halloween . . .

That's what I came to tell you, really. It isn't working out. The telephoning . . .

They let two calls get through. Detroit and Chicago. Then we tried New York and the operator couldn't get New York. Can you imagine that – couldn't get New York. We tried Denver and the line was out of order. So we got scared and quit . . .

Quit! You can't quit!

We're using long tellies. We have a few of them. But it's hard to reach their contacts. There is little use for distance telepathy and it's not practiced much.

Blaine stood in a daze.

Couldn't get New York! Line to Denver out of order!

It was impossible that Finn should have such complete control.

Not complete control, Anita told him. *But people spotted in strategic situations. For example, he probably could sabotage the world's entire communications network. And he has people all the time watching and monitoring settlements like ours. We don't make one long-distance call a month. When three came through in fifteen minutes, Finn's people knew there was something wrong, so they isolated us.*

Blaine slid the knapsack and canteen off his shoulder, lowered them to the ground.

'I'm going back,' he said.

'It would do no good. You couldn't do a thing we aren't doing now.'

'Of course,' said Blaine. 'You're very probably right. There is one chance, however, if I can get to Pierre in time . . .'

'Pierre was where Stone lived?'

'Why, yes. You knew of Stone?'

'Heard of him. That was all. A sort of parry Robin Hood. He was working for us.'

'If I could contact his organization, and I think I can . . .'

'The woman lives there, too?'

'You mean Harriet. She's the one who can put me in contact with Stone's group. But she may not be there. I don't know where she is.'

'If you could wait till night, a few of us could fly you up there. It's too dangerous in the daytime. There are too many people, even in a place like this.'

'It can't be more than thirty miles or so. I can walk it.'

'The river would be easier. Can you handle a canoe?'

'Many years ago. I think I still know how.'

'Safer, too,' Anita said. 'There's not much traffic on the river. My cousin has a canoe, just upriver from the town. I'll show you where it is.'

31

The storm sneaked in. There was no warning of it except for the gradual graying of the day. At noon the slow-moving clouds blotted out the sun and by three o'clock the sky was closed in, horizon to horizon, by a fleecy grayness that seemed less cloud than the curdling of the sky itself.

Blaine bent to his paddle, driving furiously to eat up the miles. It had been years since he had used a paddle, years since he had done anything approaching strenuous labour. His arms became stiff and numb, and his shoulders ached, and across the upper back a steel band had settled down and was tightening with every stroke he took. His hands seemed one vast blister.

But he did not slow his strokes nor the power behind them, for every minute counted. When he got to Pierre, he knew, he might be unable to locate immediately the group of parries who had worked with Stone, and even if he found them they might refuse to help him. They might want to confirm his identity, they might want to check his story, they might quite rightly suspect him as a spy for Finn. If Harriet were there, she could vouch for him, although he was not sure what her status with the group might be nor what her word was worth. Nor was he even sure that she would be there.

But it was a last, long chance. It was the final hope he had and he could not shirk it. He must get to Pierre, he must find the group, he must make them understand the urgency of the situation.

For if he failed, it spelled the end of Hamilton and of all the other Hamiltons that might be in the world. And it meant as well the end for the other parries who were not in the Hamiltons, but who lived out precarious, careful lives in the midst of normal neighbors.

Not all of them, of course, would die. But all, or nearly all, would be scattered to the winds, to hide in whatever social and economic nooks and crannies they might be able to devise. It would mean that the parries would lose on a world-wide basis whatever tacit accommodations or imperfect understandings they had been able to establish with their normal neighbors. It would mean another generation of slowly coming back, of regaining, item after painful item, what they would have lost. It would mean, perhaps, another fifty years to ride out the storm of rage, to await the growth of another generation's tolerance.

And in the long picture that stretched ahead, Blaine could see no sign of help – of either sympathy or assistance. For Fishhook, the one place that could help, simply would not care. He had gained at least that much understanding of the situation from his contact with Kirby Rand.

The thought left the taste of bitter ashes in his mind, for it took away the last comfort that he had in all the world – the memory of his days in Fishhook. He had loved Fishhook; he had fought against his fleeing from it; he had regretted that he'd left it; at times he'd wondered if he should not have stayed. But now he knew that he had stayed too long, that perhaps he never should have joined it – for his place was here, out here in the bitter world of the other parries. In them, he realized, lay the hope of developing paranormal kinetics to their full capacity.

They were the misfits of the world, the outcasts, for they deviated from the norm of humanity as established through all of history. Yet it was this very deviation which made them the hope of all mankind. Ordinary human beings – the kind of human beings who had brought the race this far – were not enough today. The ordinary humans had pushed the culture forward as far as they could push it. It had served its purpose; it had brought the ordinary human as far as he could go. Now the race evolved. Now new abilities had awoke and grown – exactly as the creatures of the Earth had evolved and specialized and then evolved again from that first moment when the first feeble spark of life had come into being in the seething chemical bath of a new and madcap planet.

Twisted brains, the normal people called them; magic people, dwellers of the darkness – and could anyone say no to this? For each people set its standards for each generation and these standards and these norms were not set by any universal rule, by no all-encompassing yardstick, but by what amounted to majority agreement, with the choice arrived at through all the prejudice and bias, all the faulty thinking and the unstable logic to which all intelligence is prone.

And he, himself, he wondered – how did he fit into all of this? For his mind, perhaps, was twisted more than most. He was not even human.

He thought of Hamilton and of Anita Andrews and his heart cried out to both – but could he demand of any town, of any woman, that he become a part of either?

He bent to the paddle, trying to blot out the thinking that bedeviled him, trying to smother the rat race of questions that were twisting in his brain.

The wind, which had been a gentle breeze no more than an hour before, had shifted and settled somewhat west of north and had taken on an edge. The surface of the river was rippled with the driving wind and on the long, straight stretches of water there was hint of whitecaps.

The sky came down, pressing on the Earth, a hazy sky that stretched from bluff to bluff, roofing in the river and shutting out the sun so that birds flew with uneasy twitterings in the willows, puzzled at the early fall of night.

Blaine remembered the old priest, sitting in the boat and sniffing the sky. There was weather making, he had said; he could smell the edge of it.

But weather could not stop him, Blaine thought fiercely, digging at the water frantically with the paddle. There was nothing that could stop him. No force on Earth could stop him; he couldn't let it stop him.

He felt the first wet sting of snow upon his face and up ahead the river was disappearing in a great, gray curtain that came sweeping downstream toward him. He could hear distinctly the hissing of the snow as it struck the water and behind it the hungry moaning of the wind, as if some great animal were running on a track, moaning in the fear that it would not catch the thing that ran ahead.

Shore was no more than a hundred yards away, and Blaine knew that he must get there and travel the rest of the way on foot. For even in his desperate need of speed, in his frantic fight with time, he realized that he could not continue on the river.

He twisted the paddle hard to head the canoe for shore and even as he did the wind struck and the snow closed in and his world contracted to an area only a few feet in diameter. There was only snow and the running waves that fled beneath the wind, tossing the canoe in a crazy dance. The shore was gone and the bluffs above it. There was nothing but the water and the wind and snow.

The canoe bucked wildly, spinning, and Blaine in an instant lost all sense of direction. In the ticking of a single second he was lost upon the river, with not the least idea of where the shore might lie. He lifted the paddle and laid it across the thwarts, hanging tightly, trying to keep the craft trim as it tossed and yawed.

The wind had a sharpness and a chill it had not had before and it struck his sweaty body like an icy knife. The snow clotted on his eyebrows, and streams of water came trickling down his face as it lodged in his hair and melted.

The canoe danced wildly, running with the waves, and Blaine hung grimly on, lost, not knowing what to do, overwhelmed by this assault that came roaring down the river.

Suddenly a snow-shrouded clump of willows loomed out of the grayness just ahead of him, not more than twenty feet away, and the canoe was bearing straight toward it.

Blaine only had time to get set for the crash, crouched above the seat, legs flexed, hands gripping the rails.

The canoe tore into the willows with a screeching sound that was muffled by the wind and caught up and hurled away. The craft hit and drove on into the willow screen, then hung up and slowly tipped, spilling Blaine out into the water.

Struggling blindly, coughing and sputtering, he gained his feet on the soft and slippery bottom, hanging tight to the willows to keep himself erect.

The canoe, he saw, was useless. A hidden snag had caught its bottom and had ripped a long and jagged tear across the canvas. It was filling with water and slowly going down.

Slipping, half-falling, Blaine fought his way through the willow screen to solid ground. And it was not until he left the water that he realized the water had been warm. The wind, striking through the wetness of his clothes, was like a million icy needles.

Blaine stood shivering, staring at the tangled clump of willows that thrashed wildly in the gale.

He must find a protected spot, he knew. He must start a fire. Otherwise, he'd not last out the night. He brought his wrist close up before his face, and the watch said that it was only four o'clock.

He had, perhaps, another hour of light and in that hour he must find some shelter from the storm and cold.

He staggered off, following the shore – and suddenly it struck him that he could not start a fire. For he had no matches, or he didn't think he had, and even if he did they would be soaked and useless. Although, more than likely, he could dry them, so he stopped to look. He searched frantically through all his sopping pockets. And he had no matches.

He plunged on. If he could find snug shelter, he might be able to survive even with no fire. A hole beneath the roots of a tipped-over tree, perhaps, or a hollow tree into which he could squeeze himself – any confined space where he'd be sheltered from the wind, where his body's heat might have a chance to partially dry out his clothing and be held in to warm him.

There were no trees. There was nothing but the everlasting willows, whipping like demented things in the gusty wind.

He stumbled on, slipping and falling, tripping over unseen chunks of driftwood left stranded by high water He was covered with mud from his many falls, his clothes were freezing stiff, and still he blundered on. He had to keep on moving; he must find a place in which to hide; if he stood still, if he failed to move, he would freeze to death.

He stumbled again and pulled himself to his knees and there, at the water's edge, jammed in among the willows, floated a swamped canoe, rocking heavily in the storm-driven wash of water.

A canoe!

He wiped his face with a muddy hand to try to clear his vision.

It was the same canoe, for there would be no other!

It was the canoe he'd left to beat his way along the shore.

And here he was, back at it again!

He fought with his muddled brain to find an answer – and there was an answer, the only answer that was possible.

He was trapped on a tiny willow island!

There was nothing here but willows. There were no honest trees, tipped-over, hollow, or in any other wise. He had no matches, and even if he had, there was no fuel except the scattered driftwood and not too much of that.

His trousers were like boards, frozen stiff and crackling as he bent his knees. Every minute, it seemed to him, the temperature was dropping – although there was no way to know; he was too cold to tell.

He came slowly to his feet and stood straight, faced into the cutting wind, with the hiss of snow driving through the willows, with the angry growl of the storm-lashed river and the falling dark, and there was another answer to a question yet unasked.

He could not live the night on this island and there was no way to leave it. It might be, for all he knew, no more than a hundred feet from shore, but even if it were, what difference would it make? Ten to one he'd be little better off on shore than he was right here.

There had to be a way, he insisted to himself. He could not die on this stinking little dot of real estate, this crummy little island. Not that his life was worth so much – perhaps not even to himself. But he was the one man who could get to Pierre for help.

And that was a laugh. For he'd never get to Pierre. He'd not get off the island. In the end, he'd simply stay right where he was and it was more than likely that he'd not be found.

When the spring floods came, he'd go down the river with all the other debris that the stream would collect and carry in its raging torrent.

He turned and went back a ways from the water's edge. He found a place where he was partially shielded from the wind by the thickness of the willows and deliberately sat down, with his legs stuck out straight before him. He turned up the collar of his jacket and it was a gesture only, for it did no good. He folded his arms tight across his chest and pinched half-frozen hands into the feeble warmth of armpits and stared straight ahead into the ghostly twilight.

This was wrong, he knew. When a man got caught in a fix like this, he kept on the move. He kept the blood flowing in his veins. He fought off sleep. He beat and flailed his arms. He stamped his feet. He fought to keep alive.

But it was no use, he thought. A man could go through all the misery of the fight and still die in the end.

There must be another way, a better way than that.

A real smart man would think of a better way than that.

The problem, he told himself, trying to divorce himself from the situation for the sake of objectivity – the problem was to get himself, his body, off this island and not only off this island, but to a place of safety.

But there was no place of safety.

Although suddenly there was.

There was a place that he could go. He could go back to that bright-blue living room where the Pinkness dwelled.

But no! That would be no better than staying on the island, for if he went he'd only go in mind and leave his body here. When he returned, the body, more than likely, would be unfit for use.

If he could take his body there, it would be all right.

But he couldn't take his body.

And even if he could, it might be very wrong and very likely deadly.

He tried to recall the data on that distant planet and it had escaped him. So he went digging after it and hauled it up from the deep recesses where he had buried it and regarded it with horror.

He'd not live a minute if he went there in his body!

It was pure and simple poison for his kind of life.

But there must be other places. There would be other places if only he could go there – if all of him could go there.

He sat hunched against the cold and wet and didn't even feel the cold and wet.

He sought the Pinkness in him and he called it and there was no answer.

He called again and yet again and there was no answer. He probed and searched and hunted and he found no sign of it and he knew, almost as if a voice had spoken out and told him, that there was no use of further call or hunting, for he would not find it. He would never find it now, for he was a part of it. The two of them had run together and there was no longer either a Pinkness or a human, but some strange alloy that was the two of them.

To go on hunting for it would be like hunting for himself.

Whatever he would do, he must do himself, by the total power of whatever he'd become.

There were data and ideas, there was knowledge, there was know-how and there was a certain dirtiness that was Lambert Finn.

He went down into his mind, into the shelves and pigeon-holes, into the barrels and bins and boxes, into the still incredible junk heap that was as yet unsorted, the tangled billions of odds and ends that had been dumped helter-skelter into him by a helter-skelter being.

He found items that startled him and some that disgusted him and others that were swell ideas, but which in no way applied to his present problem.

And all the time, like some persistent busybody, running underfoot, the mind of Lambert Finn, unabsorbed as yet, perhaps never to be absorbed but always to remain dodging in and out of corners, kept getting in the way.

He pushed it to one side, he shoved it from his path, he swept it under rugs and he kept on searching – but the dirty thoughts and concepts and ideas, the thoughts of Finn, the unraveling subject matter of that core of raging horror from Finn's nightmare of a planet, still kept popping up.

And as, for the hundredth time, he swept the dirtiness away, he caught a hint of what he wanted and went scrabbling after it – scrabbling after it through all the obscenity and evil of that core of writhing horror which he had wrested from Finn's mind. For it was there he found it – not in the bright array of junk he'd inherited from the Pinkness, but in the mass of garbage he had stole away from Finn.

It was an alien knowledge and a crooked, slimy knowledge, and he knew it had its origin on the planet that had sent Finn home a maniac and as he held it in his mental hands and saw the way it worked, how simply it worked, how logical the concepts, he grasped at least a corner of the guilt and fear which had sent Finn in raging hate up and down the land.

For with this kind of know-how the stars lay open, physically open, to all the life in the universe. And to Finn's unbalanced mind that could mean one thing only – that Earth lay open, too. And most specifically that it lay open to the planet which had held the knowledge. Not thinking of how other races might make use of it, not recognizing it as a tool the human race could use to its benefit, he'd seen it simply as a bridge between the place he'd found and the planet he called home. And he had fought with all he had to pull the old home planet back to is former smallness, to break its contact with the stars, to starve and strangle Fishhook by wiping out the parries who in the future might be drafted or invited to carry on the work of Fishhook.

For Finn had reasoned, Blaine thought, with Finn's reasoning an open book before him, that if Earth stayed obscure and small and attracted no attention, the universe would pass it by and it would then be safe.

But however that might be, he held within his mind the technique to go in body to the stars – and a way to save his life.

But now he must find a planet where he could safely go – a planet which would not poison him or drown him or crush him, a place where he could live.

He dipped again into his mind and there, hauled from the junk heap and neatly catalogued, were thousands of planets the Pinkness at one time had visited.

He searched and found a hundred different kinds of planets and each one deadly to unprotected human life. And the horror grew – that with a way of going, he could find no planet soon enough where it would be safe to go.

The howling of the storm intruded on him, breaking through the fierce concentration of his search, and he knew that he was cold – far colder than he'd known. He tried to move a leg and could barely move it. The wind shrieked at him, mocking, as it went fleeing down the river and in between the gusts of wind he could hear the dry, rattling sound of hard snow pellets shotgunning through the willows.

He retreated from the wind and snow and cold, from the shrieking and the rattle – and there was the planet, the one he had been seeking.

He checked the data twice and it was satisfactory. He tattooed the co-ordinates. He got the picture in his mind. Then slowly, piece by piece, he fed in the long-hop method – and the sun was warm.

He was lying on his face and beneath him was grass and the smell of grass and earth. The howling of the storm was gone and there was no rattle in the willows.

He rolled over and sat up.

He held his breath at what he saw.

He was in paradise!

32

The sun had passed the midday mark and was slanting down the western sky when Blaine came striding down the bluff above the town of Hamilton, walking in the slush and mud after the first storm of the season.

Here he was, he thought, almost too late again – not quite soon enough. For when the sun slipped behind the horizon All Hallows Eve would start.

He wondered how many parry centers the folks of Hamilton had been able to contact. And it was possible, he told himself, that they had done better than anyone could hope. Perhaps they had been lucky. Perhaps they'd hit the jackpot.

And he thought of another thing, of the old priest saying: The finger of God stretched out to touch your heart.

Someday, he thought, the world would look back and wonder at the madness of this day – at the blindness and the folly and the sheer intolerance. Someday there would be vindication. Someday sanity. Someday the Church in Rome would recognize the paranormal as no practicer of witchcraft, but as the natural development of the human race in the grace of God. Someday there would be no social or economic barriers between the parry and the normal – if by that time there should be any normals left. Someday there'd be no need of Fishhook. Even, perhaps, someday there'd be no need of Earth.

For he had found the answer. Failing to reach Pierre, he still had found the answer. He had been forced (by the finger of God, perhaps?) – he had been forced to find the answer.

It was a better answer than the one that Stone had sought. It was a better technique than even Fishhook had. For it did away entirely with the concept of machines. It made a human whole and the master of himself and of the universe.

He strode on down the bluff and struck the trail that ran into Hamilton. In the sky a few scattered, tattered clouds still flew across the valley, the rearguard of the storm. Pools of melt stood along the token roadway and despite the brightness of the sun the wind out of the west had not lost its teeth.

He plodded up the street that led to the center of the town and from a block or two away he could see them waiting for him in the square before the stores – not just a few as had been the case before, but a crowd of them. More than likely, he figured, here was the most of Hamilton.

He walked across the square and the crowd was quiet. He flicked a look at it, searching for Anita, but he did not see her.

On the steps four men waited, the same four he had met before.

He stopped before them.

'Good afternoon,' he said.

'We heard you coming,' Andrews told him.

'I didn't get to Pierre,' said Blaine. 'I tried to get there to find some help for us. But the storm caught me on the river.'

Jackson said: 'They blocked us on the phone. But we used long tellies. We got through to some of the other groups and they have spread the word. We don't know how far.'

'Nor how well,' said Andrews.

'Your tellies still can contact these groups?' asked Blaine.

Andrews nodded.

Jackson said: 'Finn's men never showed. And it has us worried. Finn ran into trouble . . .'

'They should have showed,' said Andrews. 'They should have turned us inside out in their hunt for you.'

'Perhaps they don't want to find me.'

'Perhaps,' Jackson told him coldly, 'you're not what you say you are.'

Blaine's temper flared. 'To hell with you,' he shouted. 'I damn near died for you. Go on and save yourselves.'

He turned on his heel and walked away, with the anger surging in him.

It was not his fight. Not personally his fight. No more his fight than any one of them. But he had made it his. Because of Stone, because of Rand and Harriet, because of the priest who'd hounded him across half the continent, he had tried to make a fight of it. And perhaps, as well, because of something undefinable, unknown to himself, unsuspected in himself – some crazy idealism, some deep-rooted sense of justice, some basic aversion to bullies and bigots and reformers.

He had come to this village with a gift – he had hurried here so he could give it to them. And they had stood and questioned his integrity and purpose.

To hell with them, he said.

He had been pushed far enough. He would be pushed no further.

There was just one thing left that was worth the doing and he would go and do it and from that moment on, he told himself, there would be nothing more that mattered, for him or anyone.

'Shep!'

He kept on walking.

'Shep!'

He stopped and turned around.

Anita was walking from the crowd.

'No,' he said.

'But they are not the only ones,' she said. 'There are the rest of us. We will listen to you.'

And she was right, of course.

There were the rest of them.

Anita and all the rest of them. The women and the children and those other men who were not in authority. For it was authority that turned men suspicious and stern-faced. Authority and responsibility which made them not themselves, but a sort of corporate body that tried to think as a corporate body rather than a person.

And in this a parry or a community of parries was no different from a normal person or a community of normal persons. Paranormal ability, after all, did not change the person. It merely gave him a chance to become a better person.

'You failed,' Anita said. 'We could not expect that you would succeed. You tried and that's enough.'

He took a step toward her.

'But I didn't fail,' he said.

They were coming toward him now, all of them, a mass of people walking slowly and silently toward him. And in front of them walked Anita Andrews.

She reached him and stood in front of him and looked up into his face.

She kept her voice low. 'Where have you been?' she asked. 'Some of us went out and scouted on the river. We located the canoe.'

He reached out an arm and caught her and swung her to his side and held her tight against him.

'I'll tell you,' he said, 'in just a little while. What about these people?'

'They are scared,' she said. 'They'll grab at any hope.'

The crowd came to a halt a dozen feet away, and a man in front said: 'You're the man from Fishhook.'

Blaine nodded. 'I was from Fishhook. I'm not with them any longer.'

'Like Finn?'

'Like Finn,' admitted Blaine.

'Like Stone, too,' Anita said. 'Stone was from Fishhook, too.'

'You are afraid,' said Blaine. 'You're afraid of me and Finn and of the entire world. But I've found a place where you'll never need to think of fear again. I've found a new world for you and if you want it, it is yours.

'What kind of a world, mister? One of the alien worlds?'

'A world like the best of Earth,' said Blaine. 'I've just come from there . . .'

'But you came walking down the bluff. We saw you walking down the bluff . . .'

Shut up, you fools!' Anita screamed. 'Give him a chance to tell you.'

'I found a way,' said Blaine. 'I stole a way, call it what you will – for one to go to the stars in both mind and body. I went out to the stars last night. I came back this morning. No machine is needed. All you need is a little understanding.'

'But how can we tell—'

'You can't,' said Blaine. 'You gamble, that is all.'

'But even Fishhook, mister—'

'Last night,' Blaine said, slowly, 'Fishhook became obsolete. We don't need Fishhook any more. We can go anywhere we wish. We don't need machines. We just need our minds. And that is the goal of all paranormal research. The machines were never more than just a crutch to help our limping mind. Now we can throw away that crutch. We have no need for it.'

A gaunt-faced woman pushed through the crowd.

'Let's cut out all this talk,' she said. 'You say you found a planet?'

'That I did.'

'And you can take us there?'

'No one needs to take you. You can go yourself.'

'You are one of us, young man. You have an honest face. You wouldn't lie to us?'

Blaine smiled. 'I wouldn't lie to you.'

'Then tell us how to go.'

Someone cried out: 'Can we take some stuff with us?'

Blaine shook his head. 'Not much. A mother could take her baby if she held it in her arms. You could pack a knapsack and strap it on your back. You could sling a bag across your shoulder. You could take along a pitchfork and an ax and another tool or two.'

A man stirred out of line and said: 'We'll have to go about this right. We'll have to figure out what we want to take. We'll need food and garden seed and some clothes and tools . . .'

'You can come back for more,' said Blaine, 'any time you like. There's nothing hard about it.'

'Well,' said the gaunt-faced woman, 'let's not be standing here. Let us get about it. Why don't you tell us, sir?'

'There's just one thing,' said Blaine. 'You have long tellies here?'

'I've one of them,' the woman told him. 'Me and Myrtle over there and Jim back in the crowd and—'

'You'll have to pass the word along. To as many as you can. And the ones you pass it on to will have to pass it on to others. We have to open the gates to as many as we can.'

The woman nodded. 'You just tell it to us.'

There was a murmur in the crowd and they all were moving forward, flowing in on Blaine and Anita to form a ring around them.

'All right,' said Blaine, 'catch on.'

He felt them catching on, gently closing in upon his mind, almost as if they were becoming one with him.

But that wasn't it at all, he thought. He was becoming one with them. Here in the circle the many minds had become one mind. There was one big mind alone and it was warm and human and full of loving kindness. There was a hint of spring-time lilac and the smell of nighttime river fog stealing up the land and the sense of autumn color when the hills were painted purple by an Indian summer. There was the crackling of a wood fire burning on the hearth, and the dog lay there sleeping by the fire and the croon of wind as it crawled along the eaves. There was a sense of home and friends, of good mornings and good nights, of the neighbor across the way and the sound of church bells ringing.

He could have stayed there, floating, but he swept it all away.

Here are the co-ordinates of the planet you are going to, he told them.

He gave them the co-ordinates and repeated them again so there'd be no mistake.

And here is how you do it.

He brought out the slimy alien knowledge and held it for them to see until they became accustomed to it, then step by step he showed them the technique and the logic, although there really was no need, for once one had seen the body of the knowledge, the technique and the logic became self-evident.

Then he repeated it again so there'd be no misunderstanding.

The minds drew back from him, and he stood alone with Anita at his side.

He saw them staring at him as they drew away.

What's the matter now? he asked Anita.

She shuddered. *It was horrible.*

Naturally. But I've seen worse.

And that was it, of course. He'd seen worse, but these people never had. They'd lived all their life on Earth; they knew nothing but the Earth. They had never really touched an alien concept, and that was all this concept was. It was not really as slimy as it seemed. It was only alien. There were a lot of alien things that could make one's hair stand up on end while in their proper alien context they were fairly ordinary.

Will they use it? Blaine asked.

The gaunt-faced woman said to him: *I overheard that, young man. It's dirty, but we'll use it. What else is there for us to do?*

You can stay here.

We'll use it, said the woman.

And you'll pass it along?

We'll do the best we can.

They began to move away. They were uneasy and embarrassed as if someone had told a particularly dirty joke at the church's ice-cream social.

And you? Blaine asked Anita.

She turned slowly from his side to face him. *You had to do it, Shep. There was no other way. You never realized how it would seem to them.*

No, I never did. I've lived so long with alien things. I'm part alien, really. I'm not entirely human . . .

Hush, she said. *Hush, I know just what you are.*

Are you sure, Anita?

Very sure, she said.

He drew her to him and held her tight against him for a moment, then he held her from him and peered into her face, seeing the tears that were just behind the smile inside her eyes.

'I have to leave,' he told her. 'There's one thing else to do.'

'Lambert Finn?'

He nodded.

'But you can't,' she cried. 'You can't!'

'Not what you think,' he told her. 'Although, God knows, I'd like to. I would like to kill him. Up to this very moment, that was what I had intended.'

'But is it safe – going back like this?'

'I don't know. We'll have to see. I can buy some time. I'm the only man who can. Finn's afraid of me.'

'You'll need a car?'

'If you can find me one.'

'We'll be leaving, probably shortly after dark. You'll be back by then?'

'I don't know,' he said.

'You'll come back to go with us? You'll come back to lead us?'

'Anita, I can't promise. Don't try to make me promise.'

'If we're gone, you'll follow?'

He only shook his head.

He could give no answer.

33

The hotel lobby was quiet and almost empty. One man was dozing in a chair. Another read a paper. A bored clerk stood behind the desk, staring across the street and snapping his fingers absent-mindedly.

Blaine crossed the lobby and went down the short corridor

toward the stairs. The elevator operator lounged beside the open cage.

'Lift, sir?' he asked.

'No bother,' Blaine told him. 'It's just one short flight.'

He turned and started up the stairs and he felt the skin tightening on his back and there was a prickling of the hairs at the base of his skull. For he might very well, he knew, be walking straight to death.

But he had to gamble.

The carpet on the tread muffled his footfalls so that he moved up the stairs in silence except for the nervous whistling of his breath.

He reached the second floor and it was the same as it had been before. Not a thing had changed. The guard still sat in the chair tilted back against the wall. And as Blaine came toward him, he tilted forward and sat spraddle-legged, waiting.

'You can't go in now,' the guard told Blaine. 'He chased everybody out. He said he'd try to sleep.'

Blaine nodded. 'He had a real tough time.'

The guard said, confidentially: 'I never seen a man hit quite so hard. Who do you figure done it?'

'Some more of this damn magic.'

The guard nodded sagely. 'Although he wasn't himself even before it happened. He was all right that first time you saw him, but right after that, right after you left, he was not himself.'

'I didn't see any difference in him.'

'Like I told you, he was all right. He came back all right. An hour or so later I looked in and he was sitting in his chair, staring at the door. A funny kind of stare. As if he maybe hurt inside. And he didn't even see me when I looked. Didn't know that I was there until I spoke to him.'

'Maybe he was thinking.'

'Yeah, I suppose. But yesterday was awful. There was all the crowd here, come to hear him speak, and all of them reporters, and they went out to the shed where he had this star machine . . .'

'I wasn't here,' said Blaine, 'but I heard about it. It must have been quite a shock.'

'I thought he'd die right there,' said the guard. 'Right there on the spot. He got purple in the face and—'

'What do you say,' suggested Blaine, 'if we just look in? If he's asleep, I'll leave. But if he's still awake, I'd like a quick word with him. It's really quite important.'

'Well, I guess that would be all right. Seeing you're his friend.'

And that, thought Blaine, was the final pay-off in this fantastic game. Finn had not breathed a word about him, for he'd not dared to breathe a word about him. Finn had let it be presumed that he was a friend, for such a presumption was a shield for Finn himself. And that was why there'd been no hunt for him. That was why Finn's hoods had not turned Hamilton inside out in a frantic search for him.

This was the pay-off, then – unless it was a trap.

He felt his muscles tensing and he forced them to relax.

The guard was getting up and fumbling for the key.

'Hey, wait a minute there,' said Blaine. 'You'd better shake me down.'

The guard grinned at him. 'No need of that,' he said. 'You was clean before. You and Finn went out of here arm in arm. He told me you was an old friend he hadn't seen in years.'

He found the key and unlocked the door.

'I'll go in first,' he said. 'I'll see if he's asleep.'

He swung the door open quietly and moved across the threshold, Blaine following close behind.

The guard stopped so abruptly that Blaine bumped into him.

The guard was making funny noises deep inside his throat.

Blaine put out a hand and pushed him roughly to one side.

Finn was lying on the floor.

And there was about him a strange sense of alienness.

His body was twisted as if someone had taken it and twisted it beyond the natural ability of a body to contort itself. His face, resting on one cheek, was the visage of a man who had glimpsed the fires of hell and had smelled the stench of bodies that burned eternally. His black clothing had an obscene shine in the light from the lamp that stood beside a chair not far from the body. There was a wide blot of darkness in the carpeting about his head and chest. And there was the horror of a throat that had been slashed wide open.

The guard still was standing to one side of the door and the noises in his throat had changed to gagging noises.

Blaine walked close to Finn and there, beside the out-flung hand, was the instrument of death – an old-fashioned, straight-edge razor that should have been safely tucked away in a museum.

Now, Blaine knew, all hope was gone. There could be no bargain made. For Lambert Finn was beyond all bargaining.

To the very last the man had stayed in character, had remained his harsh, stern self. No easy way for him, but the toughest way of all for a man to take his life.

But even so, Blaine thought, staring in chilled horror at the red gash in the throat, there had been no need to do the job so thoroughly, to keep on slashing with the razor even as he died.

Only a man of hate would do that, a man insane with the hate of self – a man who despised and loathed what he had become.

Unclean – unclean with an alien mind inside his anti-septic skull. A thing like that would drive a man like Finn to death; a fastidious fanatic who could become obsessed with his self-conceived idea of a perfect state could not live with nor survive the disorderly enigma of an alien mind.

Blaine turned on his heel and walked out of the room. In the corridor the guard was in a corner, doubled over, retching.

'You stay here,' Blaine told him. 'I'll call the cops.'

The man turned around. His eyes were glazed with horror. He wiped feebly at his chin.

'My God,' he said, 'I ask you, did you ever see a mess—'

'Sit down,' said Blaine, 'and take it easy. I'll be right back.'

Although he wouldn't be. Now was the time to blow. He needed time and he'd get a little time. For the guard was too shaken to do anything for quite a little while.

But as soon as the news was known, all hell was bound to break.

God help the parry, Blaine thought, who is caught this night!

He went swiftly down the corridor and ran down the stairs. The lobby still was empty and he set out across it briskly.

As he reached the door, it came open suddenly and someone came through it, walking briskly, too.

A purse clattered to the floor, and Blaine's hands reached out to steady the woman who had come through the doorway.

Harriet! Get out of here! Get out!

My purse!

He stooped to scoop it up and as he lifted it, the catch came open and something black and heavy fell. His free hand snapped at it and had it and he worked it back along his palm so that it was hidden

Harriet had turned around and was going out the door. Blaine hurried after her and caught her by the elbow, urging her along.

He reached his car and stooped to open the door. He pushed her to the seat.

But, Shep, my car is just a block—

No time. We're getting out of here.

He ran around the car and got in. He jerked it from the curb and out into the street. Moving far more slowly than he wanted, he eased it down the block, turned at the intersection, heading for the highway.

Just ahead stood the gutted structure of the Trading Post.

He had been holding the purse in his lap and now he gave it to her.

'How about the gun?' he asked.

'I was going to kill him,' she shouted. 'I was going to shoot him dead.'

'No need to do that now. He is already dead.'

She turned toward him quickly.

'You!'

'Well, now, I guess that you could say so.'

'But, Shep, you know. You either killed him or you—'

'All right,' he said. 'I killed him.'

And it was no lie. No matter by what hand Lambert Finn had died, he, Shepherd Blaine, had killed him.

'I had reason to,' he said. 'But you?'

'He had Godfrey killed. That itself would have been enough.'

'You were in love with Godfrey.'

'Yes, I suppose I was. He was such a great guy, Shep.'

'I know how great he was. We were friends in Fishhook.'

'It hurts,' said Harriet. 'Oh, Shep, how it hurts!'

'And that night . . .'

'There was no time for tears,' she said. 'There's never time for tears.'

'You knew about all this . . .'

'For a long time. It was my job to know.'

He reached the highway and turned down it, back toward Hamilton. The sun had set. Twilight had crept across the land and in the east one star was twinkling, just above the prairie.

'And now?' he asked.

'Now I have a story. As much of it as I ever can.'

'You're going to write it. Will your paper run it?'

'I don't know,' she said. 'But I have to write it. You understand that I have to write it. I'm going to New York . . .'

'Wrong,' he said. 'You're going to Fishhook. Not by car. From the nearest airport . . .'

'But, Shep—

'It's not safe,' Blaine told her. 'Not for anyone who has the faintest hint of parry. Even minor telepaths, like you.'

'I can't do it, Shep. I—'

'Listen, Harriet. Finn had set up a Halloween outbreak by the parries, a sort of counterintelligence move. The other parries, when they learned about it, tried to stop it. They did stop part of it, but I don't know to what extent. Whatever happens will be happening tonight. He would have used the outbreak to step up

187

intolerance, to trigger rigid legislation. There would have been some violence, of course, but that was not, by and large, Finn's purpose. But now, with Finn dead . . .'

Harriet drew in her breath. 'They'll wipe us out,' she said.

'They'll do their best. But there is a way . . .'

'Knowing this, you still killed Finn!'

'Look, Harriet, I didn't really kill him. I went to bargain with him. I found a way to take the parries off Earth. I was going to promise to clean every parry off the Earth, clean out of his way, if he'd hold off his dogs for a week or two . . .'

'But you said you killed him.'

'Maybe,' said Blaine, 'I better fill you in. So when you come to write your story you can write it all.'

34

Hamilton was silent. And so empty you could feel the emptiness.

Blaine stopped the car in the square and got out of it.

Not a light was showing, and the soft sound of the river came clearly to his ear

'They are gone,'he said.

Harriet got out of the car and came around it to stand beside him.

'All right, pal,' she said. 'Get onto your horse.'

He shook his head.

'But you have to go. You have to follow them. You belong with them.'

'Someday,' said Blaine. 'Someday, years from now. There's still work to do. There'll be pockets of parries all up and down the land. Fearful and in hiding. I have to search them out. I have to save as many as I can.'

'You'll never live to do it. You'll be a special target. Finn's men will never rest . . .'

'If the pressure gets too bad, I'll go. I'm no hero, Harriet. Basically, I'm a coward.'

'You'll promise that?' she asked.

'Of course. Cross my heart. And you're going back to Fish-hook. You'll be safe in Fishhook. Straight to the airport up in Pierre.'

She turned and went back to his car, started to get in, then turned back again.

'But you'll need the car.'

He chuckled. 'If I need one, there's a village full of cars. I can pick the one I want. They couldn't take their cars.'

She got behind the wheel and turned her head to say good-by.

'One thing,' said Blaine. 'What happened to you when I was in the shed?'

Her laughter had a sharpness to it. 'When Rand drove up, I pulled out. I went to get some help. I figured I should get on the phone to Pierre. There'd been men up there who'd helped us.'

'But?'

'The police stopped me and threw me into jail. They let me out the morning after, and I've been looking for you since.'

'Stout gal,' he said, and there was a faint throbbing in the air – a noise from far away.

Blaine stiffened, listening. The noise grew louder, deeper – the sound of many cars.

'Quick,' he said. 'No lights. Slant across the bluff. You'll hit the road up north.'

'Shep, what's got into you?'

'That noise you hear is cars. A posse coming here. They know that Finn is dead.'

'You, Shep?'

'I'll be all right. Get going.'

She started the motor.

'Be seeing you,' she said.

'Get moving, Harriet! And thanks a lot. Thanks for everything. Tell Charline hello.'

'Good-by, Shep,' she said, and the car was moving, swinging in a circle to head up a street that led toward the bluff.

She'll make it all right, he told himself. Anyone who could drive those blind mountains out of Fishhook would have no trouble here.

'Good-by, Harriet,' he had said. 'Tell Charline hello.' And why had he said that? he wondered. A hail and farewell to the old life, more than likely – a reaching out to touch hands with the past. Although there'd be no past in Fishhook. Charline would go on having parties, and the most peculiar people would continue showing up without having been invited. For Fishhook was a glamour and a glitter and a ghost. Without knowing it, Fishhook now was dead. And it was a pity. For Fishhook had been one of the greatest, one of the giddiest, one of the gladdest things that had ever happened to the human race.

He stood lonely in the square and listened to the furious sound of the coming cars. Far to the west he saw the flashing of their lights. A chill breeze came off the river and tugged at his trouser legs and jacket sleeves.

All over the world, he thought. All over the world tonight there'd be screaming cars and the slavering mobs and the running people.

He put his hand into a jacket pocket and felt the shape and the weight of the gun that had fallen from Harriet's purse. His fingers closed around it – but that, he thought, was not the way to fight them.

There was another way to fight them, a long range way to fight them. Isolate them and strangle them in their own mediocrity. Give them what they wanted – a planet full of people who were merely normal. A planet full of people who could huddle here and rot – never knowing space, never getting to the stars, never going anyplace or doing anything. Like a man who rocked away his life sitting in a rocking chair on a porch of some little dying town.

Without recruits from outside, Fishhook itself would falter in another hundred years, come to a dead stop within still another hundred. For the parries on the other planets would recruit from Fishhook even as they winnowed through the world to rescue their own kind.

But it wouldn't matter in another hundred years, for the human race would then be safe on the other planets, building the kind of life and the kind of culture they'd been denied upon the Earth.

He started to move across the square, heading toward the bluffs. For he must be out of town, or nearly out of town, before the cars came in.

And he was, he knew, on a lonely path once more. But not so lonely now, for now he had a purpose. A purpose, he told himself with a sudden flickering of pride, he had hewn out himself.

He straightened his shoulders against the chillness of the wind and moved a bit more briskly. For there was work to do. A lot of work to do.

Something moved in the shadow of the trees off to the left, and Blaine, catching the movement with one corner of his mind, wheeled swiftly.

The movement came toward him, slowly, just a bit uncertainly.

'Shep?'

'Anita!' he cried. 'You little fool! Anita!'

She came running from the darkness and was in his arms.

'I wouldn't go,' she said. 'I wouldn't go without you. I knew you would come back.'

He crushed her to him and bent to kiss her and there was nothing in the world, nothing in the universe, but the two of them. There was blood and lilacs and the shining star and the wind upon the hilltop and the two of them and that was all there was.

Except the screaming of the cars as they came tearing down the road.

Blaine jerked away from her. 'Run!' he cried. 'You must, Anita!'

'Like the wind,' she said.

They ran.

'Up the bluff,' she said. 'There's a car up there. I took it up as soon as it got dark.'

Halfway up the bluff they stopped and looked back.

The first flames were beginning to run in the huddled blackness of the village, and screams of futile rage came drifting up the slope. Gunfire rattled hollowly, torn by the wind.

'They're shooting at shadows,' said Anita. 'There is nothing down there. Not even dogs or cats. The kids took them along.'

But in many other villages, thought Blaine, in many other places, there would be more than shadows. There would be fire and gunsmoke and the knotted rope and the bloody knife. And there might be as well the pattering of rapid feet and the dark shape in the sky and a howling on the hills.

'Anita,' he asked, 'are there really werewolves?'

'Yes,' she told him. 'Your werewolves are down there.'

And that was right, he thought. The darkness of the mind, the bleakness of the thought, the shallowness of purpose. These were the werewolves of the world.

The two of them turned their backs upon the village and headed up the slope.

Behind them the flames of hate grew taller, hotter. But ahead, above the bluff top, the distant stars glowed with certain promise.

413 3467	The Godwhale	T. J. Bass	85p
413 3457	Extro	Alfred Bester	85p
417 0413	Colony	Ben Bova	£.
413 3458	The Wrong End of Time	John Brunner	
417 0208	Traveller in Black	John Brunner	75p
417 0461	Dr Futurity	Philip K. Dick	75p
417 0460	The Unteleported Man	Philip K. Dick	80p
413 3653	The Crack in Space	Philip K. Dick	
417 0197	The Simulacra	Philip K. Dick	85p
417 0259	The Man Who Japed	Philip K. Dick	85p
417 0260	Shiny Mountain	David Dvorkin	85p
417 0180	Hadon of Ancient Opar	Philip Jose Farmer	75p
417 0177	Flight to Opar	Philip Jose Farmer	75p
417 0350	Star Bridge	James Gunn & Jack Williamson	
417 0336	The Future Makers	Peter Haining	90p
417 0220	Off Centre	Damon Knight	70p
417 0222	In Deep	Damon Knight	75p
417 0221	Far Out	Damon Knight	75p
417 0190	Messenger of Zhuvastou	Andrew J. Offutt	80p
417 0215	The Castle Keeps	Andrew J. Offutt	
417 0302	The Clansman of Andor	Andrew J. Offutt	
417 0335	My Lord Barbarian	Andrew J. Offutt	85p
417 0178	Galactic Medal of Honour	Mack Reynolds	70p
417 0322	We Who Are About To ...	Joanna Russ	75p
417 0315	Across a Billion Years	Robert Silverberg	90p
413 3690	Way Station	Clifford D. Simak	85p
417 0204	Cemetery World	Clifford D. Simak	
417 0563	Time is the Simplest Thing	Clifford D. Simak	£1
413 3768	Time and Again	Clifford D. Simak	
417 0171	A Choice of Gods	Clifford D. Simak	75p
417 0236	So Bright the Vision	Clifford D. Simak	
417 0196	Shakespeare's Planet	Clifford D. Simak	
417 0217	All Flesh is Grass	Clifford D. Simak	85p